LÁ-
KÍRÍ-
BOTO

First published in Nigeria as *Lakiriboto Chronicles:*
A brief History of Badly Behaved Women in 2018
by Bookbuilders Editions Africa

Published in 2023 by Cipher Press

105 Ink Court
419 Wick Lane
London, E3 2PX

Paperback ISBN: 978-1-7392207-0-9
eBook ISBN: 978-1-7392207-1-6

Printed and bound in the UK by TJ Books Limited

Distributed by Turnaround Publisher Services

Cover Design by Wolf Murphy-Merrydew
Proofread by Odhran O'Donoghue
Typeset by Laura Jones

www.cipherpress.co.uk

Supported using public funding by
ARTS COUNCIL
ENGLAND

LÁ-KÍRÍ-BOTO

AYỌ̀DÉLÉ ỌLỌ́FINTÚÁDÉ

Cipher press

To my Ori, pathfinder, waymaker, lover and protector.
This is to Yemọja ọ̀wẹ́ẹ̀wẹ́, arẹyìn pọn Ṣàngó. To my
mothers, Ìyábọ̀dé Sànyàolú and Chris Bankole,
who taught me all I know and told me
I can always return home.

To my beautiful children,
Mofẹ̀hìntọláolúwa and Ìfẹ́olúwakìíṣá.

Foreword

In order to understand the concept of Lákíríboto, one has to understand the Yoruba way of being, of thinking. Words are not just used for communication, they are connected to the way the brain, mind and body function. Words are used for archival purposes. Yoruba words are connected to the first three sounds on the tonic sol-fa – do, re, mi – which are connected to the beat of drums, to muscle memory and dance. Dancing itself is believed to open the mind for curiosity, exploration and questioning. Words connect the Yoruba to their ancestors, their ways of being, to problem solving, society building, adaptation and possibilities of new inventions.

I've been hearing the word Lákíríboto all my life, but I never connected it to queerness because queerness was a word I came into contact with after I 'came out of the closet', even though I've been queer all my life. The word acquired deeper meanings as I sought to situate myself in my ancestry as opposed to fitting myself into Western ideas of what is 'normal' and who 'the other' is, as being othered brings with it a burden of shame and permanent victimhood.

While the English Language, the lingua franca of Nigeria, a neocolony of the United Kingdom – considered the language of 'sophistication', 'civilisation' and a mark of 'intelligence' – seeks to label and box everything in order to make sense of the world, Yoruba languages seek to question and integrate various experiences and ways of being into the universality of humanity. For to humanise every being (living, non-living and inventions) is to engineer social and environmental justice, to minimise harm in as much as it is possible to do.

My first conscious examination of the word happened in an open-air marketplace. A song recalled from my early teenage years was blasting through a loudspeaker. The musician, Alhaji Akande Abass (aka Obesere), was accusing his love interest of having same-sex leanings because they turned down his love advances. He would tell their parents that they are lesbians.

Ng ó sọ fún bàbá ẹ
Ng ó sọ fún yèyé ẹ
Pé lákíríboto lo fẹ́ yà
Pé lákíríboto lo fẹ́ yà

It is important to note that the Yoruba language is not gendered. There are no singular words for boys or girls: all children are ọmọ or the more descriptive ọmọ kékeré (a toddler or younger person), babies are ọmọ tuntun (a new child). Adults are àgbàlagbà, youths are Ọ̀dọ̀. You don't have a brother or a sister, you have an ọmọ ìyá (your mother's child) or ọmọ bàbá (your father's child). Akọ (ọkùnrin) and abo (obìrin) are the closest words to male and female in the English language. These words are, however, more closely linked to energies than gender. For example, the Yoruba will declare at the beginning of every new year that 'Ọdún á y'abo fún wa', which means the year will come with softness, creativity, endurance and abundance.

Ẹ̀gbọ́n (older sibling) and àbúrò (younger sibling) are the specific terms used for siblings. Iyèkan is a sibling born to your mother. Although they adopted unku (uncle), anti (aunty), buoda (brother) and sista (sister) from English, even the most ardent Anglophiles of us still use these words loosely, as any of the above listed titles can be applied to both family and non-family members. As family is often defined by levels of intimacy, this is an echo of pre-colonial Yoruba people, who adopted people into guilds and families freely. The only exceptions to this rule relate to matters that affect the state and its economic wellbeing, inheritance and land ownership.

The use of Lákíríboto as a specific, non-gendered descriptor of sexual behaviour can be found in Alhaji Sikiru Ayinde Barrister's song, when he describes Lákíríboto as a person who does not have sex with men. 'Lákíríboto wọn ò kí n b'ọ́kùnrin ló pọ̀' loosely translates as 'lesbians do not fuck (with) men'. For an indigenous person, who does not take their centre from Western definitions, this can be applied to any person of any gender who does not have sex with people who identify as men.

Long before queer theorists started entertaining the idea of sexual behaviour as different from gender identity, the Yoruba had made this distinction. Not only in the way Olódùmarè, the Irúnmọlè and the Òrìṣà are mostly genderfluid or non-gendered, but also in the way their civilisations are built around the protection of the most likely to be vulnerable. For example, Ọbàtálá (creator and philosopher) is the protector of neurodiverse and disabled people. Labels are not used for restriction – they are used for individual freedom, because the more aligned each person is with their original purpose on earth the healthier the larger society is.

Aside from pop culture, Lákíríboto is also a descriptor of biodiverse people. A common saying in Yoruba is 'Lákíríboto ò l'ójú awẹ́', which can be loosely translated to 'Lákíríboto does not have labia', which means it is a descriptor of trans or intersex people in medical terms.

To drive this point home, kolanuts that do not have ears like other kolanuts and that are bitter to the palate are described as Lákíríboto ... 'a pá, kò l'áwẹ́, a jẹ́ẹ́ kò dùn. This term is usually applied to women who are considered stubborn or uncontrollable. Women who refuse to be 'mounted' by societal rules or expectations.

Lákíríboto is trans, she's intersex. Lákíríboto is wild and will not bow her head in shame. She takes charge of her pleasure and is neurodiverse. Lákíríboto is the perfect descriptor of all the women in this story, because they are queer as fuck.

SEASON ONE:
A GLASS HALF EMPTY
(2005)

A DEATH

Mọremí discovered Alhaja in a sleep that was as deep as it was infinite, around 6:30am that Saturday morning. The bedsheet and blanket were tangled together to one side of the bed. It was as if Alhaja had engaged Death in a battle, and lost, because nothing Mọremí did would wake her up – despite calling her name repeatedly and shaking her, first gently and then vigorously.

Her heart raced faster than her legs as she dashed out of the house into the courtyard, hoping somebody, anybody, would join in her bid to wake Alhaja up from her death sleep.

In her eleven-year-old mind her grandmother could still be rescued, snatched out of the bloodied hands of death before her spirit crossed to the other side, a vague place that could be in the heavens above, underneath the earth or just within spitting distance.

She paused in front of the low fence that separated her home from the other houses in the neighbourhood, and stood on tiptoes. After about two minutes without even the whisper of feet, Mọ́remí ran to the gate and pulled it open, but then she remembered her grandmother's warning about gbọ́mọ-gbọ́mọ – men and women who prowled their street, turning wandering children into yams before kidnapping them.

She shut the gate and stood indecisively, for a moment, then remembered the bungalows located in the backyard. She followed a tiny path that wound drunkenly between the mango and bush cherry trees, and drew to a stop when she got to the three small bungalows fighting for space among the trees.

Mọ́remí checked each bungalow for signs of life. The doors were locked, the wooden shutters firmly closed. It was as if Alhaja had dragged every living soul with her to the other side.

Alhaja can't be dead; they had still been together the previous night watching TV, and her grandmother hadn't looked or acted like someone who was planning to die. In fact she and her brother, Olórí Ẹbí, had had a good time, taking shots from the bottle of schnapps he'd brought for her.

Mọ́remí pulled the stories of night markets where the living and dead mingled that her grandmother had told her over the years around her, a comforting blanket, because nobody ever dies, not truly.

Alhaja is not dead, she chanted, Alhaja is not dead, over and again.

She was so engrossed in her thoughts that when she stepped away from the last bungalow she tripped over the root of one of the trees and fell flat on her face. Mọ́remí tried not to cry as she pulled herself off the ground; she knew once she started, she wouldn't be able to stop.

She took several deep breaths, held on to a tree trunk and pulled herself up. She checked for bruises, there was a large one on her left shin, Alhaja will take care of it once she wakes up, she reassured herself, and called out again. 'Mama Seun! Mama Adija!'

Neither of the women who lived next door answered. She became even more aware of the silence around her, a dead silence.

Alhaja is not dead.

Mọ́remí stood under the mango tree irresolutely. Then she remembered that the day was originally meant for Olórí Ẹbí's child-naming ceremony, and lost all hope of getting help quickly. She knew everybody in the neighbourhood would be at his house, which was some distance away from theirs.

Mọ́remí would have gone there if she had known the direction, gbọ́mọ-gbọ́mọ be damned, but her grandmother had been so protective of her, she had not been allowed to run around barefooted, and sometimes, butt naked, like the other children on the street. She walked dejectedly back to the main building and settled for standing guard in front of it. She would prevent Alhaja's soul from leaving the confines of the house.

'Why the shouting-shouting?' Iya Ruka rushed up to her. 'I am hearing you from my shop.' Mọ́remí jumped off the ground and up in response and nearly collided with Iya Ruka. 'What's the problem? Kí ló dé?' Iya Ruka steadied her.

'It's Alhaja, I can't wake her up. She is on the bed with her eyes wide open, please come and help me wake her.' She tugged at the sleeves of Iya Ruka's blouse.

'Alhaja ke? Your grandmother?' Another voice joined Iya Ruka. Mọ́remí narrowed her eyes at Iya Ruka's apprentice, annoyed at the way she was craning her neck as if she could see through the gloom of the passageway into Alhaja's room.

Iya Ruka grabbed the girl's face and turned it towards herself. 'Run down to the clinic and fetch Matron, then go to Olórí Ẹbí's house and tell him to come here immediately.'

'Let's go and help Alhaja first,' Mọ́remí insisted.

'Do I look like a doctor or nurse in your eyes?' Iya Ruka snapped. She took a deep breath, softened her tone and continued in Yoruba, 'There's nothing I can do for her. Funmilayo will soon return with Matron, who is in a better position to help.'

Iya Ruka had just convinced Mọ́remí to sit down when the Matron appeared and entered the house without sparing a glance for Mọ́remí. Olórí Ẹbí soon followed after, in a flurry of neon green agbádá and self-importance.

One hour later she watched, dry eyed, as Alhaja's corpse was washed and wrapped in readiness for her burial, which was to take place at sundown according to Muslim rites.

Immediately after Alhaja's body was lowered into the earth from whence she came, the house was once again abuzz with activities in preparation for the ceremony to celebrate her life.

The first few days of preparation for the post-burial ceremony were hectic, with people coming in and out of the house as casually as they did when she was still alive. Far-flung relatives, most of whom Mọ́remí had never seen before, turned up.

Olórí Ẹbí came only once, to lock up Alhaja's room and give an order that Mọ́remí was not to be left alone. She noted that Olórí Ẹbí carried two carton boxes overflowing with papers out with him.

The women agreed it would be wrong to leave the poor little girl alone. And true to their word, they kept her company. They talked through her and about her, but none of them talked to her except to ask her what she wanted for breakfast, lunch or dinner.

Mọ́remí suffered through the invasion of her privacy in the days that followed, and a headache that was compounded by the constant wailing and whining of mourners that arrived from Alágbàdo the day after her grandmother's interment. During this period, she acquired a patina of invisibility. This newly acquired superpower manifested whenever she bumped into any of her relatives. They would look at her, apparently surprised that she was there, their eyes glazing over as they swept the compound, searching for more visible members of the family. She remained standing at the exact spot while a steady stream of commiseraters patted her on the head, before rushing off to sympathise with someone of their social standing.

On the third day, Mọ́remí wandered around the compound in a confused daze, until she found herself seated next to the mourners. Being professionals and used to seeing the dead and other invisible people, the mourners made room for her on the wooden bench.

They first studied her with caution, and then one of them asked who she was. When she told them they were at her grandmother's burial, they made mournful noises. Their tears dried up a few seconds later, and they asked if she would be returning to England or America anytime soon. They did not listen when she told them she lived here, in Idi-Ikan.

People who looked like Mọ́remí did not live in the heart of Ibadan, they lived at Bodija, or on the campus at the University of Ibadan. Posh places populated by the educated, the newly arrived from abroad, familiar strangers referred to as the àtọ̀húnrìnwá.

They told her how pretty she looked with skin so light and dark green eyes, she was òyìnbó, wasn't she? They told her how shocked they were that she could speak Yoruba as sweetly as someone licking honey. They clasped their hands to their breasts and praised this achievement. Then they complained, rather bitterly, about members of their own families who had refused to teach their children how to speak Yoruba. They listed the names of these criminals, careful not to leave any of them out.

'Ehen! See this small òyìnbó girl speaking Yoruba like a Yoruba person.' Their eyes were wide with marvel. Mọ́remí did not argue with them. She enjoyed being visible, she did not want to cause offence.

For the next few days she followed the mourners around and made certain interesting discoveries. The mourners took turns crying, and that was why it appeared that they cried endlessly. They cried in batches. They had breakfast, lunch, dinner and snacks inbetween, in batches. Whenever a fresh face appeared in the compound, the women would begin wailing and singing Alhaja's panegyrics. Even while they cried, they laughed at jokes shared in low tones among themselves. Nobody paid any attention to the mourners, except to give them money or food.

But on the day of the post-burial ceremony, Mọ́remí did not join them. Instead she wandered around the compound, a living ghost. She listened to conversations not meant for her ears.

Olórí Ẹbí has bought six big cows!

Iya Sisi has left her husband for that useless small boy.

The pots in the kitchen are not big enough, we need to get more from L'Ẹgbǎ.

Rabi is owing Iya L'Oja, you should have seen the fight! Rabi was disgraced well-well!

Mọremí was sad, then she got angry. She watched as they cooked and ate and pooped and laughed as if everything was fine. She watched as the women screamed and hugged one another, recounting stories of the last time they'd been together, at another birth, another burial, in another time, another space.

... OF GUARDIAN DEMON

Tọlá woke up from a drug-induced haze to the sound of a kitten crying persistently somewhere off to her right. She patted the bed, wondering how a kitten had gained entrance to the apartment. Something tugged at her memory but she turned her back on it, physically. All she wanted was sleep ... that's all ...

She woke up a few minutes later, an hour ... a day?

The room was dark, the blanket warm – it smelled of her. A man came into the room. He helped her to sit up and placed a mug in her hand, and she drank down the contents. It was corn-pap. The tepid semi-solid paste wrapped itself around her taste buds sweetly-sour.

She accepted the pills he offered her and swallowed them with some more pap. She lay back on the bed. Her brain was both tender and brittle, it would shatter if she was not careful. She slid down carefully on the bed, her neck held stiffly. Her head touched the pillow, it was soft, fluffy, cloudy. The cloud wrapped itself around her brain, shielding it from danger, from shattering.

The kitten was shrieking. Tọlá frowned. She tightened the blanket around her head.

Kittens shouldn't be allowed in bedrooms.

The next time she was awoken by a discomfort in her stomach. She pushed the bedclothes off, the comforting, warm bedclothes that smelled like her unwashed body. As she swung her legs off the bed, a pain like a sharpened blade jabbed at her womb. She yelped.

The man, who looked faintly familiar, like one of those faded black and white childhood pictures, stuck his head into the room. He stared at her for a while and then left.

She was relieved.

By the time she got to the bathroom, doubled over in pain, somebody was standing behind her. The woman, another faintly recognisable face, helped her to push open the door. 'Do you want to take a bath?'

Tọlá resented the woman's voice; she did not want to speak or be spoken to. The woman's voice demanded recognition, an acknowledgment.

'You should bathe.' The woman's voice was a shriek. 'You're smelling like a dead goat.'

Tọlá's resentment grew. Ignoring the pain that jabbed at her insides, she pushed the woman away from the bathroom door and returned to bed. Sleep claimed her immediately, a dreamless, dead sleep.

The kitten is mewling again … damn it! The crying was coming from somewhere near her head. Her head started pounding. Tọlá reluctantly dragged her eyelids apart. Somebody was holding the kitten. The woman whose voice demanded recognition was back, and was thrusting the mewling kitten at her. She wondered why a kitten was wrapped in a baby blanket. She turned her head away from the woman and the kitten.

'Take your baby!' commanded the woman, her voice ricocheting around Tọlá's brain. 'You cannot continue to ignore him. You cannot refuse to breastfeed him! What kind of mother are you?'

Tọlá pulled the blanket off her head and glared at the woman through eyes full of hatred. The woman recoiled. Tọlá shut her eyes and fell asleep.

The smell of something warm and tantalising woke her up. She opened her eyes and was met with a face full of worry. The face was light skinned. It wore red lipstick, blue eyeshadow deepened its brown eyes. It smiled, showing pearly white teeth.

'Hey Tọlá, it's me, Kẹ́mi.' The face had a voice, a forced cheerful voice. 'I'm your sister.' She gave an embarrassed chuckle. 'Remember me?'

Tọlá had taken a vow of forgetfulness, and she was determined not to break that vow.

'Do you mind if I sit on the bed with you?'

Tọlá nodded. Kẹ́mi sat by her legs, and fetched something from the floor. It was a tray. On it was a plate brimming with something brown and shiny, it smelled delicious.

'I brought you some fish peppersoup.' Kẹ́mi adjusted the tray so the soup would not spill and scooped some of the peppersoup. Tọlá's mouth suddenly felt funny, her tongue was bitter and furry.

'Now open up.' Kẹ́mi smiled encouragingly and pushed the spoon towards her.

When the spoon slid into Tọlá's mouth, the peppersoup

tasted as good as it smelled. She opened her mouth to receive another spoonful, then another.

'I told your husband that you might need to see a specialist,' Kẹ́mi said, as she scooped some more soup from the dish. 'I think you might be suffering from post-partum depression. But your husband says being a GP means he knows everything about everything.'

The peppersoup suddenly rushed from Tọ́lá's stomach into her throat. She jumped out of bed and ran into the bathroom. She heaved until her stomach was empty. Kẹ́mi was right behind her, patting her on the back, distracting her.

Tọ́lá shrugged off her hand and went to rinse out her mouth in the sink. She ran some water over her head and wiped her face with a towel. Ignoring Kẹ́mi, who was hovering nearby, she returned to the room, switched off the light, crawled back into her bed, swallowed two pills and tuned out all the noise. She buried her nose in her armpit. The smell reminded her that she was human.

'Enough of this!' the woman was shrieking. 'You have to take care of your husband and children!'

Tọ́lá cringed from her voice, from the words she was saying, of responsibilities, husbands, children ...

'What's all these nonsense!' The woman was in full throttle. 'You just gave birth to a baby. Are you the first person that will do operation to have a baby?' She leaned over the bed as Tọ́lá pulled the bedclothes over her head. 'I am your mother! You will listen to me!'

The bedclothes were yanked out of her hands, she was yanked out of bed. The C-section wound was still tender. It protested by stabbing her with sharpened knives.

'Five weeks after your operation and you're still lying in bed, refusing to eat or breastfeed the baby! What kind of useless mother are you?' Tọ́lá's mother stabbed her with words as she pushed her towards the bathroom. 'Depression, what rubbish. Women have had children before you, they will keep having children after you're dead and gone. You will sit up and behave!'

Tọ́lá braced herself against the frame of the bathroom door. Even though her legs were watery, she stood her ground and wouldn't budge. 'I want to be left alone.' Tọ́lá jumped in surprise as her voice came out of her throat. She tried to push her mother out of the doorway, but was shoved back forcefully. As Tọ́lá fell, she hit her head on the toilet seat, the force couched by its fake fur covering.

'I'm locking you in here until you come back to yourself,' her mother yelled before slamming the door shut.

Tọ́lá curled up on the cool marble tiles of the bathroom floor and cried. The tears were drawn out of her aching womb. She cried harder because she did not know why she was crying. She cried until she started hiccupping, but she kept at it until there were no more tears.

'E don do, stand up,' a soft, unfamiliar voice said from somewhere above her head.

Tọ́lá pushed herself into a sitting position, but was too exhausted to ask the stranger who she was, or how she got into a locked bathroom.

'I be Rita.'

She looked at the woman properly. Although she couldn't gauge exactly from her position on the floor, Rita appeared to be tall. Her curves were emphasised by the red velcro mini-dress that clung to her body, white on rice. Tọ́lá couldn't make out her features.

'Na me be your guardian angel,' said Rita.

Tọ́lá had an impression of a wink, of black matted lips forming those words, and sniggered. 'Really? I've seen pictures of angels and none of them look like you.'

Rita laughed, the sound travelling through Tọ́lá's body. 'Okay, make we gree say I be your guardian demon.' She leaned close to Tọ́lá, her face still out of focus. 'I go take good care of you.'

Tọ́lá floated off the floor, she felt like air. The desire to curl into a tight ball and seek oblivion in sleep was gone. She was born again. Old things have passed away and behold, all things have become new.

After she was done taking her bath, she knocked briskly on the bathroom door. The speed at which it was opened told her that her mother had been standing outside the bathroom all along.

Her mother peered into the bathroom. 'Who were you talking to?'

'None of your business!' Rita swept past her.

'Me?' Tọ́lá's mother smacked herself on the chest. 'You're talking to me like that? After all I've done for you?'

Rita scowled at Tọ́lá's mother. 'I did not ask you to do anything for me. I did not ask to be born!'

A FAMILY THAT PREYS TOGETHER

The meeting that would decide Mọ́remí's fate was held in the parlour of Alhaja Àdùkẹ́'s house.

The parlour was the biggest room in the house. Several old-fashioned chairs covered in forest green damask were spread around the rectangular room. The chairs were so immense that one was led to believe giants had once occupied them, and that over the years their progeny had shrunk in size.

The walls of the room held sepia-coloured pictures of long-gone ancestors, whose spirits now occupied the white space within the photographs. Further down were more recent pictures of new ancestors and aspiring ones.

The most imposing picture was that of Alhaji Muraina Alágbàdo, the family patriarch, Alhaja's grandfather. It was positioned in a corner that faced the doorway. Alhaji Alágbàdo was dressed in an agbádá made of aso-oke. He wore a thick gold necklace, dangling off which was a pendant. Both the necklace and pendant reached nearly to his ankles. On his right shoulder was a white saki, an insignia of the Ogboni Fraternity. He was staring fiercely at the camera, as if daring it to imprint his face on mere paper, with mere chemicals.

The camera won.

For this important meeting, the parlour had been transformed into a community hall. Plastic chairs were arranged facing the room's only door. Members of the family trickled in. After a while someone shooed out the children who were playing hide and seek, into the brilliant sunshine that flooded the courtyard.

The room was soon filled up with people and their chatter. The chatter started off as murmurs, then increased in intensity, a confetti of question marks, em dashes and exclamation marks clouding the air. Sentences ran into one another, bouncing off deaf ears, turning into squeals and gibberish, until every corner echoed, until it became the chaotic noise of a marketplace.

Mọremí was dressed in an ill-fitting black gown, a gift from Iya Ruka, who had decided that none of her other clothes were appropriate for the occasion. T-shirts and jeans weren't worn for mourning, and the few gowns she had were too brightly coloured. Iya Ruka had brought the gown in that morning, freshly sewn on her own machine. The gown hung down to Mọ́remí's toes, with no discernible waistline, although it bulged on one side and the short sleeves were tight around her armpits.

On Mọ́remí's feet were a pair of black Cortina shoes, which had been bought for her by her grandmother just before her death, the only things that got a nod of approval from her self-appointed wardrobe monitor.

Mọ́remí allowed Iya Ruka to drape her arm posses-sively around her shoulders as she was led deeper into the room. Murmurs of sympathy rose from the people already seated. They slowed down as each person came to either assure her that she could call on them at any time or simply pat her on the back. They told her in firm voices not to cry. Crying will not bring back the dead.

She nodded. She had no intention of crying. It was the visibility that bothered her. Her cloak of invisibility had been snatched off and she felt naked, vulnerable. Being ignored by her relatives was preferable to this obsequious performance of sympathy.

After a while, Mọ́remí got tired of standing in the middle of the room, a thing to be pitied. She detached herself from Iya Ruka and walked to the darkest part of the parlour, chose one of the chairs in a corner and squeezed herself into a tiny space. She pulled her cloak of invisibility around herself once again.

A flurry of neck craning ensued as Mọ́ríebá, a tall, dark-skinned woman with ample breasts and a neck draped in multiple gold chains, strode into the room. She was dressed in a long-sleeved shirt and trousers made out of Ankara. She wore her hair in a low cut. Her face was blank, eyes shining with fury.

'Anti Mọ́ríebá, you're back from London,' shouted one of the women who had hitherto been gossiping with her neighbour. She knelt down to greet Mọ́ríebá, who pulled her up.

'Why didn't you call me when Alhaja died? Why did I have to hear it from some busybody that lives on my street?' Mọ́ríebá's baritone bounced around the room. 'If you'd called me I would have gotten on the next flight out of London. I even missed the burial ceremony! I am particularly disappointed in you L'Ẹgbǎ, you have my London telephone number!'

'Don't be angry with me ma.' L'Ẹgbǎ hurried after Mọ́ríebá, who had made a beeline for Mọ́remí. 'I tried to call you on the number you left with me at NITEL several times, but the telephone kept saying that something was wrong with a thing called a trunk.'

Mọ́ríebá pulled Mọ́remí into a tight hug. Mọ́remí struggled for breath amid the heady perfume and enormous breasts. But she held on tightly to her great-aunt, a little flicker of hope snaking its way into her chest. Maybe things will be alright now that Anti Mọ́ríebá is here.

'We will talk later,' Mọ́ríebá whispered, and looked her in the eye, her first eye contact since her grandmother died. 'You'll be fine.'

Mọ́remí believed her.

As she turned to find a place to sit in the room, Mọ́ríebá nearly collided with Olórí Ẹbí, who was closely followed by two of his sons. Mọ́ríebá and Olórí Ẹbí ignored one another with an ease borne on the wings of long practice.

Olórí Ẹbí planted himself in front of Mọ́remí. 'Have you eaten this morning?'

'Yes sir. Thank you, sir,' she mumbled.

'Good girl.' His fatherly duties performed, Olórí Ẹbí strutted back to the front of the room, where a chair had been placed in readiness for him. His sons took up bodyguard positions on either side of the chair and glared at everybody. The family continued exchanging news about the wonderful things happening to their children, and vicious gossip about family members who were not in the meeting.

The room fell silent as Olórí Ẹbí rose to his full height. He was over six feet tall, with a girth to match. His tribal marks were deep and wide, running from the side of his head over both cheeks in the shape of Ls, just like the ones worn by his grandfather, who was also presiding over the room from his photograph. His triple chin trembled as he adjusted the abetí ajá perched jauntily on his head. So that his subjects (aka family members) would enjoy the full glory of the pink jacquard lace, he stretched out his arms and swept his agbádá gracefully back on his shoulders in the classic 'one thousand, five hundred naira' gesture mastered by all affluent Yoruba men from the womb.

Olórí Ẹbí was the only male child among his father's brood. He was also the last of the children born to the patriarch in his twilight years. This provided grist for the family rumour mill, as everyone knew that there was no way the old man could get it up, never mind impregnate a nubile young woman. Not one of them didn't believe that Olórí Ẹbí's real father was Saka, the young teacher who had been posted to the village school around the same time Olórí Ẹbí's father had married his mother. Alhaja

Àdùkẹ́ had fuelled the talk during her lifetime, when she refused to distribute the patriarch's wealth equitably after his death.

Olórí Ẹbí cleared his throat.

His subjects responded with long and loud sucking of their teeth, in perfect synchronisation.

He launched into a speech. 'We have all gathered here to execute a very painful duty. Death is a mean and vengeful master—'

He paused for effect. His inattentive audience took their cue and made sympathetic noises, hoping that would spur him to the point.

'It is the prayer of every parent that when they die their child will bury them, but it is not so in this case!' His voice rose. 'Alhaja has only one child and she is going around drinking cocaine! Drinking heroin! Having bastard children for unknown white men—'

Olórí Ẹbí was interrupted by a screech from the back of the room. Necks craned to see who was creating a scene. Scenes were good: they enlivened otherwise boring family meetings and provided fodder for gossip that could be milked for months and even years, if carefully managed.

'That is enough, Olórí Ẹbí! Please don't go there at all. It is only a dead man that knows those who will bury him!'

As soon as everybody identified the speaker they tried to keep their faces expressionless. Mọ́ríebá was not to be trifled with, at least not in her presence. She was a firebrand with a two-edged sword in place of a tongue, and was not afraid to use it.

She was one of Olórí Ẹbí's nieces. Her mother had died in childbirth, and she had spent her childhood being shunted from one family member to another. She had been, and still is, as far as most members of the family were concerned, a bloody nuisance! Always asking questions, always rocking the boat, always acting like a man! See how she's even dressed! Tueh!

It was Alhaja Àdùké who had saved her from being the prostitute they suspected she would have become, and took her in and set her up in a business. Up till a few years earlier, she had been just another struggling woman selling 'provisions' in one of the biggest markets in Ibadan. Suddenly she became the richest woman in the family, even richer than Alhaja Àdùké herself. And as was to be expected, rumours abounded: that Móríebá had used her womb for money-making rituals, that she was a drug dealer. The less vicious of the rumour-mongers offered that she got lucky when she got the sole distributorship of a new product that became an overnight success. Certain people believe it could well be a combination of the three.

'Who is the fool that dares interrupt when I'm talking?' Olórí Ẹbí barked. 'Anyway, we are here to take a decision about what to do with Móremí. Who will take Móremí home? We have searched up and down for Alhaja's will and the documents detailing her bank accounts and sundry, but we are yet to find them. Which means there isn't a lot of money available, but I promise to personally support whoever takes this girl in with money from my own pocket.'

Olórí Ẹbí's words hung in the air and for the first time since the meeting was convened, silence reigned. Nobody dared cough. He fidgeted with his necklace and cleared his throat, glanced at the doorway and continued, 'I would have taken her in by myself, but as you well know, I have healthy sons in my house, and I'd hate to cause temptation for my boys by putting a nubile, young—'

The words had barely left his lips when Mọ́ríebá jumped off her chair, her breasts threatening to burst out of the confines of her shirt. 'Ehn Ehn! Olórí Ẹbí! So you don't have any shame at all! How can you imagine that an eleven-year-old child will be tempting your boys? Something is really wrong with your brain. So, you see a temptress in a child of eleven! Will you let me have her then? At least I won't need any of your money to raise her.'

Olórí Ẹbí's face had become a mask of rage. 'Not if you are the last person on the face of the earth,' he growled. 'Rather than let a lousy and ill-brought-up girl like you raise Mọ́remí, I'd give her to a troop of monkeys!'

Mọ́ríebá sucked her teeth. 'How are we even sure you should be in charge of things sef? Where is Alhaja's will?' She turned her wrath on other family members, glaring at everyone in the room. 'And you're all going to sit down here and let this man bamboozle you with his jazz again! You're all going to keep quiet when he's obviously lying about the missing will. You will allow the fact that he's stuffed your mouth full of àkàrà sold for one kọ́bọ̀ to stop you from telling the truth!'

None of them met her eyes.

She raised her face heavenwards. 'Alhaja Àdùkẹ́, the spirit of a mother does not sleep after death, do not sleep! Come and take revenge on your enemies!'

The room trembled. Mọ́ríebá should know better than invoke the spirit of the freshly dead!

'A thousand dogs will eat that tongue of yours!' Olórí Ẹbí thundered. 'How dare you? Can you imagine this little child having the temerity to speak in the presence of her elders?'

His eyes were red, the veins on his neck stood out, his fists were bunched up. 'This is what happens when little girls have too much money: they become lippy. Who even invited you to this gathering?'

He stalked towards Móríebá. There were noises of chairs being moved out of his way, but he didn't see them. He was Moses, his anger the rod that parted the Red Sea. He loomed over her. 'Aren't you supposed to be out there with your mates playing with sand and wooden dolls?'

Móríebá sprang out of her seat, snatched L'Ẹgbǎ's scarf off her head and wrapped it around her waist. If it was war he wanted, she would give him one. She planted her feet apart, bracing herself like a sumo wrestler, held her arms akimbo, bounced on her toes, once, twice, and launched herself at Olórí Ẹbí. She had the tip of his parachute-like attire in her hands when strong arms restrained her and dragged her away from him.

He cleared his throat again and said calmly, 'If you are unmarried, a suspected or known harlot and childless, you are not allowed to take Mọremí home. It is only married and respectable people that can have her.'

He stared pointedly at Móríebá. Hisses and hostile murmurs met his announcement. Still nobody spoke up.

'I will take her,' ventured a man who had entered the room while the fracas between Móríebá and Olórí Ẹbí had been brewing.

Necks were stretched again to see the person who had spoken. It was Kasali, Olórí Ẹbí's second cousin. He worked at the Ministry of Transportation as a clerk, and was a well-respected man.

'Are you sure Kasali?' Olórí Ẹbí sounded as if he was reading from a particularly badly written script. 'What will you do with her? You and your wife have already trained all your children. Are you sure you want to start training this one too?'

'It is not me that will train her. Remember Tọ́lá, my last daughter, Dr Wálé's wife? Well, she just had another child ...'

'Eeh ẹ kú orííre o.' Voices congratulated him from around the room.

Mouths watered in anticipation of the feast that was sure to accompany this announcement. This was going to be one great month, two births and a death, food, alcohol and aṣọ-ẹbí galore. The women exchanged happy glances. Àríyá, the Óríṣà of great Yoruba parties, had sprinkled gold dust on the family.

'She needs two people to help her with simple household chores,' Kasali continued as the voices died down. 'I believe she and Mọremí will deal well together. You know her husband is a doctor.'

From Kasali's tone, it was obvious that being the wife of a doctor was a very important position. It was a thing of shame not to have at least one doctor, lawyer or engineer in the family, for such a lack suggested they were no better than savages. Even though Tọ́lá herself was viewed with a healthy dose of fear and suspicion, the fact that she had married a doctor, saving the Alágbàdo family from being considered uncivilised, more than made up for her shortcomings.

'Wait o!' Mọ́ríebá was out of her chair again. 'So, you want to take poor Mọremí to your bratty daughter's house. The one that had three children in the space of four years! You want to turn Àmọ̀pé's daughter into a slave because her mum is not around and her grandmother is dead! You human beings are wicked! If you want a slave for your daughter, Kasali, go and look elsewhere, because I'm taking this girl home with me!'

She pushed her chair out of the way and tried to reach out to Mọ́remí, who had flung off her cloak and jumped to her feet. But chairs and bodies mysteriously blocked Mọ́ríebà's path, while an old man grabbed Mọ́remí's arm in a steely grip, forcing her to sit down. For long minutes, Mọ́ríebá struggled, then stopped when it dawned on her that she would have to fight in order to take Mọ́remí out of that room. She smiled grimly.

'I've had it with you and your disrespect,' Olórí Ẹbí started in triumphant tones. 'Must you have an opinion about everything? For once in your life can't you just shut up?'

Yes, the room murmured, nodding in time to the beat of connivance and duplicity that Olórí Ẹbí was drumming.

'This is unacceptable behaviour and I will no longer stomach it! Little wonder no man has deigned to put you in his house. You are an unrepentant witch! Lékan! Kunle!' Olórí Ẹbí called his two sons who looked exactly like him, except where he had run to fat they were packed with muscles. 'Throw that woman out and don't let her back in here!'

The boys approached Mọ́ríebá as they would a spitting cobra. Mọ́ríebá stooped to pick her bag with unhurried grace, her body daring the boys to draw near her. She sashayed towards Olórí Ẹbí and stood in front of him, matching him foot for foot, her eyes trained on his. 'This is a long ass-series, Raufu, and this is just episode one of season one.' She moved closer to him and whispered, 'You will not finish watching it.'

Olórí Ẹbí smirked back.

As Mọ́ríebá exited the sitting room, the gathering burst into a round of applause – an overreaching woman had been put firmly back in her place.

... AND ANOTHER DEATH

The night had been accompanied by a heavy rain that had lulled the village to sleep with its savage drumming, paving the way for a sunshine-filled morning. While birds chirped busily at one another, the village square gradually filled up with communal goats, chickens, dogs and sundry domesticated animals, rumoured familiars of Alágbàdo's witches and warlocks.

A scream tore through the air, scattering the animals that had been up all night (if rumours are to be believed) into different parts of the square.

Less than thirty seconds after the first person ran helter-skelter into Mogaji Alágbàdo's compound, a crowd had gathered around Iya Kudirat. She was in the grip of a sadness so deep she left sympathisers bereft of words. She looked so tragic sitting on the floor of the passageway that most of the women joined their voices to hers in heart-rending wails.

The threads formerly wrapped around Iya Kudirat's hair in pretty cornrows were tangled together. Her blouse was torn and her wrapper askew. She pulled the body of Ìṣọ̀lá to her bosom. The boy's head lolled back, his eyes staring into the netherworld.

'Ìṣọ̀lá! Ìṣọ̀lá! Answer me Ìṣọ̀lá! Please Ìṣọ̀lá!' As she shook the boy's body, his head flopped against her chest. 'Just answer me. Don't do this to me Ìṣọ̀lá! Aaah!'

Some men tried to take the boy from her, but she held on tightly and growled at them.

'Leave her alone!' Kudirat ran at the men, headbutting one of them. She yanked at his trousers in an attempt to drag him off her mother. The man hit her with the back of his left hand without even a glance. She yelped, stepped back and stumbled on someone's outstretched legs.

'Get out of here,' the man barked at her.

One of the weeping women helped Kudirat to her feet. As Kudirat was being led out of the house, L'Ẹgbǎ ran into the passageway, screaming like someone whose body had been drenched in hot oil. She tore off her scarf, tied it around her abundant waist, threw herself on the floor and started thrashing about. Once again, L'Ẹgbǎ was in character as one who mourned louder than the bereaved. She was that peculiar relative who always showed up when there was an urgent need for wailing and gnashing of teeth.

'Orí mi ò! Aiyé! Aiyé mi ò! Orí mí ti burú o!' L'Ẹgbǎ wailed as she rolled on the floor.

Her arms were wrapped around the head that she claimed has been destroyed by misfortune. She jerked around so violently that other sympathisers quickly moved out of her way before she did somebody bodily harm.

Iya Kudirat's head jerked up, her eyes two chips of ice. She wiped the tears off her cheeks and dropped Ìṣọlá's lifeless body on the floor. Before anybody could react, she'd pounced on L'Ẹgbǎ and started pummelling her.

'Witch!' She smacked L'Ẹgbǎ across the face.

Whack!

'You've eaten all my children.'

'Whack! Whack!'

'When your poisoned womb can't produce boys, why won't you go and kill mine? Today is the day you will meet your maker! When you get to hell, you can have a reunion with your dead mother who gave you witchcraft to eat!'

The crowd of spectators were frozen, not only by the way Iya Kudirat had attacked her co-wife, but by the methodical way she went about beating her up. The calmness in her voice, the almost soothing cadence of her violence.

'Stop it, Iya Kudirat! Stop it now!' an authoritative voice rapped out. The voice snapped the crowd out of their inertia and they turned referees, scrambling to be the first to separate the women.

Iya Kudirat, by that time, had sunk her teeth into L'Ẹgbǎ's neck, aiming for the jugular. L'Ẹgbǎ sputtered and flailed. Screaming had not helped her.

Kudirat stood by the door leading out of the passage-way, arms akimbo. She shook her waist martially, nodded in satisfaction. 'That serves you right, witch. You have finished eating all my mother's children. Now it's time for you to be eaten!' She rained half-understood curses down on the woman from the safety of the doorway. 'Oloriburuku, Oloshi! You will never do well all the days of your life!'

A noise snagged Kudirat's attention. She looked over her shoulder and caught sight of her father headed towards the house, whip in hand, his dark face rendered even darker by a fierce scowl. His tribal marks stood out in relief against his cheeks. Sweat dripped off his face. He looked like the image of Satan that the new pastor had been trying to paint for the villagers since he arrived at Alágbàdo to establish his church.

The last time her father looked like that, he had nearly killed the man who stole his pregnant nanny goat. Kudirat knew that if she stepped out of the passageway it was likely she would be the first recipient of the whip, so she jumped through the closest window and peered over the windowsill.

She watched her father storm the passageway. She watched as he whipped her mother and L'Ẹgbá. She watched how people ran out of the house as speedily as they'd entered it.

Her eyes were still locked on her father as he dropped the whip, picked up her brother's dead body and sat on one of the benches placed against the wall. Her heart thudded against her chest. He only had to look up to spot her, but she couldn't take her eyes off the man she could no longer recognise.

He was holding the corpse of her brother to his chest, in a way he'd never held him when he had been alive, in a way he'd never held her: lovingly, tenderly. He buried his face in Ìṣọ̀lá's chest and wept. She sat on the ground and joined her silent tears to his.

In the days that followed her brother's death, Kudirat kept her chatter to herself. She slept on a mat that had suddenly become empty. There was nobody putting their legs on her, pinching her, waking her up in the middle of the night demanding water.

Ìṣọ̀lá's death had turned her mother into a shrivelled-up woman who refused to sleep or eat. Women of the village came into their home on silent feet. Whispers, sniffles and quiet sobs took the place of the cheery conversations and laughter that used to fill the house.

On the fifth day, the heaviness became too much for

Kudirat. She ventured out of the house and was soon deeply involved in the games played by the children who, like her, were on holidays. She and her friends had sat for their Common Entrance Exams the previous month, and all of them waited anxiously for the news that they could proceed to the new secondary school that the government had built next to their primary school.

Kudirat loved school, she loved reading. She'd read the few books she'd found in the school 'library' – a shelf full of worn books that she and a few others had read over and over until their covers had become tattered. She wanted to meet with the children having adventures on English moors, those blonde children on the cover of *Famous Five* books who seemed not to have any problems in the world except solving mysteries and eating gooseberry jam, scones and chocolates (whatever those were).

But her life was in this village, in a house that had become a shrine to her dead brother. She waited for what she knew not, a life-changing event she couldn't put a name to. Her anxieties peaked when she caught her father giving her furtive glances.

By the evening of the seventh day, when Kudirat was at the tip of screaming, her father summoned her into his room. He patted a space on his six-spring bed, indicating that she should sit beside him.

'Kudi-Owo,' he called her, his pet name for her.

She met his eyes, then dropped hers, remembering her mother's injunction never to look into the eyes of an adult. Things like that were pretty difficult for her. She mulled over her name as she studied her intertwined fingers. Kudi-Owo means 'bringer of wealth'. She did not think the name suited her because her parents did not have a lot of money. If they did, they would have bought that chocolate thing for her, and they would have taken Ìṣọ̀lá to the hospital in Ibadan when he had started convulsing.

'I know that sometimes you think I'm a bad father,' he continued. Kudirat resisted the urge to look into his eyes again. 'But all the discipline I give you is because I want you to grow up to be a strong woman. The kind of woman that will make a success of her married life and have healthy, well-behaved sons and daughters for her husband.'

He paused as Kudirat's head jerked up, all attempts at not staring at him thrown to the wind. Why is he talking about marriage and children? Her heart thudded loudly in her ears. She yearned for so many things she could not name, but marriage and children were definitely not on the list. She'd never even thought of herself in those terms. She wanted to do ... things.

Aren't I too young to be married gaan sef? She swallowed the question when she remembered Birikisu, one of her friends from primary school. The girl had been married off as soon as she sprang a pair of breasts in primary five. For nearly three months after Birikisu's wedding, Kudirat had tied a cloth around her chest, Ṣàngó forbid they start bouncing!

'I also want you to have a very good education,' he interjected into her thoughts. 'You know that these days whether you are a man or a woman, if you don't have an education your life will be miserable. Look at Ìyá Wálé, the village àmẹ̀bọ: her problem is a lack of education. If she had gone to school like your mother did, she would have learnt how to mind her own business.'

Kudirat's heartbeat slowed. He was still talking about education. Forgetting herself, she relaxed and informed her father that some of her teachers were gossips, and they were educated. What has education got to do with being a gossip? Either you were or you were not. Her words dried up as her father's face tightened.

'What I am trying to say is that I have found a very good opportunity for you to make something of yourself. If you allow your head to rest in one place, you might even marry a doctor.'

Baba Kudirat rose from his bed and shut the bedroom door, he threw open the windows in order to monitor passers-by.

Kudirat followed him around. 'Doctor, Bàámi that one is a good thing! Everybody will be looking at me with respect. Everybody will call me Dr Kudirat, just like Dr Wálé, Anti Tọ́lá's husband.'

Kudirat's imagination took wings. There it was! That thing she wanted so badly. This was the opportunity she had been waiting for, a chance to get out of this small village. She would finally prove to her father that she was better than ten boys put together! Maybe she'd find out why her brother had died, why so many children die. And if she played her cards right, she might even go to London and eat that chocolate thing and scones and gooseberry jam.

Her father sat on the lone chair in his room. Kudirat knelt beside him.

'But before you can get to the point where you can marry a doctor, you have to work really hard and go to a good school. That is why I want to send you to Lagos so that you can live with Tọ́lá and her doctor husband.'

Her father had barely finished talking when Kudirat leapt to her feet. What did it matter that her father thought she wanted to marry a doctor and not become one? She was going to live in LAGOS! The most beautiful place in the world! Lagos was filled with shiny things and shiny people. Everybody in Lagos was rich. They all drove big cars. Lagos was a tiny step away from London. She would become world-famous Dr Kudirat Alágbàdo! She danced a little jig.

That stupid Mulikat girl who had gone to spend one week in Ibadan during the last holiday had not allowed anybody to forget it. Every conversation was peppered with 'Ibadan this, Ibadan that', but she, Kudirat, was not going to stupid Ibadan, she was going to live in Lagos – the richest city in the whole world, except for London.

According to legends, the chickens in Lagos were as big as houses. All the houses in Lagos were tall, crafted from gold. There were a lot of bridges over the sea. She had seen pictures of the sea: it was big, bigger than the river that ran through her village. The books said so.

Another thought then occurred to her, damming her joy. 'Bàámi, what about Maami? Who will help her around the house when I'm gone? Won't she be sad?'

'Don't worry about your mother, Kudirat, I will handle her. Just go and pack your things. First thing tomorrow morning we will travel to Ibadan so that I can hand you over to Kasali, who will then take you to Lagos.'

Kudirat sighed and knelt again to thank her father. He placed a palm on her head.

'As you are travelling to Lagos, do not forget that you are my child. Morally upright, kind, submissive. You must never forget all the training we gave you.'

'Yes Bàámi.' Kudirat made her voice as humble as she knew how, even managing to lower her eyes. Then she jumped to her feet, ready to fling herself out the door, to announce the good news to the whole world.

'You are not to tell anybody about this.' His voice stopped her. 'Let them find out after you are gone. It's only the things done in secrecy that have any value.'

Later that evening, Kudirat was passing by her mother's room when she heard her parents talking in low tones. Her mother sounded like she'd been crying. Kudirat paused and put her ear against the wooden door.

'It is for our safety,' she heard Baba Kudirat say. 'Didn't the pastor tell us she is a powerful Emèrè, that she's the one that blocked your womb? Remember he told us to remove her from our house or something calamitous would happen? Well, Ìṣọ̀lá is dead. Do you want to spend the rest of your life as the woman who bore only one child, a female one for that matter! Let her go, Àbẹ̀ní, let Kudirat go.'

'But nobody in my lineage has ever been a slave to another.' Kudirat's mother sounded outraged. It was the first time in days that Kudirat had heard her mother's voice clearly. She moved even closer to the door. 'You are saying I should send my daughter off to Lagos as a housegirl. No, Baba Kudi, never!'

'Have you forgotten that she would be sent to school? Tọ́lá is a nice girl. She will never treat your child badly.' Baba Kudirat's tone changed. 'If you refuse to send her, both of you can move back to your father's house so that I can marry another wife.'

Kudirat strained her ears but heard only the whisper of silence.

SEASON TWO:
INTERESTING TIMES
[2005–2007]

CHIEF WHO IS CHIEF...

Olórí Ẹbí's face was inscrutable as he watched man and woman grovel before him. While they were telling him how magnanimous he was, he was thinking about the fickleness of human beings, their disloyalty.

He knew the couple too well. They were exactly like the others who had gone before them, men and women who had been in that same position at one point or another, begging, singing his praises, but that was where it ended. They knew nothing about loyalty. They were pigeons who would eat with you, drink with you and, as a matter of course, shit on you and then take off in times of trouble.

'Olórí Ẹbí, if you give us this loan, I promise to refund it to you as soon as the shipment of my goods lands.' The man's eyes were trained on his, as if that would work. 'You know I've never asked anything of you before. But this is the only opportunity my son has to read law at the University of Ibadan. He is a very brilliant boy and we need this fifty thousand naira to pay his registration fees and buy him a few things.'

Olórí Ẹbí also knew the boy in question, and he was far from brilliant. Since he had started primary school, the boy had been notorious for repeating each class twice, and how he had managed to pass his school certificate (and so well!) baffled everyone. In fact, Olórí Ẹbí and Kasali had a bet riding on the boy – that he would be expelled before finishing his secondary school education – but since Elédùwà has decreed that wonders should never cease in the land of the living ...

'Tobi is a very good boy, I know he will never forget you if you do this for him, my in-law,' said the kneeling woman.

Her voice grated on Olórí Ẹbí's back teeth. He looked her fully in the face, and slowly hardened his eyes. The woman swallowed, shifted from one knee to another and finally dropped her eyes.

'Àdèlé.' Each syllable of the man's name dropped like boulders off Olórí Ẹbí's lips. 'If you were a woman, I'm sure you would be named "Ruth of Moab". I am surprised that a man of your stature would come to my house to beg for money and still be shameless enough to carry his wife with him.'

He watched emotions chase themselves over Àdèlé's face, from embarrassment to anger, a struggle that went on before the mask of politeness was pulled back.

'I am sorry for bringing my wife along with me.' Àdèlé turned to his wife. 'Mama Tobi, I think you should leave.' The woman rose off her knees without a word, her body stiff.

'Don't worry about that: it's already too late.' Olórí Ẹbí waved a dismissive hand. 'It is men like you, who have no secrets from your wives and go around showing your lack of manliness that have given women the power to be talking back to other men. Anyway, how you run your household is none of my business. What is it to me if your wife wears the trousers?'

Àdèlé shrivelled up at the insult. His wife remained suspended in motion, tears gathering in her eyes, though Olórí Ẹbí noted from underneath his bushy eyebrows that they did not flow down her cheeks. Olórí Ẹbí grunted in disgust.

'I will consider giving you the loan, but as you both know, things are not as rosy in the country as they used to be and the farmland has not been yielding as much ... but I will see what I can do for you. Send the boy to me tomorrow.' He waved them off, a pair of pesky flies.

Olórí Ẹbí knew that he would give them the loan. It was his role, his duty. He was the head of the family, the provider. The money would become what tens of other loans he'd made to other members of his family had become: a bad debt, never to be paid back, never to be asked for.

Sometimes he resented the yoke of leadership the Óríṣà placed on his shoulder, but he would bear it. His ancestors had not gone around whining about family responsibilities. They had performed their duties without a second thought. He would prove to the Alágbàdo family that he was a worthy son. Let them bring all their problems. He would solve every single one!

'Thank you sir, he will be here tomorrow,' a subdued Àdèlé answered as he rose from his supine position.

Olórí Ẹbí dropped his head to his chest in pretend slumber and watched the couple troop out of the sitting room. He knew the two were going to start quarrelling as soon as they got home, and that was enough. He chuckled. As soon as they shut the door behind them, he lifted his head off his chest and sighed deeply.

What short memories people have! So Àdèlé can come to me for money!

Àdèlé's father was Olórí Ẹbí's uncle (may Allah rest his soul), his father's immediate younger brother. The one who Olórí Ẹbí had run to when he could no longer bear living in the village. In those days motor transportation had been scarce and expensive. Olórí Ẹbí remembered the hard trek from Alágbàdo to the man's house in Ibadan, his only companion the small bagful of boiled corn he had had the foresight to steal from one of his stepmothers.

Àdèlé's father had not even offered Olórí Ẹbí a cup of water. He did not ask how he had made it to Ibadan. He had disregarded the fact that it was already after 6pm and ordered him back home. That evening, a tired and hungry Olórí Ẹbí had spent his first night in a motor park, the first of many, swearing revenge on everybody who had brought him to that point.

Olórí Ẹbí looked up as the door to the sitting room was thrown open. Kasali bounced into the room in his usual ebullient fashion and started dancing as soon as his eyes lit on him. Olórí Ẹbí smiled genuinely for the first time on that hellish Saturday morning. It had been one dreary meeting after another, mostly members of the extended family coming with their insatiable demands: My wife is in the hospital. I need a job. My family has not eaten in two days. My children's school fees ...

Not a single one of them had asked after his own

pocket. About how he made the money he doled out to them. About how his immediate family were doing. It was all about them.

Kasali was the only person who cared, the one man he could rely on. Kasali had never asked anything of him but friendship. He reminded Olórí Ẹbí of his first and only dog, Bingo. That animal had been loyal to him. Kasali worshipped him, paid attention to every word that fell from his lips as if he was an oracle.

'Congratulations on executing such a great and wonderful family meeting, Olórí Ẹbí.'

'The success belongs to both of us. That Mọríebá girl nearly ruined everything.' Olórí Ẹbí was magnanimous in victory.

'Ah, but you put her in her place, Olórí Ẹbí, right where she belongs,' Kasali beamed.

'So, when are you taking that child to Lagos?' Olórí Ẹbí asked as soon as Kasali made himself comfortable on the chair next to his. 'Doesn't your daughter need help again?'

Kasali looked uncomfortable.

Olórí Ẹbí's heart went out to him. 'How's Tọlá now? Don't you think we need to take her to see Bàbá Lálúpọn?'

'It's not me,' Kasali frowned. 'It's that husband of hers.' He sighed dramatically. 'He wouldn't even listen when I suggested that we should take her to see Bàbá Lálúpọn. He said he's a doctor and a born-again Christian, that Jesus will take care of everything.'

'Is that why you have not come to pick up Mọremí?'

'Actually no.' Kasali was studying his interlocked fingers with the concentration of someone who would be interrogated on their length and width in a short while. 'Tọlá is much better now, in fact her mother has returned home. It's just that I think it's a good idea if I can find someone else to go along with her.'

Kasili brightened up and looked at Olórí Ẹbí. 'I've been able to talk Bàbá Kudirat into giving me his daughter. She's presently at my place.' His face fell again. 'It's that son-in-law of mine. He said the timing has to be right, that he doesn't want me to just be bringing people to his house. He said Tọ́lá needs to be a little more stable.'

Olórí Ẹbí moved to the edge of his seat; he nodded and made sympathetic noises. He sent a basketful of thanks to Elédùwà, who had blessed him with sons. He couldn't imagine how it felt having a child that might strip herself naked at any point and take to the marketplace. Watching the dance of a madman in the marketplace is fun, except when the man is one's child.

'It's not that I'm pressurising you, but I want Mọ́remí out of Ibadan as soon as possible.' He tried to get the urgency of the situation across to Kasali by gripping his arm. 'I've been told that Mọ́ríebá woman visits the girl every day. I don't want her to influence the child with her wickedness or kidnap her. Please do this for me and you'll be adequately compensated.'

'Haba Olórí Ẹbí.' Kasali pried his fingers off his arm. 'I'm not expecting anything from you – after all, you're doing me a favour. Don't worry, I will take care of it. By the end of this week, the girl should be in Lagos.'

Olórí Ẹbí stared at him a tad longer and suddenly flashed him a smile. 'Quadri!' he yelled, pulling the door open. 'Quadri!'

'Bàámi!' Quadri yelled in reply.

A thin glasses-wearing boy of about fourteen entered the room, an open book in his hands.

'Silly boy! Ọ́yá put down that book. Go and bring me the half-bottle of Schnapps from my wardrobe.' Olórí Ẹbí handed Quadri the keys to his room.

'Yes sir.' Quadri placed his book on the glass-topped table and made to exit the room.

'Don't break it o! And don't drink out of it, I know the exact amount of Schnapps in the bottle.'

'Yes Bàámi.' Quadri closed the door quietly behind him.

'You and these your sons,' Kasali, who had been delighted by the performance, laughed.

'Don't mind them, all of them are drunkards.' Olórí Ẹbí sounded more proud than annoyed. 'Any time they lay their hands on my drinks they just finish it. One of them has been sneaking into my room, drinking my spirits and refilling the bottles with water. The day I catch the culprit ehn?'

I'M A VERY GOOD GIRL ... FATHER

Tọ́lá dragged herself out of bed, a chore as tasking as preparing Jésùtitófúnmi and Jésùwálayé for school. As exhausting as cooking. Breathing itself was a chore.

Her formerly slim body had thickened in the months that followed Jésùlayomi's birth. Her breasts drooped heavily, her arms floated on the mass of fat that had accumulated underneath her armpits, her waistline was thicker than it had been when she had been pregnant. Her face was puffy and mottled with eczema and pimples.

Sloth, wanton, slut.

Traces of the beauty she had been at seventeen, when she was a spanking new-bride, could be found in her thick lashes, her dark eyes, the tiny nose that sat between her high cheekbones.

Slattern, sluggard.

She had doubled in person, in personality. Tọlá had swallowed and birthed Rita and it showed in the stretch marks that mapped suffering on her stomach, arm and hips. She drew open the blinds, and the sight of the rutted road and filthy masses that passed along it like an army of ants met her eyes. All those dirty, desperate-looking people, always needy, demanding shit she did not have from her with their eyes. They filled her with dread.

She shut her eyes against the image and took a deep breath. The stench of an open sewer filled her nostrils. She stepped back and closed the blinds.

As she turned away from the window, the baby started screaming. She let out an exasperated breath; he had been screaming all day. She tuned out the racket. It baffled her that people have six or seven of them when she knew for a fact that she had three children too many.

All those people who go on about how beautiful babies were, their wonderful smell and so on and so forth should have their heads examined. Here she was praying for a few minutes of soul-saving solitude before visitors came banging on her door, and there he was screaming as if somebody had lit a fire under him.

He's been fed, diapered and watered, what else does he want from me?

His screams pierced through. She tried to focus on other things, but it seemed that the harder she tried, the louder he cried.

Smashing his head against a wall will be highly satisfying.

She ran into the room and stuck a pacifier in his

mouth. Slipped into the toilet and fetched her stash of cigarettes from the tank. She lit the first one and drew the smoke inside her lungs. That first inhalation always hit the right spot. She welcomed the lightheadedness that accompanied the smoke as it filled her. She closed the toilet lid and sat on it. Her shoulders drooped as she took another drag.

Tọ́lá wondered why people placed such ridiculous demands on her. They wanted her to marry, to have children, to be a slave, a lover, a good friend. To be supportive, to love her children unconditionally. She was supposed to be gracious, to be happy all the time.

She flicked cigarette ash on the tiled floor, took another drag and rested her head on the toilet tank. She wanted to be all those things so badly. She wanted to feel, to love her children. She wanted to genuinely experience that rush of love she had witnessed on people's faces when they looked at their children. She had prodded and poked her insides, but there was nothing but despair inside her. A deep darkness, hunger for something she had no words for.

How was she supposed to give what she does not have? Why did people insist on having children? Weren't there enough people on the miserable face of the earth to share the darkness?

The emptiness gnawed at her heart and she wanted to bawl her head off, to join her baby in crying at the unfairness of it all.

All I've ever asked for is freedom.

For a heartbeat she considered sliding to the floor of the bathroom, curling up in despair and moaning till she felt better.

'Abeg stop am!' Rita, her guardian demon, materi-
alised. 'Wetin dey do this one? Wanting to cry, wanting to
love … nyeh, nyeh, nyeh,' she whined in a high falsetto.
'Who needs love? Dem dey carry am go market? Abeg light
another cigarette – you go dey alright.'

Tọlá lit up as she stared at Rita. She had stopped
wondering why Rita had no features.

'Ehn ehn, see how your bodi come chillax. Make I
come list the things I no understand, since this world is
such a confusing place. I don't understand why you have
three children, when you're obviously the worst mother in
the world. I don't understand why you take all the bullshit
that idiot you call a husband—'

'That's enough!' Tọlá jumped up, took a last drag of her
cigarette and dropped the stub in the toilet. She sprayed
the room generously with a lavender air freshener and
opened the windows to let the smoke out. She brushed
past a giggling Rita into the children's bedroom, grabbed
the baby and looked into his eyes.

He cooed at her.

He is such a happy child, poor ignorant thing.

'Just you wait,' Tọlá whispered. 'Wait for the world to
snatch your innocence—'

She swallowed the rest of her tirade. *I won't be that kind
of mother. It stops with me.*

She examined him thoroughly, as she'd done a hundred
times before, as she'd examined her other children when
they were babies. He was the picture of health, with shiny
eyes and chubby cheeks. Her father said he looked like
her. She sincerely hoped that was not the case. The baby
smiled at her toothlessly and she allowed him to curl his
little fingers around her index finger. She smiled back

at him and waited, no, yearned, for that rush of tender feelings. But nothing happened.

She hurriedly fed him and changed his diaper. She patted his back gently until he gave a loud burp and she smiled ... smelly little thing.

She jumped as the bell rang.

'Who is it?' Her fingers nervously flittered to her uncombed hair. She rushed to her room and pulled a comb through it while changing into a clean gown.

'It is us,' her father responded from the other side of the door.

'I'm coming.' She picked the baby up and then took her sweet time opening the door.

Her father was there with his ever-present pleasant smile. His name suited him perfectly: Kasali Alágbàdo, Kasali the corn seller. A man of average height, he wore his potbelly comfortably on his stocky frame. His eyes flashed merrily. Tọ́lá wondered how many shots of schnapps had gone into making him that happy.

Two girls cowered behind him. She forced a smile for her father and opened the door wider to let them in.

'Ẹ káàbọ̀ Bààmi.' She sketched a kneeling to him as the three trooped into the sitting room. Her eyes widened as she took a closer look at the girls. *They are so young, too young to be placed in my care.*

One of them was short, dark and slight. Everything about her was dainty. Her face was oval, her nose tiny and pointed, her mouth wide and smiley. Her eyes danced with mischief. She reminded Tọ́lá of herself about that age – the only difference was that the girl looked happy. She couldn't remember the last time she'd been that happy.

The girl who stood beside her was tall and rangy, with disproportionately long arms and legs that put Tọ́lá in mind of stick insects. Her hair was a full mess of thick curls shot through with red highlights. Her mouth held a pair of full lips that looked as if they pouted a lot. She stared at Tọ́lá through a pair of wary green eyes, the other feature, besides her creamy skin, which gave her away as biracial. The girls carried their worldly goods inside black polythene bags.

'You must be Baba Mogaji's daughter, Kudirat.' She put as much warmth as she could into the smile. 'And you,' she said, as she took Mọ́remí's limp hand in hers, 'are Anti Àmọ̀pé's daughter, Mọ́remí. I am pleased to meet both of you. I hope we will all be happy living together.'

'Yes ma,' Kudirat said eagerly.

Mọ́remí grunted something Tọ́lá couldn't catch.

'Please do sit down. I made some lunch because I knew you would be hungry by the time you get here.'

Her father made himself comfortable on one of the chairs. Kudirat made to take the baby from her.

'No, it's alright, you guys are tired, you will have more than enough time to carry him.' She turned a chilly smile on her father, who had started pontificating about the names Nigerians gave their children.

'Can you imagine naming a child Mọ́remí? You just stick the poor girl with a name that will stand out and probably embarrass her for the rest of her life. As if her white skin is not bad enough. What happened to solid names like Adéọlá, Àmọ̀pé, Fèyísará, Ìṣọ̀lá and co? Some people don't even know what to name their children these days.'

He grabbed the baby from her and tickled him.

Bàámi was not one for seeking consent.

The baby giggled, and her father threw him in the air, catching and tossing him again and again. Tọ́lá felt apprehensive, the root cause of which she refused to examine.

'See me complaining to somebody who named her children Jésùtitófúnmi, Jésùwálayé and Jésùlayomi.' Her father gave her a sly look.

'Haba Daddy, you know I did not name the children by myself.' She sat next to him, her eyes eagle sharp. 'Left to me I will call them by the nice solid names you gave them – Tọ́pẹ́, Àṣàkẹ́ and Fẹ́mi. But I am a woman, what rights do I have?'

'All these Kiriyo people just give names to children without checking if it will suit the head of the child it is being given to,' her father continued, enjoying his audience.

She switched her attention to the girls who were still cowering near the doorway. 'Let me show you girls to your room and then we will have lunch.' She grabbed the baby out of her father's arms. 'After Daddy leaves, I will show you around. My husband has arranged for a nice school for you around the corner, you will start on Monday.'

She showed them a room off the kitchen. The room was small but she had put in shelves and hangers for their clothes, a carpet and a fan.

The mattress was on the floor, covered by a blue bedsheet, with a pink duvet folded on top. She remembered how lost and lonely she had felt when Wálé brought her to Lagos. She did not want the girls to experience that pain. That was why she'd gone out of her way to make their room as comfortable as possible.

She studied them closely. Kudirat was obviously pleased but Mọ́remí was shuttered, her eyes darting from one end of the room to the other. Tọ́lá could almost spot the curling of the tips of her lips.

She'd heard a lot about Mọ́remí, how spoilt and surly she was, and it appeared the reports were true. She remembered her mother referring to Mọ́remí as emèrè, a wood spirit who'd been sent to the world to torture the Alágbàdo family by Karishika, queen of the underworld. Tọ́lá was determined to like the girl. Anybody whom her mother disproved of must be an interesting person.

They moved to the kitchen and she showed them where the plates and cutlery were. She started dishing the food.

Kudirat broke the silence. 'I like your house.'

'Thank you, Kudirat.' Tọ́lá was genuinely surprised at the compliment. She tried to look at her house through Kudirat's eyes, but all she could see was the puke orange and green that had been used to paint it inside out. Wálé had chosen the colours, specifically, she suspected, to annoy her.

Her mother had also told her about Kudirat, whose only failing appeared to be that she was raised in a bush village that couldn't even boast of a major road. Her mother had described the girl in terms of a workhorse. She'd been advised to keep her husband and all her things away from the girls when they eventually arrived because all house-maids were stealers of 'worldy goods' and spouses.

I wish someone would steal Wálé from me.

They settled down at the dining table and devoured the food.

Tọ́lá's father belched and scratched his crotch. Tọ́lá hoped her disgust did not show on her face.

… here we fucking go!

'So, children, this is your new home. You must promise to make your aunty very happy.' He rose from the dining table and stretched. 'I don't want to hear of any bad thing happening between you and her. Tọ́lá is a very good girl and has never given us any trouble. That is why I know both of you will be happy here.'

Yes, I'm a very good girl, father.

Tọ́lá had reconciled herself to the condescending manner in which her father spoke to her. A dumb woman who has never done anything with her life. She was as delicate, and as useful, as a rose bush in the middle of a cassava farm.

'Girls, please clear this place and wash everything in the kitchen sink,' she said, rising from the dining table. It was time to dismiss Kasali Alágbàdo.

'Tọ́lá, I know I don't have to lecture you about how to treat the girls.'

But you will, won't you?

'You have to hold them with a firm hand. But be kind, and feed them regularly.'

I don't need to water them too?

'You know how children can be a handful. You just have to call me anytime they start acting up.'

Tọ́lá stared at him, deadpan, as he went on and on.

'I have to leave now for a meeting in Ibadan. I promise to drop in once in a while to keep an eye on all of you.'

Oh yes, we need eyes kept on us since we can't take care of ourselves.

When Tọ́lá still did not say anything, he changed the subject. 'So, how's your husband? I spoke to him on the telephone before we embarked on our journey.'

'He's fine.' Tọ́lá threw the baby over her shoulder. She

had no intention of discussing Wálé with him. He never listened anyway. 'Give me a minute.'

She went to her bedroom and picked the envelope full of five hundred naira notes Wálé had told her to give to her father that morning. It amused Tọ́lá that everybody assumed that, because her husband was a doctor, they had a lot of money. Nobody knew about her husband's cocaine habit or that they were living on the edge of bankruptcy. But she had learnt how to take care of herself. Rita had taught her how to siphon money from their joint account. She had opened another account in her own name and kept money there.

'No take too much o! Small-small, a ten thousand naira here and there per week. You see that time we he go drink so tey, e go don roll inside gutter, increase am to twenty thousand every day until him eye clear.'

She returned to the sitting room and handed the envelope to her father. Her father's eyes lit up as he pulled out its contents and started counting. Then his face fell.

'I thought he was going to leave me more than this.'

She could almost touch his disappointment. She wore her best impression of surprise and dismay as she took the envelope back from him, pretending to count the money. 'I'm sorry, sir, but that's all he gave to me.'

'Do you have anything for your mother?' he asked hesitantly.

She turned a glassy-eyed stare towards him and lifted a hand towards her temple.

'I'm sorry ...' Kasali backed away from her.

Her mother had left the house over two months ago, and Tọ́lá had refused to speak to her since. Even Kẹ́mi had given up on pleading with her to forgive their mother.

'Now that we have the girls here our expenses will increase,' Tọ́lá said, as if her father had not just ruined an already ruined day.

A perfect day. No noise, no children, no husband, just me and my pillows and a good novel ... every fucking day is ruined already!

'I have told you that you needn't spend too much on them,' he said. 'Simply register them in a government secondary school. They don't need to pay school fees.'

'But there's no more free education, and we need to buy their school uniforms and textbooks,' she said.

'Textbooks ke? You don't have to waste money on that one. Buy them the basics: English and Maths. They can borrow the rest from their classmates.'

She returned the envelope, turned abruptly and made for the door.

'I thought Olóri Ẹbí would have sent the money for Mọ́remí's upkeep to Wálé's account,' Kasali said, not budging from his position in the centre of the sitting room.

Tọ́lá turned towards him, hand on the doorknob. 'We just paid our house rent, you know how expensive that is, and that's beside the fact that our children are also in school. Everything is expensive in Lagos.' The crestfallen look on his face made her soften her voice. 'Things are not as easy as they look, Bàámi.'

She made a mental note to withdraw some more money from the joint account before Wálé blew it.

'It's alright. What about you? Don't you have anything for me?' He flicked his tongue over his lips, the way a snake would dart its tongue out to taste the air.

'Bàámi!' Tọ́lá's laughter rang false, even to her ears. 'You know I don't have a job.'

'But that has not stopped you from giving me something in the past,' he whined. Flick, flick, his tongue went again.

'Like I said earlier, things are much tighter now.' Tọ́lá walked casually towards him. 'We are just managing.' She reached out for his hand and gently, but firmly, dragged him through the door. 'Don't worry. Once I have something I will send it to your account.'

She pulled the door shut and ushered him down the flight of stairs, hand firmly planted on the small of his back. When they got to the road, she hailed a taxi. As she waved him off, the tight knots in her stomach loosened.

DỌ̀KÍ OLÓYÈ

It was a beautiful Saturday morning in Lagos. The sky was a bright orange. The sun shone merrily overhead, covering everything it touched with its warm, golden fingers. But all its warmth and shine did nothing for Mọ́remí as she washed soap suds out of another child's garment. Did it belong to Jésùtitófúnmi, Jésùwálayé or Jésùlayomi? Mọ́remí could not have cared less.

The darkness in her heart rivalled the sun. Helplessness, frustration, tiredness and a sadness she had been unable to shake off since her first arrival in Lagos. Every muscle on her face pulled tightly into a frown. Today made it two years since she had discovered her grandmother's stiff body in her bed. Two years since she became a drudge. Alone, abandoned, unloved. Two years of learning to take care of herself, learning to live by her wits.

She wasn't allowed to celebrate this milestone by curling up in bed, a blanket drawn over her head, to wallow in self-pity and mourn all she had lost. Instead she was seated in front of a mound of dirty clothes.

Scrubbing, scrubbing, scrubbing.

She scrubbed every morning: clothes, floors, walls, shoes. No breathing space, no leisure, no breaks. Her free moments continually interrupted by children nearly her age needing to be cleaned, to be comforted, to be fed, children who needed her attention because they couldn't get it from their parents.

I'm a child too! I'm just a child!

Her once soft and pink palms had hardened into pads, the wrinkled backs of her hands testament to her drudgery. Tears threatened at every turn, a cascade that would easily fill up the fabled fountain of tears located at the point where the earth met the heavens. She embraced the coldness within and hardened up her heart.

She used to cry before. Every night she would rock and rock on the bed, crying for the girl she used to be, the home she'd lost, her absent mother, for a former life in which she had been the pampered grandchild of an indulgent woman. She would cry until Kudirat wrapped her in a tight embrace. Kudirat's breath warm against her neck, whispering strengthening words. *We'll be fine, nothing lasts forever, we will survive this.*

'You're still here, Miss Slowcoach.'

Kudirat sauntered over to her. She was carrying two buckets full of washed clothes. She took a look at Mọremí's face and immediately dropped them.

'Here, let me finish doing this for you.' She sat down beside Mọremí on the bench and tried to push her aside.

'It's alright, Kudirat, I'm nearly done washing them.' Mọremí's voice came out husky.

Kudirat looked at the mountain of dirty clothes and then, seeing the pout on Mọ́remí's lips, she shrugged and rose from the bench. She walked the short distance to the lines and started hanging out the clothes to dry.

Mọ́remí concentrated on a dark green spot and scrubbed it. In the early days, when she still had hope that something could happen, whenever she was washing or scrubbing her fingers would turn red and then bleed. Kudirat would bring out her precious package of shea butter and rub it on them.

As she'd lost her hopes, her hands had lost their tenderness. Her muscles, which used to ache every night, had toughened.

Mọ́ríebá usually visited her anytime she was in Lagos, the last link to the life Mọ́remí used to know. She would bring a pile of books, chocolates, clothes and money for her. She would bring laughter and good memories of her grandmother.

The first time Mọ́ríebá came to the house, Mọ́remí's heart had nearly flown out of her chest. She had thought she would be rescued from Lagos, that Mọ́ríebá was her fairy godmother. But her aunt had shaken her head as they descended the staircase.

'I'm so sorry, Mọ́remí, I don't want Olórí Ẹbí's wahala,' she said, avoiding Mọ́remí's eyes. 'It's good that you're living with a family, every child needs the steadiness of a family with a male figure. You know I'm single and I don't plan to marry any time soon. I'm so sorry.'

Mọ́ríebá had looked at Mọ́remí then, and her eyes were full of words her lips were not speaking. She cleared her throat and continued in a firmer tone. 'But if you're being maltreated, just call me.'

The question was what constituted maltreatment – was it not being allowed to sit on the chairs? Or sing or watch TV? Was it the invasion of her privacy, when a drunken Wálé would burst into her room just after she'd taken her bath? Or when Wálé took the gifts her aunt brought for her?

Was maltreatment when Wálé insisted that she scrubbed the kitchen floor, the bathroom and the toilet every morning? On her knees, the scrubbing brush held at ninety degrees, the muscles in her arms contracting painfully from the pressure, because it must be clean! A speck of dust found on the floor meant she had to do it all over again.

How could you put all these into words without sounding like a brat? Wasn't this what other girls in her position did every day of their lives without complaining?

Tọ́lá was, of course, an angel. She was the one who returned your gifts to you on the sly, who spoke to you like a human being. She would, on her good days, laugh with you, talk about the books you'd shared. She would tell you not to scrub the floor anytime Wálé was on call, make you special meals. But Tọ́lá also came with her burden of secrets.

I should be used to secrets by now. Mother taught me about keeping secrets. I'm a secret keeper.

Mọ́remí hardly ever permitted herself to think about those days, her Peckham days as she called them. She locked them away in a dark corner of her heart. The same way she helped Tọ́lá ... no, Rita ... lock away her clothes and shoes and that penis-shaped rubber thing. But since she'd started living in Lagos, her Peckham days would no longer be denied. They took over the good memories of the years she spent with her grandmother.

Peckham was dirt, it was hunger. Peckham was mummy dearest telling her to hide in the wardrobe anytime someone came to the door, to keep quiet and listen to the creak-creak of the bed. It was wearing extra layers of clothes underneath her own clothes, inside the dressing room of big department stores. It was mummy dearest dropping bars of chocolate, necklaces and wristwatches in her pocket, her heart beating like a drum as mummy dearest told her to wear her prettiest smile for the uniformed man at the door so he wouldn't search her pockets. It was the day she was arrested, taken into a room and shown a video of herself, mummy dearest sniffling into her sleeves. Being taken away and having to live with a bunch of other children and a strange white woman, who looked at her with eyes full of pity.

For a heartbeat she thought she would choke on air, die from breathing.

She threw the cloth she was washing on the ground and stomped on it, tore at it. When she heard a ripping sound, something in her lightened. So she took another one and ripped it in two, and then another one ...

She could breathe better by the time she heard the snap of buttons popping off a shirt. She looked at the work her hands had wrought, a small heap of torn clothes on the ground. She nearly felt guilty.

'Hey slowcoach!' Kudirat was back. 'Nice work.' She nodded at the pile of torn clothes.

'It's "slowpoke", not "slowcoach",' Mọremí snapped.

'Whatever. Grammar no be my language.' Kudirat dragged a low stool in front of Mọremí and started rinsing out the clothes in a huge plastic bowl. 'I wonder why Tọlá didn't allow you to go for your grandmother's remembrance ceremony.' She squeezed out soapsuds from a torn gown.

'I didn't want to go,' Mọremí muttered. She hated it when Kudirat tried to draw her out. Somehow the girl thought she could make things better by saying a lot of rubbish and sounding all-knowing.

'Liar! You so wanted to go.'

'No, seriously, I didn't.' Mọremí turned cat-green eyes on her. 'Olórí Ẹbí said they are only frying àkàrà and there is no point in me coming.'

'But if Anti Mọ́ríebá had been around, I bet she would have insisted that you should be there even if they're only distributing cups of water.'

Mọremí shrugged and continued scrubbing. Within a few minutes the girls were spreading out the last of the clothes, both whole and torn, on the lines.

'Good morning, your royal majesties.'

The girls froze.

Wálé walked towards them, jangling his car keys. Dòkí olóyè, the chief doctor, was the name Kudirat had given him in their early days.

Wálé was a man of average height, who would have been considered handsome if not for his perpetually red, rat-like eyes and the bags underneath them. His fair skin was as smooth as a baby's bottom, testament to the fact that hard living had nothing to do with skin condition. His expression was lofty: he knew everything, and he knew it. His lips were thin and cruel, often twisted into a sneer. He had started nurturing a potbelly that made him look like a malnourished, pregnant goat.

dòkí olóyè the donkey, because of his sticky fingers that wandered all over your body. His perpetually hard cock, that he would find ways of rubbing against you, particularly when he was 'punishing' you.

Mọ́remí grunted in disgust when she remembered the day he had cornered her in the short passageway that linked the master bedroom with the children's room. He'd stepped out of the bathroom directly into her path, and without a word he'd grabbed her hand and forced it towards his cock. 'Rub it,' he'd growled into her ear.

She had stubbornly refused to. What stupidity is that? Rub what? A silent struggle had ensued, with Wálé trying to force her hand towards his cock, and Mọ́remí resisting with all her might.

She'd been saved by Kudirat, who had burst onto the scene and inserted herself between them, shouting for the neighbours at the top of her lungs.

Of course they'd been punished for it.

After that day, Mọ́remí had started carrying a sharp knife around with her. She swore to use it on him if he so much as smiled at her again.

'So, this is what you do instead of doing your chores?'

The girls stared at the ground and genuflected to him.

'Good moring sah.' The girls spoke in the worst English they could muster, because he hated it when they spoke good English to him, answering them with a mocking laughter and a 'What do we have here? The Queen of England herself.' He would tear their words apart, pointing out each grammatical error.

Wálé took pleasure in humiliating them. He would deny them meals or force them to eat leftovers when he felt offended. He would mock Kudirat's Alágbàdo accent, whereby she replaced 'ch' with 'sh'. Kudirat had worked hard to get rid of the accent, but still slipped into it whenever she was upset.

'Will you get out of this place?' he yelled at the girls as they scrambled to clear the buckets and sundry things they'd been using for their laundry. He stalked off towards the staircase that led to the flat. 'I want breakfast and I want it now!'

Mọ́remí made to rush after him but was held back by Kudirat. 'Where do you think you're going?'

'Where do you think I am going?'

'Calm down, Mọ́remí.' Kudirat folded her arms across her chest. 'You can't be going around fearing someone just because—'

'Mọ́remí! Kudirat!' Wálé was back. 'Why are you still standing there?'

'Yessah! We her comin sah! We are a pack the buckets ni sah!' Kudirat responded in a singsong voice.

Mọ́remí had once compared Wálé to Olórí Ẹbí, the symbol of darkness and evil in her life.

'Wálé is not like Olórí Ẹbí at all,' Kudirat had said. 'Olórí Ẹbí is a hawk that would snatch a chick from underneath its mother's nose, but Wálé is a vulture, a bottom feeder. He's the henchman who's always getting shot in movies.'

'Don't let me have to call you again!' Wálé shouted, and left as abruptly as he'd appeared.

They rushed upstairs. After cleaning up and preparing some boiled yam and fish stew, they took out their portion first and hid it in their room, then they dished Wálé's food from the warmer. Kudirat spat into the stew and stirred it with her fingers, the way Ngozi had shown them when they'd been holding one of the 'housegirls meetings' at the public tap, where they usually congregated in the evenings, ostensibly to fetch water.

The housegirls meeting was better than ten schools combined. It was where they shared tips on how to steal money without being detected. How to spit into the food of your mean bosses, the appropriate amount of spittle, or, if you're daring enough, just the right amount of urine that would not show up in the taste of the food. How to deal with brats making your day horrible. Where to find the cheapest foodstuff so you'd be able to make profit when you were sent to the market. It was where they learnt about cocks, and fucks, and sexing.

Wálé was glued to CNN when they placed his food on the dining table. The girls hovered near the kitchen door as he ate it. Mọremí's face was pulled into a mask of disgust while Kudirat giggled quietly. The housegirls had taught them how important it was to witness and enjoy the humiliation of their tyrants.

THE COSMOPOLITAN HOUSEMAIDS OF LAGOS

Kudirat watched from the corner of her eye while pretending to read a book as Mọremí tiptoed to Tọ́lá's room. She pretended not to see the bundle of clothes underneath Mọremí's arm when she emerged a few minutes later and ran out of the flat.

She and Mọremí had been lounging in the sitting room, reading some books borrowed from Wálé's bookshelf. It was during one of those stolen moments, when they got some other housemaid to babysit for them, that Mọremí's phone started ringing.

She had come to recognise the look that crept up on

Mọremí's face, the one she wore whenever she felt she was being burdened. Her cheeks would flush red, her irises would deepen to a darker shade of green. Mọremí couldn't keep a secret to save her life but Kudirat indulged her. She enjoyed knowing what was going on without letting on.

Three years of living with somebody is no joke.

She was watching a fashion show on E! when she heard heavy footsteps mounting the staircase.

Kudirat wondered why Mọremí was returning home with Tọ́lá so early. She hopped off Wálé's favourite chair, straightened the throw pillows and removed the books she and Mọremí had been reading from the floor.

She had just made it into their small room, which had grown even smaller over the years, and shut the door, when she heard the front door being pushed open.

She wondered how badly damaged Tọ́lá was this time around.

'I need your help, Kudirat.' Mọremí was in the room with her, her eyes brimming with tears.

'Oh god, what has she done now?' Kudirat jumped off the mattress that Mọríebá had bought for them a few weeks ago, after Kudirat had contrived to show her the state of the flattened mattress they'd been sleeping on for three years while ostensibly giving her the recipe for her special melon seed soup with bush meat.

'Just come with me!'

Within a few minutes Kudirat and Mọremí were in the bedroom with Tọ́lá. She was spreadeagled on the floor, moaning. When she'd left earlier that morning to go shopping, she had been wearing an iro and buba, with a headscarf. But the Tọ́lá that Mọremí asked Kudirat to help lift off the floor was wearing a body-fitting black gown with a deep neckline. The gown was stained with patches of dirt and blood. She had a small gash above her brow.

'Shouldn't we call Dr Wálé?' The sight of blood sent panic screaming through Kudirat's system.

'Don't call him!' Tọ́lá slurred her words like someone who'd been at a huge quantity of spirits. In fact, she reeked like she'd taken a bath in a tankful of ogogoro. Kudirat wondered where she could have been.

Tọ́lá didn't have friends, and in the early days she never used to go out except on the odd Sundays Dr Wálé bothered to show up. But in the past year she'd been going out regularly. She would leave home in the morning, happy and glowing, and sneak home in the evening, Mọ́remí, the accomplice, ferrying mysterious bags up and down the staircase. Sometimes Mọ́remí would disappear for hours and return home, Tọ́lá in tow. After her outings, Tọ́lá would be depressed for several days, refusing to come out of her bedroom.

Mọ́remí stripped off Tọ́lá's clothes, then she and Kudirat helped her into the bathroom. They turned on the shower and held her up. Mọ́remí fetched some disinfectant and used cotton wool to wipe the wound on her head, the big scratch on her arm, the one near her ankle. After giving her a bath, they dragged her back to her room and helped her on with her nightgown, then they put her into bed.

'We have to fetch the children from Ngozi's place,' Mọ́remí said as they left Tọ́lá's room.

'You stay with her, I'll go,' Kudirat replied, and wandered out of the flat in a haze. She was tired of living with the Roberts, bone tired. She was tired of having to look after children she was barely older than, tired of picking up after them, cleaning their snotty noses, taking them to school, entertaining them, chiding them and mothering them. She wanted her mother too. Back in the village she used to help around the house and keep an eye on Ìṣọ̀lá, but here she was a full-time caregiver to three children and two grownups.

To think I'd been so happy when I was coming to live in Lagos.

She smiled when she remembered the girl she had been. The one clutching her dreams of the future along with a plastic bag full of her best clothes, the two careworn Nancy Drew novels she had inherited from her mother and her firm belief in the chickens of Lagos that were as tall as houses, of streets paved with gold, bridges built over an ocean that wrapped itself around the world like women wrapped their heads tightly with scarves.

In spite of it all she still held on to her dreams, that Lagos would smile on her and choose her as one of those special ones who made it. She would graduate as a doctor, she would gain her independence.

When she had got straight As in her JSS3 exams everybody had congratulated her except for Wálé, who sneered, 'Are we getting ideas above our station?'

She had laughed at all of them. She knew what she had done: given the examination council what they wanted, almost exactly. Her photographic memory had replicated those words on paper. It had worked for her in primary school, and it would see her through medical school. She wasn't in school to get an education: she got that from the streets.

She was soon at Ngozi's place, which was five houses away.

'Thanks for watching over the children,' Kudirat said, as the buxom girl threw open the door.

'Did you bring it?' Ngozi demanded, stretching her hand out.

Kudirat took a small bottle of oral contraceptives out of her pocket and placed it on Ngozi's palm. Kudirat got her education from girls like her.

Ngozi's madam's husband had been raping her since she started duty at their house as an eight-year-old. The previous year she had got pregnant and the man had taken her to have an abortion. Kudirat and Mọ́remí had met Ngozi the day after the procedure, when she had fainted at the public tap. The other girls had turned to them since they served a doctor, the closest they would get to any kind of medical attention. Although they had not been of much help except to give her some painkillers, when Ngozi had come around she had been effusive in her thanks.

It was then that she had told them the story of her boss and his wife, who had turned a blind eye to what was taking place under her nose. Kudirat was determined to help. Even if she could not prevent the rapes from happening, she could stop pregnancies and abortions. So, she decided to get Ngozi some contraceptives.

It had taken a lot of sneaking around, reading Wálé's medical books and asking Tọ́lá seemingly innocent questions about reproduction. After a rather longwinded and disjointed lecture about the evils of sex, Tọ́lá had eventually shown her 'the pill' and where she kept them.

Kudirat supplied Ngozi with the pills, stolen from Tọ́lá's bedside drawer.

'Thank you so much for these, ehn?' Ngozi said as she tucked the small bottle into her bra. 'The work I am using them to do, you won't understand.'

Kudirat narrowed her eyes at the girl. Ngozi was not to be trusted.

'What kind of work do you use them for?'

Ngozi moved so close to Kudirat they were breathing in the same air. 'I juss crush two of them' – she jiggled her breasts as she spoke, and the pills shook in rhythm – 'and put it into my Oga's food, the guy will just be walking up and down like zombie. Sometimes he will sit down on one chair and be looking at wall like say feem dey there. Sometimes he will not even come out of his room at-all-at-all!'

She stepped back and gave Kudirat a beatific smile that dimpled her cheeks. 'Even now I no tink the man remember say I dey im house again, this ting, ehn? E better pass juju, those medicine people get better juju!'

Kudirat frowned. 'I don't understand. They are contraceptives, not sleeping pills. And why would you give it to your Oga instead of using it yourself?'

Ngozi's face shuttered. 'Shebi it's that I don't pregnant again.'

Kudirat paused. 'I tink you be proper winsh Ngozi.'

'Eh? Me? I reject it in Jesus' name!' Ngozi snapped her fingers over her head.

'The tin I wan say be, you dey very very intelligent,' Kudirat said hurriedly. 'Ah! Asanwa! This your idea ehn! No sexing, no pregnant!'

'Exactly! No sexing, no pregnant!' Ngozi beamed and jiggled her breasts. 'I dey sleep every night. I no dey even bother to put chair behind my door again!'

'Omalicha! Asampete! Ọmọ tó dùn! Ọmọ tó ṣan!' Kudirat hailed Ngozi as she did a little jig, turning on one spot. She twerked for Kudirat, who pretended to spray money on her buttocks.

Ngozi stopped mid-dance and turned serious. 'You know sometin? Come!' She grabbed Kudirat and steered her towards the room where the children were making a racket. She clapped twice and the children froze.

'The three Jesu, prepare to dey go your house! But first, we dey come!' The children looked at her in fear and trepidation. She dragged a baffled Kudirat through the passageway and the kitchen to the backyard.

'Wait here.' Ngozi dropped Kudirat's arm and ran to the adjoining flat and peeped through a window. 'Esther, Esther, Ọya come!'

Kudirat watched the drama from afar. The tiptoeing, the closing of doors quietly, the whispers. She had met Esther the week before, at the public tap. The girl was a new housemaid, a tiny thing who reminded her of the way she used to be when she'd newly arrived in Lagos.

'Ehn, ehn, this is the Kudirat I tell you about.' Ngozi pulled the girl towards Kudirat. 'Tell am.'

Esther twisted her fingers and stared at her feet.

'Make I tell am?' offered Ngozi. Esther nodded.

'The ting is you know Sylvester nah, the boy that lives with Esther's madam.'

Kudirat tried to recollect the boy, but failed. She nodded anyway.

'He sex Esther last night. She too she want the medicine. I give her one today so that the boy will leave her, but she want her own and I cannot be sharing the small one you're giving me.'

Kudirat realised that there was an unspoken rule that once you were a housemaid you would also become a sex slave for all the men around you. Her mother had taught her well, about men who liked little girls, about how to make sure they never come near her.

'They don't like you Kudi-Owo. They like power. They want to control you and your body, they want to own you.' Her mother had turned away from the open fire on which she had been cooking and trained a hard look at her. 'Anytime a man says that you should come and enter his room, just smile well-well and tell him you want to go and bring your mummy.'

Kudirat missed her mum so badly at that moment, but on the heels of that feeling always followed resentment, an anger that burned in her chest so fiercely she wanted to combust.

She turned her attention back to the girl standing in front of her, eyes averted, shame stamped on her posture. She touched the girl on the arm, and whispered, 'I'm so sorry about the ting wey happen.' She bent closer. 'E nor be your fault, the shame na for the idiot wey sex you. I go soon bring something for you ehn? But is it still paining you down there?'

The girl remained mute.

'I have give her paracetamol, it was really paining her this morning,' Ngozi said.

Kudirat thought about the girl till she got home, her mute embarrassment, her rape, like so many others.

SEASON THREE: PLAYING WITH ÈṢÙ'S TITTIES (2008–2011)

UNDERGROUND SPIRITUAL GAMES

Olórí Ẹbí straightened up, spread his agbádá out, and wore his most forbidding expression as the door was pushed open. His chest tightened at the sight of his niece, Mọ́ríebá. She was dressed in her usual masculine garb: today it was a pair of jeans and an outsized t-shirt. Olórí Ẹbí was sure that if he listened carefully enough he would hear the clanging of the multiple chains draped around her neck. The largest one had her name stoned across the pendant.

She brought a smell of foreign trips, expensive perfumes and wealth into the room. Her strides spoke of her self-confidence, something that always disconcerted him. Most people who came into his home usually had an air of diffidence around them, but not Mọ́ríebá. She strutted around like a cock, except she was a hen. When she knelt to greet him, the proper way it should be done, he was slightly mollified.

'Good afternoon, sir.'

He took note that she didn't stay long enough on her knees, but one couldn't expect too much of a girl like that. He'd asked himself several times why he disliked her so intensely, why her presence made him so uncomfortable. If she was a man, he would have thought it was envy, but a woman! He was sure it was because she talked back. She couldn't seem to keep her opinions to herself, and he resented her for it, the same way he resented the easy way she wore affluence, her confidence. He resented the breadth of her shoulders, the thickness of her arms. Her haircut, the car keys dangling casually from her fingers, the way she sat, legs spread apart – like a man!

'I hope you and the boys are fine, sir?' she asked politely after making herself comfortable on a chair close by.

Olórí Ẹbí grunted and leaned back, his fingers splayed across his mouth and nose, his eyes watchful, wary.

'I met Ìyàwó on my way in. She's looking really well, Ẹ̀gbọ́n mi, you're taking—'

'Stop there! Just stop it!' He jerked up from his slouch and leaned towards her. 'Why are you here? What do you want?'

Mọ́ríebá bared her teeth at him in the parody of a smile. 'I actually want you to listen to what I have to say, because I know how you switch off when you don't want to hear the truth.'

Olórí Ẹbí `arched his eyebrow, but he swallowed the bile that threatened to burst out of him. The truth. He wondered what she knew about those words. Whose truth? Hers?

'I was in Lagos to see Mọ́remí. Actually I had just returned from one of my business trips to India—'

'Young lady, do not come here with your ill-mannered

boasts about world travel, we have heard. We know you went to India and China and Dubai and New York. Just tell me exactly what you want.' He saw the quickening anger in Mọ́ríẹbá's eyes and grinned inside. He loved a good fight. He loved when he had a worthy opponent. Mọ́ríẹbá was one of the few worth crossing swords with. 'Why are you here?'

Mọ́ríẹbá moved closer to the edge of her seat, making small growling noises in her throat. 'I will never insult an ancient man like you, or else I would have considered your remark fuelled by jealousy. But since I'm a well-brought-up woman, who knows her own worth and does not cringe from bullies—'

She took a deep breath, swallowing the rest of her words. 'Don't let us quarrel, Olórí Ẹbí.' Her tone was conciliatory. 'You're like my father, you have done a lot for me.' She paused. 'Even if I do think you could have done more.'

Olórí Ẹbí shook his head, Mọremí obviously hadn't learnt how wicked the world could be, and she was about to find out.

'Alright, go on,' he said. He placed his elbows on the armrest of his chair and covered half his face with both hands.

'I have a business proposition for you,' she started.

Olórí Ẹbí sat up straighter and listened.

'I don't like the way Mọremí and Kudirat are being treated in Lagos. I don't like it at all.'

Olórí Ẹbí didn't move a muscle. She was beyond redemption.

'And I think it's more Wálé's fault than Tọ́lá's.'

He wondered about her mental health. The way she switched from one emotion to another couldn't be normal.

'You should have seen them – particularly Mọ́remí. Her hands are red and raw from washing clothes, her clothes are torn.'

The more Mọ́ríebá talked, the louder her voice became. She seemed to be in the grip of hysteria. He shook his head in sympathy. *Poor child.*

'I've bought clothes for her in the past few years, but I don't think she's allowed to wear them. Her hair, my goodness! She's all skin and bones.'

When she stopped talking, he waited for more, but she was taking deep breaths.

'Let me get this straight, you came here to tell me how Wálé and Tọ́lá are maltreating Mọ́remí.'

'No, Olórí Ẹbí, it's more than that. Children should live with people who care about them. For one, I don't think Tọ́lá has recovered from the episode she suffered after having her last child, and Wálé is the most irresponsible man I've ever seen. In the past three years I've been to their house more than twelve times, and I've never met him at home, not even once.'

He was truly baffled. *Why were women like this?* 'Correct me if I'm wrong, but are you saying that you expect Wálé, who is a doctor, to be at home just because you're visiting?' he said in his most reasonable tone. He didn't want to trigger her again. 'None of the things you're saying makes any sense, or is it that those children are telling you tales so you can feel sorry for them?'

Mọ́ríebá expelled an impatient breath. 'They've not told me anything! They don't need to tell me anything. I've been there, I've spent time with them. I saw them three days ago. For the first two hours, Tọ́lá didn't even bother to come out and say hello, and that's not the first time she's done that. I eventually went into her bedroom because the girls claimed she was indisposed. My goodness, it was horrible. The room stank like a gutter and Tọ́lá was in bed with clothes and shoes piled all around her, she wouldn't even say hello to me.'

He tried to listen, especially to the things she wasn't saying, like jealousy – after all, Mọ́ríebá wasn't married and Tọ́lá was.

'We need to sort that girl out! The most bizarre aspect of the visit happened when I was about to leave. Tọ́lá came out of the room, all dressed up and greeted me as if I'd just arrived. We need to get those children away from her and get her away from that man! She needs to see a proper doctor.'

Olórí Ẹbí held out placating hands.

'Calm down madam! Firstly, I don't know what "episode" you're talking about. See, let's not get all confused.' He sat back in his chair. 'Let me understand this. You claim that Mọ́remí and Kudirat are not being taken care of, yes?'

Mọ́ríebá nodded.

'You forget they were not sent to Lagos to be taken care of: they went there to learn about responsibility and hard work. You weren't raised by your parents, were you? Neither was I. You didn't turn out too badly. Look at how far you've come due to hard work.'

Olórí Ẹbí was deliberately being obtuse, and he knew that she knew.

'Kudirat and Mọ́remí are children!' Mọ́ríebá's voice was pitched to the highest volume possible, and it grated on his nerves. 'They shouldn't be made to take care of other people's children!'

Olórí Ẹbí sucked his teeth. 'I can now see what all these travelling up and down has done to your brain. Is Mọ́remí the first person to go and live with other people? Have those other people died? And those girls are not children, aren't they in SS2 now? Some of their age-mates are already married with children sef!'

Mọ́ríebá suddenly looked unsure of herself. He relaxed against his chair; he'd won another round.

'Okay, let me put it this way,' she said. 'A few years ago, Alhaja and I went to her lawyer's office.' Her voice was low and full of menace. 'I was the other witness, and I do have a rough idea of what is contained in the will.' She was looking directly into his eyes. 'I will stop searching for Alhaja's will – in fact I will not bother you about the will again – if you let me have Mọ́remí. I will personally hire a housekeeper for Tọ́lá and pay her a salary.'

Olórí Ẹbí was done. 'I can see that you are not only stubborn; you are also hard of hearing.' He jumped out of his chair with an air of finality. 'In one sentence you've made some veiled threats and at the same time you've tried to bribe me with something you don't have!'

He towered over her, his agbádá spread out like the wings of a hawk about to dive on a chick. 'Listen to me very well. If your empty womb is crying for a child, I'm sorry but you can't have Mọ́remí. Go and born your own! I know all your secrets, Mọ́ríebá, don't push me!'

He turned and pulled open the door, particularly proud of the way he swept his agbádá after him. 'By the way, good luck with finding the will. Haven't you been searching for it for the past four years or so? I'll be very happy when you do!' He shut the door behind him, then went directly to his room, pulled off his agbádá, turned on the fan and sat at the foot of his bed.

Mọ́ríebá was a true Alágbàdo and never made idle threats. If she'd made up her mind to find the will, that was exactly what she would do. It no longer mattered that she had been unable to get a hold of Alhaja's lawyer. She knew the old man would back Olórí Ẹbí up, even if she got to meet him.

Olórí Ẹbí went back downstairs and met Ìyàwó shutting the front door.

'Anti Mọ́ríebá was really angry,' she said as she turned the key in the lock. 'I don't know why you people squabble like little children—'

'Nobody asked for your opinion. Go and get me some of the àkàrà you fried this morning, and a bowl of palm oil. Put them on that wooden tray and bring them to my room.'

Ìyàwó stepped back, clasping her hands to her chest. 'Sorry o, the owner of my bride wealth.'

Olórí Ẹbí sucked his teeth at her sarcastic tone, stomped back to his room and changed into something more comfortable. By the time he had finished dressing in an ankara shirt and matching trousers, Ìyàwó was knocking on his door. She placed the things he'd requested on a table and gave him a hard stare before leaving.

He slid his feet into a pair of rubber slippers and pulled open the toilet door. After locking it securely behind him, he grabbed the torch beside the toilet bowl, switched it on and balanced it carefully on the tray. He opened a smaller door that led from the toilet into the older part of the house, which had been sealed off years ago.

The house had been originally built by his great-grandfather, who had raised it from a bungalow into a two-storey building. Olórí Ẹbí's father had 'modernised' it by adding a new wing, using it as his base whenever he came to town from Alágbàdo.

As he went down the passageway, the thin white light of the torch periodically lit up the blackened mud walls, scampering rats and thick dust motes that tickled the back of his throat. He took a right turn and carefully descended the rickety wooden staircase that led to the lower part of the building. He expelled an angry breath with each step.

He leaned on the banister for a few seconds. He resented that he had to make these pilgrimages. He had done nothing to be ashamed of, but that was the way things had to be. In the days of yore, you put your Órìṣà out in the sun, displayed their beauty for everyone to see. There were constant offerings and annual celebrations of your ancestors, your Òrìṣà and your ẹgbẹ́. Members of your family were Ifa scholars and Órìṣà adepts, who used their knowledge to make new inventions. You thrived and proudly bore the names of your ancestors. You were Èṣùbìyí, Ṣàngówánwá, you were Ọyáfúnmi, Òòṣágbèmí. But the imported religions and their fanatics had put an end to all that.

You had to hide your knowledge of the Órìṣà so nobody would call you evil. You had to blend with the crowd. The days of tolerance were long gone, those days when you could be an Ògún devotee and a chaplain at the same time. Nowadays, anything relating to ancestor veneration was viewed with suspicion. No longer could the Imam carry his mother's Egúngún: you were either one or the other. So, you took your Òrìṣà underground and served them on the sly.

Olórí Ẹbí placed the tray in front of the Ìbejì icons mounting guard to the shrine that had been in the family from time before history. He crouched in front of the statues and offered each one the àkàrà, all the while chanting their panegyrics.

> Ẹ̀jìrẹ́ ará-ìsokún
> ẹdúnjọbí
> Ọmọ ẹdun tíí nṣ'eré orí igi
> Ófesẹ̀ `méjèèjì bọ́ sílé alákìísa;
> Ó s'alákìísà d'onígba aṣọ

Accept this offering and let the ears of the Óríṣà be attentive to my petitions.

He rose to his feet, dusted off his clothes and entered into an even darker room. He switched off the torch and reached out for a clay lamp above the doorpost, took a box of matches off the post and lit the wick The lamp flickered its orange flames, casting long shadows against the walls and the icons of the Óríṣà.

He stepped further into the room, and made for the statue of Èṣù seated in the left-hand corner. He placed the oil lamp on the ground and lifted the clay pot full of palm oil from the tray. He dribbled the oil on the statue's head and knelt in front of the messenger of Elédùmarè.

> Láaróyè
> Adíjàálẹ̀ ta'kété Bàbá òríta
> A fi'bi díre, a f'ire díbi
> Má ṣe mí o
> Má sọ bẹ́ẹ̀ni mi di bẹ́ẹ̀kọ́
> Má sọ bẹ́ẹ̀kọ́ mi di bẹ́ẹ̀ni

'Láaróyè, I've brought evil reports of Mọ́ríebá, the daughter of Olúrónbí, to you. Mọ́ríebá came into my house to threaten me! After eating my pepper and oil, she had the guts to come into my own home and threaten me!'

Sweat dripped down Olórí Ẹbí's back, so intense was his anger. His voice bounced off the walls into Èṣù's ears.

'There's no hiding the truth from you because you're the all-seeing one. Àdùkẹ́ the daughter of Àjọkẹ́ was the one who first stole my inheritance. Instead of allowing me to take charge when I came of age, the woman called me a criminal and gave me two buildings and a piece of land deep inside one bush village to shut my mouth. I had to send her to an early grave because it is the person who makes enquiries about how we will complete our task that we show how it is done. Instead of leaving well enough alone, her apprentice, Mọ́ríebá, the daughter of Olúrónbí, has threatened to go and search for a will that I have decided has to remain missing, just because she wants the custody of Mọ́remí, Àdùkẹ́'s granddaughter.'

As Èṣù fully apparated in a room filled with the smell of ancient offerings and heartfelt pleas, they allowed themselves to soak in the history of the people who had intertwined them with the Alágbàdo lineage. They scrolled through the archives of Àjà, and pinpointed the exact moment the first Alágbàdo had accepted them as one of their many Óríṣà. Through the millennia, through war and famine and displacement, the Alágbàdo had carried them around. Although things had changed with the arrival of the missionaries, the Alágbàdo had kept them close until the great-grandfather, who had converted to Islam for economic reasons. Now their progeny had forgotten most of their own histories. They were mixing foreign ideas with authentic ones.

Èṣù was slightly amused by the young man sweating so passionately in front of the soapstone statue that represented them and reflected on how they used to be annoyed with the way people kept conflating them with the European Satan. But these days they found being thought to be what they were not interesting; mischief making had just been made easier. After permitting themselves a faint smile, they paid attention to the things the young man was not saying.

Olórí Ẹbí paused to catch his breath. The room had grown stuffier. He was sweating from every pore. He used the hem of his shirt to wipe his face. 'Here is my errand, and here is the palm-oil.' He dribbled some more palm oil on the statue. 'I want you to dodge Mọ́ríẹbá's footsteps with all manner of ills. I want you to make sure disfavour and ill-will follow her around. That she will be so busy with all the trouble you will visit upon her, she won't have time to go about searching for stupid wills. That you, Oníléorìtàa, Ológiri Òkò, will dodge her footsteps with illnesses and disease. That her business will fail and she'll turn destitute. And if she persists, I want her to die. Yes, Èṣù, I want her to die a sudden death, the same way her mentor died. I am ready to pay any price you demand of me, just do as you have been told and do it within the week. Ase!'

Èṣù was so delighted by his performance that they burst into a round of applause. They admired Olórí Ẹbí's willingness to take risks. His ability to play Ludo with his own life.

Olórí Ẹbí felt lighter as he put out the lamp and climbed the staircase back into his room. He fell into a deep sleep as soon as he hit his bed, only to be woken up by a loud hammering on his door.

'Bàámi! Bàámi!'

'You are a big fool!' Olórí Ẹbí yelled as soon as he pulled open his door. 'How dare you come to my door and start shouting like the house is on fire? Haven't I told you that you are not to come near this room except when you have been summoned? Answer me. Lékan!'

'Bàámi, I'm sorry, but I have important news,' the boy mumbled.

'By Ògún, I hope the news is important enough or I will skin you alive!'

'It is Baba Kasali, sir. Tọ́lá just phoned now. She said he's dead: he was involved in a car accident—'

'T' FOR TROUBLE

'Oyinbo, come and cut the grass over here!' Mr Hakeem beckoned at Mọ́remí.

Back in her grandmother's house, she'd not been aware of the difference between her and other children in the neighbourhood. She knew she was special, but it wasn't because of the colour of her skin. She had been special because she was rich, had too many clothes and toys and was her grandmother's precious eyes. That had changed when she moved to Lagos. In Lagos she acquired a new cognomen, 'oyinbo', but more than that she was treated with a combination of disdain and fascination. She was always treated differently.

It had got worse as she grew older. Her skin, defying her refusal to apply any kind of cream to it, shone as if the sun itself had taken refuge underneath it. She'd grown taller, the rest of her body finally catching up with her outsized arms and knobbly knees. Her breasts were small and perfectly rounded, her stomach flat, her hips as slim as those of a young boy.

She'd been told by many, both strangers and familiars, that she was beautiful, that she should become a model. Mọ́remí didn't want beauty. Beauty was a burden she refused to bear. She'd rather have Kudirat's melanin, her shiny, blue-black skin that bestowed belonging, anonymity, a beauty that had nothing to do with the colour of her skin. She did not want to be an exotic species, something not totally human.

'I'm talking to you, Mọ́remí!' Mr Hakeem snapped.

She stood to attention. 'Me sir?' She heard muffled laughter from her classmates. They had learnt over the years that she never answered to 'oyinbo'. Mọ́remí sauntered as slowly as she dared over to where he he stood, all six feet of him.

Mr Hakeem was a tall drink of water, who has been drunk, and drunk. He had boyish good looks, which he complemented with a well-groomed beard. Mr Hakeem was a believer: he believed he was god's gift to Bariga Comprehensive High School, and maybe he was. According to gist, he was passed around the school on a regular basis from teachers to senior students and back to the teachers in an endless ping-pong game. He was the school's one-man welcoming committee, gifted to guests interested in such things as cocks. A generous transmitter of STIs.

'Just one kiss,' he whispered, as she drew close to him. 'Not even a kiss – one peck, and you can return to your classroom.'

Mọremí was not in the least surprised. She'd heard worse pick-up lines from people who didn't even have the tenuous claim of familiarity that Mr Hakeem had, who at least had sometimes crossed her path in the school corridors. But she had also been well tutored by Kudirat. She could ad lib.

'I can't hear you, sir,' Mọremí said calmly, as she took a step away from him. 'Can you speak louder?'

'Come on, don't be stubborn,' he whined close to her ear, bringing to mind mosquitoes singing their malaria song while they prepared their needle-sharp proboscises to feast on her blood. 'You know I love you, I want to even marry you.'

'Mr Hakeem, sir,' she pitched loudly as she took another step away, 'you still haven't shown me the patch of grass I'm supposed to cut, sir! If you point it out I'll be able to see it, sir! I can't hear what you're saying, sir!'

'You really are as arrogant as everybody says you are,' he hissed. 'So, because you're oyinbo, a broke one at that, who is even a housemaid, you still go around with your shoulders raised up.'

Mọremí gave him her trademark deadpan stare. 'Where did you say I should cut, sir?'

Mr Hakeem realised that he wasn't getting anywhere with her. He growled and pointed at a dense bush far away.

'Thank you, sir!' Mọremí shouted. Her classmates, who had been pretending to be interested in cutting grass rather than enjoying their bit of afternoon entertainment, tittered.

Mọremí approached the grass cutting with the same dedication and intensity she applied to her household chores. Her long arm brought down the machete on the grass with precision, and each time she raised it up, it flashed in the midday sun like Ogun's avenging machine. She soon developed a rhythm, accompanied by a long stream of curses that Èṣù thoroughly approved of.

Èṣù was on an evidence-gathering trip, examining the life and times of the Alágbàdos in the story Olórí Ẹbí had shared with them. So far, Èṣù approved of all the women they'd been asked to visit.

Mọ́remí had run out of steam and was deep in conversation with her classmates when the bell for closing hours rang. She dropped her machete in the storeroom and went to wait for Kudirat at the school gate.

She should be mad at Kudirat because it was her fault that every single girl in their grade had been punished, all because of hairstyles. But she wasn't. She was amused.

Mọ́remí didn't have any problems with her hair: she had a problem with the hairdresser, a middle-aged woman who was rather fond of shoving Mọ́remí's head in between her thighs, the stink of her badly bleached skin nearly choking Mọ́remí to death. She gave her hard knocks if Mọ́remí so much as moved her head to breathe in some clean air. One day she'd headed to the barber's and had it cut as low as possible. Although Wálé had told her how ugly she looked when she got home, Mọ́remí knew that it was one of the best decisions she had ever made.

Kudirat on the other hand loved her long, thick, hair. She cared for it as a mother would a new-born baby. She wore it in beautiful styles, and during the holidays and on weekends she would condition it with shea butter and coconut oil. She would comb it until it floated, nimbus like, on her head. She and the hairdresser had a mutual-admiration society going on. The hairdresser plaited her hair lovingly, and she claimed that inhaling the stink of her skin was a small price to pay for a headful of beautifully plaited hair.

Kudirat had always resented the way the school dictated hairstyles to the students. She hated it more because erring students were punished with a blunt pair of scissors. She had one of her brilliant ideas on the day a girl was given a shave at school assembly. The JSS1 girl had been blubbering, tears of humiliation and snot running down her face. Kudirat had launched a campaign among the SS2 students. She told them how unfair the school policy was, how it was humiliating: why couldn't the girls wear any hairstyle they wanted as long as it was kept clean and neatly done? There had to be a protest, a mass thing that would shock the school authorities.

The girls had decided that the next Monday they would all wear their hair in a style that wouldn't pass. Mọremí thought they would not have the liver to push through, but she had underestimated the resentment for authority that hid in the hearts of fifteen-year-olds.

She had been surprised when every single girl in their grade who did not wear their hair in low cuts came in that Monday with their hair either floating freely on their heads, like Kudirat had done, or woven into tiny, complicated styles that had the school authorities calling an emergency meeting. Kudirat and the other ringleaders were carted off to receive special punishment from the principal, while Mr Hakeem had been delegated to mete out punishment to the minions.

Mọremí waited for nearly an hour before an exhausted Kudirat, clothes stained and awry, showed up. Her eyes were puffy and red.

'We were made to cut some elephant grass at the back of the junior classes with blunt cutlasses,' she answered Mọremí's unasked question. 'Then she got Mr Shaba to cane us.'

She showed Mọremí the raw bruises on her palms. Mọremí grabbed the bruised hands and made to kiss them.

'Idiot, get away from me!' Kudirat pushed her away.

'You stink!' Mọremí announced gleefully.

'So do you, Miss Ring o' Ring o' Roses. That's not all.' Kudirat pulled a neatly folded note out of her pocket and handed it to Mọremí, who quickly scanned it, wincing at the typos.

'What is this? You have to bring our parents to school tomorrow morning or you will face expulsion?'

'Yes. So, how has your day been?' Kudirat asked in a false cheerful tone.

Mọremí shrugged. 'Not as bad as yours. At least the grass we got to cut was not elephant grass, our machetes were rather sharp and I also got a marriage proposal.'

'Mr Hakeem!' Kudirat burst into laughter. 'You lucky girl, you.'

'You don't know how lucky I am,' she said, po-faced. 'After marrying my broke-ass teacher, I will never do another day of work in my life, except maybe cook, wash and bear many, many children … by getting sexed every single night.'

The girls stood in the middle of the walkway and laughed. They leaned into each other and laughed so hard tears were streaming down their faces. They laughed so loudly that other pedestrians gave them a wide berth, and a bus conductor yelled directions to Yaba Psychiatric Hospital to them.

'Is this how we are going to spend the rest of our lives?' Kudirat hiccupped.

'How else are we to live? We are expected to spend our entire lives dodging penises and drudgery. It's why we were born, what we were born to do. We are girls, we shall not be sexed!' That thought sobered them up faster than a bucket of cold water. They crossed the road and embarked on the final stint of the trek that would take them to their street.

'You are in deep shit though.'

Kudirat curtsied. 'Thanks for that piece of wisdom, oh great one.'

Mọ́remí ignored her tone. 'Tọ́lá is out, or we might get home and she'll be in her room with the windows and doors barred.'

'Or she might have gone to one of her ogogoro joints and is preparing to call you to come and rescue her,' Kudirat added sneakily.

Mọ́remí eyeballed her and sucked her teeth loudly, then continued talking. 'Wálé is hardly ever at home, and even if he is, he'd not go to your school out of spite, which you should be thankful for, because if he did, he'd not only get you expelled, he'd also have your name stricken from the school register.'

'It seems,' Kudirat said, mimicking Wálé's deep tones, 'we are getting ideas above our station, aren't we, your royal highness?'

Mọ́remí suddenly remembered Ortega, one of their classmates. 'I have an idea though, how much are you carrying on you?'

Aside from the money they stole from both Tọ́lá and Wálé, the girls were doing a brisk business with the Housemaids Cabal (as Kudirat referred to Ngozi and her gang). Ngozi had suggested that, instead of just giving the pills away, they should make some profit from it. Since Ngozi's genius idea to feed their bosses the contraceptives, housemaids from as far as Ikoyi were now patronising them, buying the oral contraceptives as quickly as they could steal them. They supplied Ngozi with the pills, she supplied her chain of housemaids and remitted their cut to them. Typical of Tọ́lá, she had turned a blind eye to their activities because there was no way she wouldn't have noticed the frequent disappearance of her pills. So far, there had been no complaints, not even from dòkí olóyè. Everybody was happy and that was that.

Kudirat rifled through her pinafore pocket and pulled out a wad of notes. 'I found about ten thousand naira in dòkí olóyè's pockets yesterday when Tọ́lá asked me to do the laundry.'

'Good, give me five k and follow me.' Mọ́remí stretched out her hand to receive the money, and turned towards the seedier part of their neighbourhood.

'Where are we going?' Kudirat asked apprehensively.

'To see Ortega,' Mọ́remí replied, jumping over the huge gutter that separated them from relative safety.

'When did you become friends with Ortega?' Kudirat snatched her hand out of Mọ́remí's. 'When did you start keeping secrets from me?'

'Ortega and I are not friends,' Mọ́remí snapped.

'But you know the way to his house?'

Kudirat sounded jealous. Mọ́remí had no intention of telling Kudirat that she'd been to fetch Tọ́lá from a beer parlour in that part of the neighbourhood several times.

'If you don't want to go, we can always turn back. After all, it's your problem, not mine.'

Kudirat glared at her. 'My problems are yours.'

Ortega was the toughest and roughest boy in their school. If somebody was being bullied or a mean prank was being played on a teacher, he would be leading the pack. Rumour had it that he smoked weed with a bunch of other miscreants behind the boys' toilet during school hours. Mọremí knew that it was no rumour, and that Ortega not only smoked weed, but also sold it alongside other hallucinogens that helped students cope with their messed-up lives. It was a wonder that he hadn't been expelled, but in fact he hedged his bets, selling drugs to the teachers and helping them to 'leak' exam papers.

The girls walked past houses built so closely together there wasn't space to walk in between them. Most were unpainted, and the ones that were had faded to a filthy version of their original colours. The houses looked dejected, as if they were well aware of their condition.

After a few minutes of dodging drying laundry, open sewers and other things best left unexamined, they finally slowed down in front of a ramshackle aluminium building which, incongruously, had a satellite television dish hung on one of its outer walls.

Mọremí was still wondering where she should knock when Ortega came out, using the ratty curtain that hung on the door to cover his body.

'Hi Ortega,' she said brightly. 'It's me, Mọremí.'

'And so what?' Ortega sneered. 'The great white girl has come to visit the poor black boy so we should throw a party.'

'Ortega why now? Wetin I do wey you dey talk like this? I wan ask why you no come school today.'

'Why you like to dey ask those kind questions? How

he take consine you whether I go school or I no go school, you be my mother?' He scowled at them. 'How you take know my house sef?'

'Don't be like that, Ortega.' Mọremí wasn't surprised at his hostility. The last time they had spoken he had asked her out, and she'd turned him down. 'I get better deal for you. At least come outside make we yarn better thing. I no come here with dry mouth o.' She dipped her hand inside the pocket of her school uniform and brought out a wad of one hundred naira notes.

Ortega quickly dragged her inside the house, Kudirat at her heels. 'You should never wave money around like that in this neighbourhood. We nor dey joke at all!'

He turned on the light and a naked bulb flooded the room, a perfect square with a queen-sized bed taking up most of the space. A couch along one wall had a direct view of a huge television set on the other side of the bed. A pot sat empty on a stove beside the couch. Ortega picked up a faded blue t-shirt draped over a chair and covered his bony chest with it.

'I have a job for you,' said Mọremí, 'and we will pay you very well. We need to rent parents for Kudirat tomorrow. Tell them to dress nicely but not too nicely. They have to convince the principal not to expel Kudirat. I will give you an envelope tomorrow morning which they'll give to her. I am sure she won't do anything further to Kudirat after she gets a bribe.'

'No lele Mọremí.' Ortega's eyes filled up with mischief, his earlier hostility melting in the sun of naira notes. 'You know say that be my job. Kudirat's parents go dey the school gate tomorrow morning.'

He turned to face Kudirat. 'Make sure you come in

early so that you can get to meet them before you go in.'

'Okay, thanks,' Kudirat mumbled, and shifted from one foot to another.

Mọremí went to the heart of the matter. 'How much you go collect?'

'The parents will take fifteen thousand naira and me I go collect five thousand naira finder's fee.'

'Don't be silly. Seven and a half k each for just thirty minutes' work? Lai lai, even ọlọṣọ nor dey cost reach that.' Mọremí pulled the money from her pocket. 'Let's do this quickly. I will pay Mr and Mrs Mogaji five thousand naira each and pay you a three thousand finder's fee.'

Ortega accepted the cash and counted it. 'Wey the balance?'

'After dem complete their work successfully.'

'Mọremí baby, the only Mọremí that ever liveth. Paddy mi!'

'But you were calling me names earlier!' she snapped.

'You know as e dey go nah.' He sobered up. 'I'm sorry, I shouldn't have.'

'It's alright.' She smiled at him. 'I know say anybody wey give you money na im be your best friend, until you've finished spending it.'

'You know that's how I roll.' His voice took on a bus conductor's gruffness.

'Don't forget the name: Dr and Mrs Roberts,' said Mọremí, as they stepped out of the room. Ortega wrote it on a piece of paper.

The following morning Kudirat's parents turned up at the gate as promised. The middle-aged couple wore matching Ankara outfits, Kudirat's mother plump and smiley, her father thin and stern looking.

Mọ́remí's respect for them grew as Kudirat entered their class later looking properly humbled and sad. The illusion was dispelled as soon as Kudirat passed by her table and flashed a saucy smile.

'Did you notice that they didn't cut anybody's hair? We won!'

Her whispered words lingered with Mọ́remí all through that day.

THE SLEEPWALKER...

Tọ́lá knew the exact moment Wálé rose from the bed. She knew this because he wasn't there when she rolled over to check he'd really gone. He'd been getting up from his side of the bed regularly for a whole week and she would follow him with her mind, eyes tightly shut.

He would first go to the sitting room and walk around for a while, then to the kitchen where he would open the fridge and never shut it. Then he would head for the toilet, and finally the children's room.

After a week of following him with her mind and studying the patterns of his midnight wanderings, she had gone to the children's room and peered at him through a crack in the door, because he had stayed in there for longer than usual.

He was standing still at the foot of the bed the three Jesus shared. He leaned over and placed gentle kisses on the children's foreheads. He straightened the rumpled bedsheet, covered them with their bedclothes and adjusted their pillows.

On the surface, he looked like a caring father, but she knew him better than that. She knew he couldn't be trusted, not around children. Wálé cared for nobody, not even himself. He was a pleasure seeker who did whatever it took to get him high whenever he wanted to. He was also smart and cunning. He groomed his victims until they were willing slaves to whatever depravity he had in mind.

She had thought all that had ended when one of their neighbours had confronted him, claiming that he had made her little child fondle his penis. There had been a lot of shouting and denials, but things got so bad they had been forced to move from their palatial residence in Ikoyi to a cramped flat in Bariga.

He's turned his attention to the children.

The possibility was horrifying, reminding her of her own childhood. 'Uncles' with groping fingers, uncles who wanted you sitting on their laps, uncles kissing you on the lips, warning you to tell nobody.

Nobody was going to do that to her children. It would be over her dead body.

In the past few years, when she'd pretended not to see how he touched Móremí and Kudirat, it had never occurred to her that he would eventually do that to his own daughter. The following night Tọ́lá was pretending to be asleep when she thought she heard whimpers. She jumped up and burst into the children's room, just as Wálé straightened and rose from the children's bed.

Jésùtitófúnmi's nightgown was scrunched around her waist, her pants pulled down to her thighs.

Wálé brushed past her without a word. She sat in the space Wálé just vacated and straightened her daughter's clothes. When she was finally able to look up, her eyes met Jésùtitófúnmi's, which were full of fright. Tọ́lá's tummy turned water.

'Daddy was touching me. I told him to stop,' Jésùtitófúnmi whispered.

Tọ́lá wept as she lifted her daughter out of the bed and carried her into the sitting room. With trembling arms, she pulled Jésùtitófúnmi into a hug, her daughter's tears soaking through her gown. After a while, Jésùtitófúnmi's trembling subsided. So did hers, and so did their tears.

Tọ́lá whispered the question that had been on her mind for over a week. 'Has he touched you before?'

'Yes. He puts his tongue in my mouth. He said I shouldn't tell anybody, that he loves only me.'

Tọ́lá's stomach churned. Her throat closed up with revulsion at what she'd allowed to happen. She pulled herself together. *This is not about you, Tọ́lá!*

She waited, but Jésùtitófúnmi did not say anything further. 'He will never touch you again, I promise you that,' Tọ́lá said, more to herself than to her daughter. 'I will protect you, I promise. I won't let him hurt you again.'

Tọ́lá knew she was babbling but didn't know what to say. There was no handbook to guide her, nobody had prepared her for this. Nobody had told her what to do if her children's father decided to assault his own children. What could she say?

She felt a movement against her shoulder. Jésùtitófúnmi was saying something.

'What did you say?' Tọ́lá pulled her daughter's head off her shoulder.

'Is it true that you're mad, mummy?' her daughter asked earnestly. 'Daddy said you have mentallo; he said your head is not correct and that is why he loves only me.'

Tọ́lá froze. *Am I mad?*

'Yes,' Tọ́lá's voice wobbled, 'I am mad.' Her voice

grew firmer. 'But your Daddy is madder. His madness is incurable. He should be locked away.'

'That's what Kudirat said too,' Jésùtitófúnmi whispered.

Tólá wanted to howl, to let out the pain that was tearing at her insides. But she had to feel the pain, to let it eat at her so she would never forget this moment. Her pain would be a memorial of the horror she'd put her daughter through.

'I don't care if you're mad,' Jésùtitófúnmi said fiercely. 'I love you, mummy.'

Tólá rocked Jésùtitófúnmi until she slept. For once her demons, the voices, were banished. For once she would listen to her daughter's heartbeat, she would listen.

In the early hours, when she heard Wálé moving about in the master bedroom, she returned Jésùtitófúnmi to her room and went to the kitchen. Still quiet inside, she fetched some beans and started the process that would turn it into àkàrà.

She poured herself into the preparations, peeling, blending and frying the bean paste. She whipped up the pap in no time and had the dining table set by the time Wálé emerged from their room, all dressed up.

It was 4:30am.

She nodded at the table and watched him sit down. Still without a word, she sat across from him and waited until he'd taken a bite of the àkàrà before speaking.

'Why are you such a bastard?' Her tone was conversational, almost casual. 'In the paedophile's bible I guess there's no such thing as incest.'

Wálé considered himself to be poker faced, but Tólá had lived with him long enough to recognise the little signs. A flicker of something akin to panic skittered through his eyes.

'I don't know what you're talking about,' he shrugged.

'I saw you in the children's room last night, and Jésùtitófúnmi told me it wasn't your first time sexually assaulting her.' She choked the words out of a dry mouth.

'I don't know what you are talking about.' He frowned a little and continued with his meal. With a mouthful of pap he said, 'Maybe I was sleepwalking. I am known to sleepwalk on certain occasions, under certain circumstances.'

'I never knew you sleepwalked,' she said softly.

'You know nothing my dear wife, so let's just keep it like that.' He gave her his most charming smile and dropped his spoon. 'How are you sure about the things you claim to see? Are we sitting at the dining table? Are you holding a conversation with me or one of your imaginary friends? You know your delicate condition, Tọ́lá, your tendency to see things, to hear voices. Am I even in this flat?'

He leaned close to her. His lips hovered over hers. 'Calm the fuck down, baby,' he whispered. 'What you need to do at this point is what you usually do, watch Africa Magic and drink vodka.' His voice became a growl, 'And don't fuck with shit you can't handle!'

He straightened his tie, gave her a contemptuous look and turned to leave.

Tọ́lá saw red. The voice that had been silenced since she married Wálé at seventeen burst through the barriers that had been imposed around it: her mother telling her that a woman should do everything in her power to keep her marriage, the church telling her that she was the neck and her husband the head, society telling her that divorced women were the whores of the earth, that her ailing mental health was a thing of shame.

'I have taken a lot of shit from you, Ọláwálé Roberts.'

Rita's voice blocked his path.

'I know you mess around with little children.'

Wálé opened and closed his mouth like a fish that had been taken out of water. His deadpan, seen-it-all mask had fallen off.

'Don't fucking mess with my children again.' She walked up to him. 'You can mess with my head, finger my brain, but if I catch you touching any of my children again, you won't live to regret it!'

Wálé grabbed her shirt. 'Did you just threaten me?' he yelled. 'Did you just say you're going to murder me if I touch my own children?'

His sharp eyes looked into her soul. 'So, I should not play with my own children again. I do hope you listen to yourself, Tọlá. I've been telling you that you're totally bonkers, totally. All these years I've helped you to hide your shame by not having you committed to an asylum. I help manage your sickness. I supply you with meds. But all you do is—'

Rita grabbed his shirt. 'Meds Wálé? What meds have you been giving me? You've been giving me meds without my knowledge?'

Before she could say anything further, Wálé sent her head spinning with an open palm slap, pushed her away from him and slammed his way out of the flat.

Tọlá lay on the floor, refusing to give in to tears. She pulled herself up and went into her bedroom, shut the door after her and began to hyperventilate.

I nor know why you nor wan make I take care of this bastard!

'No,' Tọlá said firmly. She now knew well Rita's method of 'taking care' of things. It usually involved Rita doing things Tọlá couldn't remember, things that led to wounds all over her body, getting stuck in strange neighbourhoods and having to call Mọremí to come and pick her up in a taxi. Things that involved high-heeled shoes, short gowns, dark rooms, strange men that smelled like dirt and sweat.

Things she didn't want to recollect. Things that were best left behind in dark, dangerous rooms, or stuffed into nylon bags by Mọremí and hidden away in dark, dangerous cupboards located somewhere in the kitchen.

Who will believe me? Who can I call?

Tọlá's hand shook as she dialled Kẹmi's number. Her older sister picked up after the first ring.

'Hello Tọlá, how are you? This is a pleasant surprise!'

The words got stuck in her throat. Where should she start? Would Kẹmi even believe her?

She'd never been close to her sister, not even during their childhood. Especially not after her episodes started at the age of eight, when she would refuse to sleep, eat or go to school for days.

'I'm fine. I just thought it's been too long since I spoke to you.'

'How are your children and husband?'

'Fine, they are all fine.'

Tọlá was saved by the doorbell. 'Kẹmi, let me call you back, someone's at the door.'

Her heart sank as she pulled open the door to Mọríebá. She had never particularly liked the woman who walked through her door as though she owned the house, but then she'd never particularly disliked her either. She glanced at the clock. It was 5:45am.

'Good morning, Aunty Móríebá,' she said, careful to place an emphasis on the 'morning'. 'I'll go wake the children up.'

'No, please, not yet,' said Móríebá. 'I came to talk to you.'

Tọ́lá didn't feel like talking to Móríebá. She wanted to go into the bedroom and close the door. She wanted a smoke and a shot or two of vodka. But nobody cared what she wanted, so she sat down. Today was a very important day, and she would strive to be normal. She would do things that 'normal' people do, like sitting down with guests and arranging their clothes just so. Normal people didn't yell at visitors or slam the door in their faces. They wore expressions showing how interested they were in whatever bullshit their guests had to say.

'Can I get you something to drink ma?' she asked politely.

Móríebá shook her head. 'We need to talk.' She patted a space beside her. 'Would you mind coming closer?'

Tọ́lá shifted a little closer to her, wondering why the woman was being so dramatic.

'I am sorry if in the past I made you feel as if it's your fault your parents treated me less than human when I came to live with you as a teenager.'

Móríebá was well known to be tactless, so Tọ́lá was not surprised by her words.

'It was not your fault. You had nothing to do with it. I know that you have your own problems, but I want to talk to you as a woman, and a mother.' Móríebá raised her hands and smiled ruefully. 'I know I don't have children of my own, a choice I made many years ago, but that doesn't mean I don't have human feelings.'

Tọ́lá wondered where the conversation was headed. She also found it weird that Mọ́ríebá was the first woman she had sat that close to for the first time in a long while, and her skin wasn't crawling.

'Let me just get straight to the point.' Mọ́ríebá patted her hands, which were folded primly on her lap. 'You're the first person I'll be telling this, but I've found Alhaja's will.' She grinned. 'Not only was I made the sole executor, but I'm also Mọ́remí's legal guardian.'

The last sentence ricocheted around Tọ́lá's brain like a bullet. 'Please, not Mọ́remí.' She gripped Mọ́ríebá's hand and made to kneel down. 'Please don't take her away from me.'

Tọ́lá heard the desperation in her own voice but she didn't care. She was beyond caring. Mọ́remí was her secret keeper. Mọ́remí grounded her. She loved Mọ́remí in ways that she'd never thought it possible to love another human being who wasn't her blood. Mọ́remí and Kudirat were the closest she'd had to friendship since childhood. They never judged her; even at her lowest they were there. They shared a love for reading and watching films.

'I have no intention of "taking Mọ́remí away from you", as you put it.' Mọ́ríebá was implacable. 'Mọ́remí is not a thing to be given or taken.'

Tọ́lá recoiled at the accusation in her voice. The shame of the past, of her parents treating Mọ́ríebá as a housemaid, a slave, then sending her away because she was too headstrong, mixed in with the unacknowledged guilt of the present. Here she was, an adult, enslaving a girl for close to five years. For the first time, the saying about apples not falling far from the tree made absolute sense to her.

I'm a hypocrite, just like everybody I'd ever judged, a bloody hypocrite!

'More importantly,' Móríebá continued, her voice gentle again, 'Móremí is no longer a child. She will soon leave, whether you like it or not.'

Tọ́lá swallowed the truth of those words, bile in her throat.

'Here's what we are going to do,' Móríebá said, as Tọ́lá turned watery eyes towards her. 'You, the children, Móremí and Kudirat will come and spend part of the holidays with me. By the time you return home, I would have found you a proper housekeeper, someone who will take good care of both you and the children. I will pay you and her a monthly salary.'

A lifeline had just been thrown to her, without her asking. Here it was, a chance to get away from Wálé, to get her children away from him. Tọ́lá burst into tears.

Èṣù raised a toast to the women. For all his faults, Wálé had great taste in brandy.

SEASON FOUR:
THE WIND, THE DAMN'D
WHIRLWIND (2011–2012)

A WHIRLWIND CARRIED OFF THE BENENOISE KING

Kudirat clicked-clicked on killer high heels towards the venue. She walked dreamily, her short gown floating on a cloud of chiffon, the exact way it had happened in her dreams. Dreams she had kept for so long in a secret compartment in her heart. A secret she hadn't dared share in case the evils of the world, those who performed terrible deeds in the dead of the night, snatched it away and killed it with their stabbing knives. She felt lush. She was lush.

Her D-cup breasts, which had been banished underneath layers of clothes ever since they'd started growing, were on display, wiggling and jiggling. Breasts that she had previously kept hidden away from eyes that would lust after them, eyes that would judge her as loose just because of the way nature had made her. She pushed out her chest.

Her buttocks were shaken, those that had shamed her when she boarded a bus or taxi, people shouting about tiny girls with fat buttocks. Her rounded stomach, which she'd wanted to exchange for Mọ́remí's flat, iron-board stomach, was not sucked in. Her hair was combed out, the way she'd always wanted it to be: thick, dark and bushy, and softened with shea butter. She wore it – a crown. A touch of colour on her lids, purple, her eyes lined with kohl, her lips coated black. Lush.

Mọ́remí had not wanted anybody mucking around with her face. 'No make-up please, not even a light touch, thank you.' The make-up artist whom Mọ́ríebá had employed to prepare them for the party had left in a huff after sorting Kudirat.

Even at the tailor's, Mọ́remí had insisted that she didn't want a gown; she was never wearing another gown again. Gowns symbolised sadness. They reminded her of the black, shapeless one she had to wear during Alhaja's burial, of the washed-out ragged gowns she wore at Tọ́lá's house. No more gowns! They made her a pair of trousers and a loose shirt.

But Kudirat was wearing magic in Ankara and chiffon. Barely three weeks ago, she'd been a housemaid, stealing money, selling contraceptives, running after snotty-nosed kids, waking up at 4am to clean and wash and prepare for school. A few weeks ago she had been a slave.

But Kudirat had remembered. She remembered the rites of propitiation. After her ordeal with the school authorities, she had started offering the Òrìṣà some of the little she had. She gave Èṣù palm oil, she offered Ṣàngó bitter kola. She'd given Ọya, her personal Òrìṣà, black-eyed peas and corn.

Ọya, the all-seeing, all-knowing whirlwind, had seen to all that. She had spoken to the cold, harsh wind that had been Kudirat's life for the past five years. Ọya had ordered the storms to cease and had given her a warm, comforting breeze. She had decided to place her on a loving lap, the lap of luxury.

Kudirat was not one to go examining the teeth of a gift horse. She would seize the moment, make use of every advantage thrown her way. She would be smart.

Kudirat was her mother's daughter.

The people of Alágbàdo village had called her mother a whore, a husband snatcher, but her mother had seen a chance to leave the poverty of her life behind, and had seized it. Not a husband snatcher: she was an opportunity snatcher. She'd left the decrepit old farmer she'd been married to as a teenager for a younger man searching for a son. Although Kudirat hadn't seen her in over five years, the edicts her mother had passed down to her were her daily mottos. Be kind, but do not allow anybody to make a fool out of you. Work hard, but better still, work smart. Take advantage of any opportunity that comes your way, but don't be greedy. Nothing lasts forever.

I am my mother's daughter.

She had taken the news that she and Mọremí would be leaving Lagos for Anti Mọ́ríebá's house with a shrug. It was life, and didn't life have a way of throwing surprises your way? She had been somewhat bemused by the speed at which Tọ́lá had asked them to pack their things and the children's luggage for a holiday in Ibadan. It was as if somebody had injected new life into Tọ́lá. By the third day, their things were ready, hidden away in a corner of the kitchen where Wálé never ventured

'I'll be spending a week in Ibadan,' Tọ́lá said to the girls as she fetched her suitcase out of her room too.

Three weeks later, Tọ́lá and her children were still at Mọ́ríebá's. It appeared they had moved permanently into the little flat on the ground floor.

Mọ́ríebá had made them dump everything they'd brought from Lagos and had taken them shopping. Kudirat and Mọ́remí had been hesitant when they saw the price tags. The clothes cost more than the money they'd been able to put together in all their years of stealing. Mọ́ríebá had started picking clothes for them, and when the girls realised she was not going to stop, they had gone to choose the things they wanted for themselves.

Kudirat, being of a practical turn of mind, decided to take everything happening to her as a dream, so she acted the way she would have done in her dreams – like a queen. She stayed in bed and ordered breakfast from the cook, she ignored the children's screams, she watched TV in the afternoon! She wore brand-new clothes and new underwear, every day! She sat in a car and was driven everywhere. The closest she'd come to doing any household chores was putting her clothes in the washing machine and picking them up later, ironed and neatly folded. She was living the dream and for as long as it lasted, she would.

Within the week, Mọ́ríebá had gone to register them in a school – a private school, with well-laid out classes in beautifully painted, airy classrooms. They had to drag Kudirat away from the science laboratory.

Kudirat's fingers were perpetually crossing, her breath in a state of suspension, afraid that if she breathed in too deeply she might wake up.

She crossed them again as they arrived at the red carpet. They were about to walk past the cameramen and photographers. Kudirat stopped.

'What is it now?' Mọremí sounded exasperated.

'It's the red carpet. We have to wait for our photographs to be taken and then we'll get interviewed.'

Kudirat's eyes were huge. She'd seen this done on TV before and had always wondered how it would feel standing in front of a camera. She flashed her most charming smile at the interviewer, a young man with a beard and a yellow bowtie. She pointed at Mọremí, who was rolling her eyes at her antics. 'We are the celebrant's daughters.'

The interviewer's eyes lit up as he scrutinised the girls. 'We have a pair of angels on our hand,' he murmured to the cameraman, who asked them to stand in front of a giant portrait of Mọríebá with 'Happy Birthday Pappy' splashed across it in bright red.

'I don't want to do this,' Mọremí whispered to Kudirat.

Kudirat tugged at her arm. 'But you will do this, for me.'

They stood in front of the camera, Mọremí scowling at her sneakers while Kudirat chatted and laughed and flirted.

'Pinch me, quickly,' Kudirat whispered as they went in.

'Uh?'

'I said, "Pinch me", so I'll know this is not a dream.'

Mọremí's squeezed-up face relaxed into a smile. 'Of course it has to be a dream. Stuff like this doesn't happen in real life.'

Kudirat moved closer to Mọremí, suddenly nervous. 'Do I look alright?' Mọremí took a long look at her, and Kudirat could see how beautiful she was in her eyes.

'shouldn't even be asking you, you're prejudiced.'

'And you are gorgeous,' said Mọ́remí, making heat rush up Kudirat's face. 'If this is a dream, I don't want to wake from it because of you. I've never seen you so happy before, and I want you to be happy.'

Kudirat felt tears burn her lids, but she pushed them back. 'You're just mean, you want to spoil my make-up because you are not wearing any.'

They descended the staircase leading into the hall, Kudirat gripping Mọ́remí's arms so she wouldn't fall over in her heels. As soon as she stepped off the last stair, she turned towards Mọ́remí and yelled, 'I want to dance.'

'But shouldn't we find a table first?'

'Not if this is a dream. I don't want Ọya or whoever is in charge to wave her wand and make it all disappear before I dance in front of a live band led by Alhaji Igi-Sekele.'

'What in the world are you on about?'

'You won't understand,' Kudirat murmured.

Ngozi would. They shared a love for Fújì music and filled their phones with songs from different Fújì musicians. Kudirat had grown up on Àpàlà and Fújì, which her father played early in the mornings and in the evenings, whenever there was power supply. The beats of wéré and talking drums comforted her, took her back to her days of innocence when her biggest worries had been whose compound she and her friends would steal mangoes from.

She suddenly missed Ngozi and the rest of the gang. She wanted to share her good fortune with them, show them what real happiness meant. She would show them the washing machines and hoovers, all sorts of appliances that made the jobs they spent their days slaving over so easy. She would tell them that there were people trained to do all those jobs they did, people who made a good living from this and got days off. She wanted to tell them about being a teenager and being free from toil.

Mọ́remí protested all the way to the stage where the musician was singing about a Benenoise king who was carried off by a whirlwind, to the frenetic beat of snare drums.

> Ewo ji toja togb'Oba aganyin
> Ogbe Kofi, Nene,
> I don't know,
> I don't care ...

Kudirat threw herself into the beat. It had been too long since she had danced, too long since she had let herself go and allowed the music to dictate the movement of her body. Women in colourful Ankara and lace joined them on the dancefloor. They wore outlandish gowns made in mad designs. Their titties were out, draped with jewels. They wore make-up like superstars and had stashes of naira notes in their tiny bags. These women were free and confident. It showed in how they carried their gèlè, twisted into mind-bending designs, on elegantly held heads. They gyrated and twirled their waists to the music.

Not long afterwards, men in flowing agbádá joined them and started pasting their foreheads with brand-new naira notes. The women were provoked into frenzied dance steps, hips swaying, bosoms shaking, while their gèlè gleefully defied the law of gravity.

Kudirat and Mọ́remí climbed up the stage and started spraying the musician with freshly minted hundred naira notes, given to them earlier by Mọ́ríebá. Kudirat was happy that she had been able to convince Mọ́remí to let them keep some of the money underneath their mattress before coming to the party. She knew if she had more, she would have sprayed it all.

The band segued into another song, praising them to the high heavens. Nothing less than new naira notes would do for Alhaji Igi-Sekele.

Owó tuntun l'èmí nfẹ́
Kudirat ó jẹ náírà,
O jẹ Euro,
O jẹ Pounds,
Ótún jẹ dollars rẹpẹtẹ

Not to be outdone, a gentleman who looked danger-ously close to delivering a set of triplets joined them on stage and started throwing hundred naira notes. Kudirat and Mọ́remí stepped away from the melée as people scrambled for the money, tucking it into their pockets and bras.

'Kai but you girls are slow o! See how you were looking on like Lukman while those women grabbed the money that the man was spraying,' said a voice by their shoulders.

It was Tolú, Kudirat's stepsister. Tolú was the daughter of the woman her mother had snatched her father from. She remembered Tolú's mother as Anti L'Ẹgbă, the trouble-maker who usually came to bug her dad about school fees. Tolú and Kudirat had met for the first time earlier in the week in the company of L'Ẹgbă, who was handling the catering for the party. L'Ẹgbă had simply pointed at Kudirat and said, 'That's your sister. Her name is Kudirat.'

Tolú had shrugged and walked away. It surprised Kudirat that she was suddenly being friendly.

'You guys look alike,' Mọremí said softly.

The similarities in the line of their jaws and dainty noses, and even in their height and blue-black skin hue, were so pronounced they could almost pass for twins.

'We should. After all we share the same father,' Tolú said dismissively.

Kudirat looked away in embarrassment. Nobody talked about stuff like that; there was too much history. Too many people had been hurt by decisions taken by the adults in their lives. She felt that Tolú resented her, but she shouldn't have bothered wasting her emotions. After all, their dad had practically sold Kudirat into slavery.

An uncomfortable silence descended on the trio as they dragged chairs around an empty table. Kudirat's stomach reminded her that she had barely eaten all day, so she waved frantically at one of the servers bearing a tray full of food. The server ignored her.

'What's this nonsense? I'm hungry!' she protested as another tray was carried past their table.

'You girls are truly learners. You'd better go to one of the serving points and order what you want, or you're going to be ignored all night,' instructed Tolú.

Of course we are learners, we've spent the past five years cooped up with a perv and his mad wife! The words sprang to Kudirat's lips but she swallowed them. She was ashamed of calling Tọlá mad, even in her mind.

Kudirat jumped out of the chair and tottered towards one of the serving points scattered around the tent. 'Helluur,' she said in the fakest Lagos accent she could summon. 'My muom' – she swept the room, spotted

Mọ́ríebá at a table filled with fat yellow women and all kinds of alcohol and waved at her – 'said I should cuom and tawk to you, that you'll take gewd currof uz.'

The young man nodded, and before long Kudirat was leading, triumphantly, a train of servers bearing different kinds of food and drinks. The servers laid out the table while Kudirat returned to the drinks stand. She was back a few minutes later, grinning like the cat that got the cream.

'Okay, tell me what you've done,' said Mọ́remí.

Kudirat pulled her arm from underneath the table and flourished a bottle of Irish cream under Mọ́remí's nose. 'We are fulfilling another fantasy tonight.'

'I'm not drinking that,' Mọ́remí protested.

'Oh yes you are!' Kudirat poured generous shots into three glasses. 'Remember the night you convinced me not to drink too much of the one on Dr Wálé's liquor shelf ...' She trailed off, remembering him. She wondered again, as she had repeatedly since they arrived in Ibadan, if he knew where his wife was.

'I remember no such thing,' said Mọ́remí.

Kudirat had lost the heart to hound Mọ́remí, so she fell quiet. She shivered with trepidation at what could happen if Dr Wálé didn't know his wife was in Ibadan. Kudirat dropped the bottle on the table and sighed.

'I suggest you hide that bottle, because here comes Anti Mọ́ríebá,' Tolú said, her eyes fixed on her phone.

The girls turned guiltily, but instead of Mọ́ríebá they found Quadri the Bookworm standing behind them.

Quadri was another person they'd met at Aunty Mọ́ríebá's house. He was one of Olórí Ẹbí's sons, a frequent visitor they ignored. Kudirat had decided that she didn't like him because Mọ́remí said the son of a snake was a snake.

He flashed them a snakey smile. 'Am I not the luckiest man in the world? Finding a bevy of beauties sitting all by themselves, who are feeling lonesome and unappreciated, is a rare honour.' He sat down and beamed at them.

'Stuff your cheesy words jọ!' Kudirat said contemptuously. 'We are your cousins. You're not supposed to be looking at us like that, and I don't remember anybody asking you to sit on that chair.'

'Kudi baby, even though you're my second cousin twice removed or something of that nature, I don't think it's fair that you'd deny me the pleasure of basking in the light of your beauty and eating part of this spread.' He paused. 'Tasting the Irish cream you're hiding under the table will also be nice.'

Mọremí scowled at him. 'Are you for real?'

'Oh, yes, I am for real, my third cousin Mọremí, whatever that means, and I can always call Anti Mọríebá to seek her opinion on this matter, since she's standing right over there.' Quadri waved at Mọríebá, who smiled at him and waved back.

'Stop teasing the girls, Quadri,' Tolú admonished. 'Don't mind Quadri. He might be one of Olórí Ẹbí's sons, but he's totally cool.'

The girls relaxed and started heaping food onto their plates. Within a short while most of the food on the table had disappeared and the bottle of Irish cream was nearly empty. They were all giggling and talking affectionately to one another.

Quadri disappeared and after a while he returned with a bottle of wine.

'Good boy Quadri,' Kudirat said as he sat down.

'I haven't seen your dad tonight,' said Tolú.

Mọ́remí's expression froze.

'Oh, he's not coming. He hates Anti Mọ́ríebá too much to watch her being happy. She's the antithesis of everything he believes a woman should be. She's rich, young, unmarried and independent. She doesn't need him. To worsen things, she has just snatched darling Mọ́remí, with all her gorgeous money, from underneath his nose' He added casually, 'He told members of the family not to attend this party and threatened to place curses on anybody who dared to.'

Quadri looked around the tent and laughed. 'I guess he's not as feared as he imagines himself to be, or the lure of Àríyá has been more powerful. Isn't that table filled with the Alágbàdos both home and abroad?'

The three girls strained their necks towards the table Quadri was using his chin to point at, and truly the table was filled with people they were familiar with. Family members from Alágbàdo village were even present.

Quadri shrugged, popped some fried meat in his mouth and continued talking as soon as he swallowed. 'He's just jealous. He wants all the money in the world to belong to him. He has control issues. He loves it when people are dependent on him.'

'Don't be silly, your dad is not that bad,' Tolú said, in a tone that implied she did not mean what she was saying. She had even taken her eyes off her phone.

Quadri uncorked the wine. 'Oh yes he is. He's worse than you'd imagine. You obviously don't know him.'

'And you're being so casual about it?' Mọ́remí was baffled. 'Isn't he your father?'

Quadri raised an eyebrow. 'How else should I be? Go around scowling and being generally unhappy because my father is a mean bastard? I refuse to be like my brothers, who pretend to be like him so that he will love them. The only person my father loves is himself.' He smiled. 'You people are young, so you wouldn't understand.'

'It's good that you're all happy about the way your dad goes about destroying people's lives, taking things that don't belong to him, but I don't think I'll ever forgive him for what he did to me,' Mọ́remí said hotly.

'Don't get all worked up: what he's done to you is mild stuff compared with what he's done to other people. I can tell you stuff about Bàámi that would make your toes curl. Do you know I met my mother for the first time this year? I'm nineteen years old and for most of my life I actually believed she was dead because Bàámi told me so.'

He picked up a piece of chicken and passed the bottle of wine to Tolú. The girls stared at him goggle-eyed.

'What? Why are you all staring at me like that?'

'You're talking about Olórí Ẹbí.' Kudirat whispered the name as if saying it any louder would summon the man into their presence.

'I used to believe everything he told me, until I met my mum. I've discovered that the only way to make my father powerless against you is by being indifferent to him and his theatrics.' His voice deepened into a whisper, and he turned serious all of a sudden. 'You plan your moves against him quietly. Never show your hand, prepare to fight dirty and, when you're ready … go for the jugular.'

Three jaws went slack.

'So, are you going to move in with your mum?' Mọ́remí asked after a heartbeat.

'No.' Quadri straightened up and took another sip of his wine. 'He doesn't even know that my mother finally found me, or that I know that she's alive. She's afraid of him. I will stay with him until I collect my admission letter and then I'm off. He's made it clear to us all that he's not going to pay our fees past secondary school anyway, and he has many sons, I don't think he'll be too worried about me.'

He looked straight into Mọ́remí's eyes. 'By the way, Mọ́remí, I'd be careful. Bàámi doesn't give up easily, and I know he's up to something.' He leaned in and whispered, 'Watch your back!'

Èṣù drew up a chair and sat beside Àríyá, the Órìṣà of great Yoruba parties, who was ensuring that the celebration was going as smoothly as possible by sprinkling excitement and giddiness intermittently in the air.

'These Alágbàdos really know how to throw it down! Abeg, pass me that Cîroc.'

BACK TO REALITY...

Tọ́lá walked around Agodi Gardens, marvelling at how much things had changed. She felt as if she was seeing Ibadan for the first time. Everything her gaze fell upon had a patina of glitter.

She could truly see; she was looking around instead of constantly looking inside. The windows of her mind were thrown open, and she gloried in the sunshine.

Her sneaker-clad feet danced down walkways. She gave them freedom to lead her where they would. And they remembered her favourite places, they led her to the little corner where she used to feed the monkeys, to a tree that she climbed as a child. Her feet knew her path to happiness, so she followed them.

The garden was one of the few places in Ibadan (or anywhere else for that matter) that held good memories. Memories of Easters past, when, as a child, her family would picnic in the garden. Because the church posters always described the picnic as 'Going to Galilee to watch Jesus rise from the Grave', for a long time Tọ́lá believed that Agodi was the town of Galilee.

It was the only place where she had been allowed to be a child. She and Kẹ́mi would chase each other around, play hide and seek with other children, feed the animals and climb the trees.

As she grew older, she not only discovered that Agodi was not Galilee, but also found out that she didn't like being with the others. She began taking explorative walks into its heart, further and further away from her parents, the church, her sister. She would lose herself in the trees and flowers, in the chirping of birds, the howling of monkeys, only returning to the group when it was nearly time to leave.

A monkey chattered at her from one of the trees that populated the nature conservatory. Tọ́lá chattered back to it and threw it the rest of her biscuits.

Oh to be free!

Lagos had become a distant memory, her brain shutting down that part of her life with Wálé as if it had been a dream, an insubstantial nightmare.

Her phone jangled. It was Kudirat.

'Anti, you'd better come home now, now, now!' Kudirat's panic reached through the phone.

'The children—'

'The children kẹ̀? Anti this one pass the children o! There is fire on the mountain! Your mummy and Uncle Wálé are shouting—'

The sound of scuffling filled Tọ́lá's ears as Kudirat's voice faded.

'Hello, hello, Kudirat, are you still there? Kudirat!'

Suddenly Mọ́remí's calm voice came over the phone. 'Hello, Anti Tọ́lá, it's me, Mọ́remí.'

'What's going on there?'

'I think you should come home. Some people are asking for you.'

'And they are shouting at Aunty Mọ́ríebá,' Kudirat yelled into the phone.

'Anti Tọ́lá just come home—'

Tọ́lá was already at the exit and on her way.

She waited for a taxi. She could leave now and never look back. She could hide and wait them out. She could return to Agodi Gardens and take out her SIM card, the way she'd replaced the one she was using in Lagos.

But that wasn't the way to treat a woman who had given her a chance, no questions asked, and Wálé would win, he would get the children. She died a little inside. That wasn't a thought she even wanted to contemplate.

More importantly, where would she go? Yes, she had some money in her bank account, money she'd siphoned from their joint account over the years, but what about headaches? What about Rita?

In the past few months, she had somehow managed to control Rita and her appetites. She still had days when the whisper of feet on the floor would send her scurrying into the bedroom, doors locked, windows barred. But it was somehow not as bad as it used to be. It was like the top layer of darkness had been lifted off. Nobody came to tell her to stop it or get out of bed. She didn't know what miracle Mọ́ríebá had performed but even the children seemed to be more understanding. They had so many people doting on them they weren't as desperate for her attention. Mọ́ríebá had made it okay for her to stay in the darkness and feel safe.

She hailed a taxi.

Tọ́lá got out in front of Mọ́ríebá's house, bracing herself for the onslaught of the high Italian opera she was about to participate in.

'Grandma and Dr Wálé and Olórí Ẹbí are waiting for you,' said Kudirat, opening the gate for her. Mr Sule, the gateman, hovered in the background. Tọ́lá stepped into the compound.

'The children are in your flat with Mọ́remí.' Kudirat lowered her voice. 'We've told them to keep quiet or Ojuju-Calabar will carry them off.'

Tọ́lá smiled faintly. Not one but three Ojuju-Calabar were already waiting to swoop them back to a dungeon. Her children's greatest enemies were not some mythical masquerade from Calabar: they were much closer.

'There she is!' her mother shrieked from inside.

Tọ́lá was suddenly surrounded.

'Where are the children?' asked her mother, Olórí Ẹbí and Wálé, all in different tones: her mum's a shriek, Olórí Ẹbí's a deep boom, Wálé's icy.

Tọ́lá tried to shut out their voices and walk towards the house, but she was pulled back roughly by Wálé.

'You are not taking another step until I see my children.'

'Jesus, my saviour, my Lord, who has done this to my child?' Tọ́lá's mother had taken off her scarf and wrapped it around her waist. 'This is the handiwork of my enemies.' She shut her eyes and started praying. 'Oh Lord of Esau, Lord of Jacob, Lord of Israel, bring fire down and consume all my enemies. All those who are jealous of my child's marital success shall die by fire. Bring down the mountains oh lord and they shall become like mud underneath my feet, let my enemies die, by fire, die! Die! Die!'

Tọ́lá expelled a breath of disgust and stepped away from her mother, who continued her shrieking. Èṣù stepped closer to Iya Tọ́lá and studied the different expressions on her face.

'If there's any witch or enemy here, it's you, mother,' Tọ́lá said, when she couldn't take it any longer.

Her mother stopped mid-tirade, her mouth agape. She held her breasts in consternation. It was an unspoken rule that nobody interrupted when she was praying. People were expected to stand in awe of her prowess, her use of words a sword of righteousness, of judgement.

'Iya Tọ́lá,' Olórí Ẹbí interjected, 'I've told you that Mọ́ríebá's juju is strong. We need to get your poor daughter and her children away from her before it's too late.'

'I am not going anywhere,' said Tọ́lá.

'What did you just say?' Olórí Ẹbí growled.

'You are coming with us whether you like it or not.' Wálé was still in character as the hard-done-by, valiant man.

Tọ́lá looked at him fully in the face. 'Is it so that you can have access to the children and do your evil with them?'

Wálé looked at her with contempt. 'I told you Olórí Ẹbí, this girl is mad. Can you imagine what she's saying?'

'You know what?' Olórí Ẹbí lowered his tone so it became a soothing rumble. 'I think we should all calm down.' He turned towards Tọ́lá with something that might have been a smile. 'We'll go to my place and discuss this.

At the end of the day, you can either decide to either stay here or to return to Lagos with your husband.'

Tọ́lá looked at each of them. A determined look was on their faces. They were ready to make trouble. Maybe it was even better this way. 'Okay, let me go and inform Anti Mọ́ríẹbá tha—'

Wálé dragged her back. 'I want my children, and you're not leaving until I see them.'

'Calm down, Wálé.' Olórí Ẹbí patted him on the back. 'Legs are removed from a pair of trousers one after the other. We will sort everything out.' He gave Tọ́lá the tic pretending to be a smile again. 'You may go and tell her. We'll wait here for you. Please don't take too long.'

Mọ́ríẹbá met Tọ́lá at the door. 'What have you decided?'

'We'll be going to Olórí Ẹbí's house for a meeting,' she replied, taking Mọ́ríẹbá's hand in hers. 'I'm sorry about the embarrassment.'

Mọ́ríẹbá squeezed her hand. 'It's alright, Tọ́lá, if they'd been civil, I would have been surprised. You're an adult and should be allowed to make your own decisions.'

'I have made up my mind. I'm not returning to Lagos. They can't make me.'

Mọ́ríẹbá snorted in disgust. 'Just take care of yourself and watch your back. That old man can't be trusted.'

Tọ́lá pulled the door shut, closed her eyes and leaned her head against it, a dull throbbing behind her eyelids. She was ill prepared: she'd naively assumed she could hide out in Mọ́ríẹbá's house forever.

She took a deep breath, straightened up and went back outside.

'I'll sit in front with Wálé, you sit in the back with your mother,' Olórí Ẹbí ordered as they got to the car.

The drive to Olórí Ẹbí's house in the heart of Idi-Ikan would have been deathly quiet if Iya Tọ́lá hadn't been muttering prayers.

'I am not returning to Lagos with Wálé,' Tọ́lá said as soon as they were all seated in Olórí Ẹbí's parlour. 'As far as I'm concerned our marriage is over.'

Tọ́lá's mother jumped out of her seat. 'That will not be your portion in Jesus' name! My daughter will not be a single parent or a divorcée! I serve a living God, and he shall not allow my feet to be moved, the God of Israel does not sleep nor slumber, a thousand shall fall—'

'Ah, that's enough,' Olórí Ẹbí hissed impatiently.

Wálé watched all of them with an air of cold detachment.

'So, Tọ́lá, what led to this decision?' asked Olórí Ẹbí .

Tọ́lá knew the answer. She didn't love Wálé, she'd never loved him. She had married him because her parents had told her to. But they wouldn't care. They didn't hold truck with such nonsense. Marriage was for procreation and for women to have a crown on their heads, the husband being the crown, of course.

Should she tell them about Jésùtitófúnmi? But what evidence did she have? And what about the meds? Why did she need to justify herself? Why couldn't they just accept her decision?

'He's been giving me medications without my knowledge,' she blurted out.

'Ngbọ́ Wálé?' Olórí Ẹbí turned towards him.

'I don't know why we are holding this meeting when you all know quite well that she is mental!' Wálé's air of disinterest had hardened into cold rage. 'How can a woman leave her marital home, with her children, without informing anybody? She just disappeared. I've nearly gone mad searching for her all over Lagos. It wasn't until yesterday that her mother called that I found out she'd been in Ibadan all along.' He narrowed his eyes at Iya Tọ́lá. 'I am not even sure this was not a plan between mother and daughter!'

Iya Tọ́lá was out of the chair in a flash. 'Wálé, how can you say such a thing?'

'Sit down, woman!' Olórí Ẹbí barked. 'Continue what you were saying my dia son-in-law.'

Tọ́lá's heart sank. Of course she knew the outcome of this meeting. She tightened her face. *I won't let them bully me.*

Wálé pointed a dramatic finger at her. 'This woman is an ingrate! She has not only accused me of molesting my own daughter, she's also threatened to kill me. In fact she can stay in Ibadan for all I care! I just want my children back.'

Tọ́lá cringed as her mother knelt in front of Wálé. 'Don't be like that, my son-in-law, please don't let her foolishness separate you.'

'Mama, please stand up,' he said, pulling her up.

Tọ́lá wanted to tear out her hair, she wanted to throw herself on the ground and weep. Her mother's pleading was a taste of the humiliation she knew was in store for her. The oasis of the last few months had in fact been a mirage.

I'm so fucked.

Wálé flashed her a triumphant look. 'As I was saying, Olórí Ẹbí, we all know about Tọ́lá's condition. I knew about it before I married her. I thought I could manage it.' He turned towards Iya Tọ́lá. 'Am I lying?'

Iya Tólá shook her head mutely, her head downcast.

'Six years sir! Six years of managing her ... her ...'

'You don't have to say it,' Olórí Ẹbí said sagely.

You married me off at seventeen because you couldn't bear me. The churches, the deliverances hadn't worked.

A memory peeped through, of being tied down, a live cock rubbed over her naked body by an old man in sultana with rotten teeth.

Olórí Ẹbí sighed loudly. 'It is in a bid to eat yam that the fingers get stained by palm oil. It is quite entertaining watching a mad man dance naked in the market place.' He gave Tólá a meaningful stare. 'But a mad man is not a thing to be desired as a child. Wálé, please go on.'

What the fucking hell is he on about?

Tólá shushed Rita.

'I took her to see a psychiatrist after she had our last child and fell into deep depression.'

Tólá looked at Wálé. It was the first time she'd heard that she'd been to see a psychiatrist. Was he telling the truth?

'I even took her to see a female psychiatrist! One of my colleagues, Dr Adejana,' Wálé continued. 'She was the one that recommended the meds to her, these are just ordinary multivitamins and antidepressants. We started out with benzodiazepines, but when that wasn't working, she said that we should put her on a course of Zyprexa or Seroquel.'

Olórí Ẹbí cleared his throat. 'Ekùn! That's my doctor! See how he's speaking big-big grammar.'

Tólá's head began to pound in earnest. She stepped aside for Rita.

'In the past six months, it appeared that the medicine was actually working! I had hopes that things would turn around, but I was wrong!' Wálé shifted his attention and turned to face her. 'Here's the thing: I will not force you to return to Lagos with me. However, I'm taking my children, because I cannot allow them to be raised by a psychotic woman.'

'My in-law, you don't have to say anything further,' said Olórí Ẹbí. He turned to face the woman he presumed to be Tọ́lá. 'I think you've heard all the things your husband has said, and as your father's best friend and also the head of this family, I order you to return to your husband's house!'

Olórí Ẹbí's voice rose in volume, and he moved to the edge of his seat. 'Do not allow a jealous woman who has neither husband nor children ruin your marriage. A woman without a husband is like a king without his crown. Do not allow someone use jazz to spoil your head.'

Rita studied him closely: the frantic manner his Adam's apple ran up and down his neck, his dark, thick lips, his surprisingly white teeth, those plump cheeks, his pink tongue dotted black in patches. She giggled. 'I'm so fucked.'

Iya Tọ́lá burst into tears and started praying. 'All you spirit of wickedness, the spirit of madness that wish to take over my daughter, I bind you in Jesus' name! I bid you depart!'

'I told you, Olórí Ẹbí, she's mad.' Wálé jumped out of his seat. 'In fact, I'm leaving, I will go and pick up my children.'

Rita kept on laughing. She laughed so hard tears were streaming down her face. She was laughing at herself, at the corner into which she'd been boxed. She laughed at them, because they had no idea. 'I don't know what that woman has told you to make you think you can leave with my children!'

'I will take those children from you! You will never see them again!' Wálé blazed at her, ignoring Iya Tọ́lá, who was clinging to his leg, tears running down her cheeks, words of self-abasement spilling out. She was promising him heaven and earth, if only ...

Olórí Ẹbí, who had been staring at Rita wide-eyed, shouted, 'Enough of all this! What is funny about us? You think we're here to play?' He rose from his seat and loomed over them all. 'I have heard that you're mad, but now I can see how very mad you really are!'

The hysteria in the room rose a notch more as Wálé turned towards Olórí Ẹbí. 'I already warned you, sir, this is what I live with on a daily basis, and I'm done!'

Madwoman ... Crazy girl ... Medicine ... Seroquel ... Delusional ...

Then, to Tọ́lá's surprise, Rita burst into tears.

'This matter has passed "be careful" o.' Olórí Ẹbí looked at her warily. 'I hope she won't start tearing her clothes off now.'

'She's not been taking her medicine,' Wálé said.

Olórí Ẹbí looked at him in admiration. 'Ah Wálé, so you've been managing this madness all these years without complaining?'

'I'll return to Lagos with you,' Rita muttered. She straightened her spine, wiped her face and looked at them soberly. 'I'll return to Lagos with you.'

'Praise God!' Iya Tọ́lá shouted.

PHOTOGRAPHS IN SEPIA

Mọ́remí envied Kudirat. She envied the easy way she had settled into their new life, taking the ups as easily as she had taken the downs. She envied her laid-back, shit-happens and we-are-all-going-to-die-someday attitude.

She acknowledged the huge thing that kept her awake at night – anxiety. How she felt everything, how she bottled up everything. Everything included her mother: an abiding, hour-on-the-hour fear that her mother was dead, or that she'd overdosed on heroin and was now a vegetable, rotting away in some dank corner of Nigeria. Or worse still, that she was one of the teeming masses of junkies that littered the streets, begging, stealing, prostituting. That one day, she'd run into her and her mother wouldn't recognise her.

She bottled up those moments when she missed her grandmother so painfully that her chest would contract, her lungs gasping for air. Inside too there was also her deep-seated hatred for Olórí Ẹbí and Wálé, and her resentment of Tọ́lá, who had burdened her with more secrets – as if she did not have enough of her own.

She hadn't even known how to name all these emotions until she'd met Miss Akunne, the counsellor at her new school. The feelings just roiled and bubbled inside her, and sometimes the pressure would build in her head until it was fit to burst. It was during those moments that she lashed out at the nearest object, or person, who was usually Kudirat, her whipping boy.

When they had started at their new school, Mọ́remí had been so sullen and uncommunicative in class that she'd been sent in to see Miss Akunne. She had been going to see the counsellor regularly, for fifteen minutes every day. The woman had given her books to read and new words to express how she felt. Miss Akunne would listen, whether she spoke or not, and gradually Mọ́remí talked:

about her grandmother and her mother, about Tọlá and her years of servitude.

Her sessions with the school counsellor added to the list of things she worried about, because the school was a far cry from Bariga Comprehensive High School.

The school itself was built in the form of a square around a vast field, where students played games in the afternoon. There were different buildings and classes for different subjects. The teachers were polite and well educated. They even seemed to enjoy teaching. Instead of blackboards, there were white boards connected to the internet. iPads had replaced textbooks and notebooks. Instead of getting caned, they were sent to see Miss Akunne. Their science laboratories were actual laboratories, with gleaming equipment. Where Bariga Comprehensive High School housed broken dreams and desperate hopes, Berger High School made dreams come true. Students were friendly, speaking a language so advanced that Mọremí sometimes wondered if she was still in secondary school. Terms like intersectionality, politics of colour and race, radicalism and feminism were casually thrown around.

The other students asked Mọremí the meaning of her name. 'Were you named after that Ife Princess/warrior/ spy? Or does the name have other meanings?' They wanted her to talk about being biracial ('We are all mixed you know'). They held group discussions about being part Russian, Eriterian or Igbo, and how that affected their way of seeing the world.

Sometimes she missed Bariga Comprehensive, with its uncomplicated students.

Everything about the new school whispered sophistication, wealth, international travel. On Fridays, the school dressed in a wild array of colours. The other students casually dropped the names of designers she'd only watched on E!, the same way they dropped the names of Nigerian one-percenters in the most harmless of conversations. They loved Kudirat because she was so 'quaint' and 'traditional', said she was lucky to have lived an 'authentic African lifestyle', that her Yoruba was so 'effortless'. But Kudirat lapped it up, hamming it up any time they were in the cafeteria. She would drop her aitches, indiscriminately, like soft-boiled eggs, and on her good days she'd throw in a little capering, mocking their mockery of them.

There were wild parties on weekends where everybody got high on love and other illegal substances. Parties that Mọ́remí attended for two reasons: to watch Kudirat dance and to kiss girls in dark corners.

'I love, love your aunt,' a girl called Trixie had sighed one morning as they walked through the school reception area together. 'In fact I think I have a little crush on her. She's so butch.' She skittered away at Mọ́remí's stony visage. Nobody talked about things like that in the light of day, not even in the hallowed halls of Berger High.

Mọ́remí's new anxiety had started insidiously enough, but the longer she stayed with Mọ́ríebá, the realer it became. She worried about the money Mọ́ríebá was spending to keep them in the school, the amount she spent on the new designer clothes she kept buying for them. She even worried about the amount of food she and Kudirat were eating.

On some days, she suspected Mọ́ríebá was doing these things more for herself than for them. The seriousness with which she'd taken up her role as an adoptive mother to two teenage girls spoke of careful planning, years of secret yearnings.

'I've been reading up about teenagers, and according to the book, this is when you're at your most vulnerable. We need to work on your self-esteem,' Móríebá had said.

Móremí's fortunes had finally changed. But they weren't hers. She worried that Móríebá's resources would soon be depleted, and she would come to resent them.

In the Roberts household, money was a tangible thing, discussed in raised voices behind closed doors, accompanied by slaps, screams and the slamming of doors. With Móríebá, money was simply there: in the quality of the food and the battery of maids who came and went with quiet politeness. It was in their bank accounts with alarming regularity. It wasn't discussed. But Móremí and Kudirat quietly talked about it. Móremí's grandmother had told her that if something appeared to be too good to be true, then it must be.

As she walked down the long corridor to Móríebá's room and knocked on the door, she thought about Miss Akunne, who had insisted that fears were to be faced, because what was the worst that could happen?

'Come in,' said Móríebá cheerfully from inside her room.

Móremí pushed open the door and stepped in.

'Good morning, Móremí!' Her aunt smiled at her. She was in bed with the curtains drawn. The air was crispy and scented with the expensive perfumes she wore. 'Shut the door after you and come and lie beside me.'

'Good morning, Anti'. Móremí climbed into bed with her aunt. She pulled the covers over herself and snuggled into Móríebá.

'I love having you here with me.' She pulled Mọremí closer. Mọríebá was always saying things like that. She called it positivity, speaking love.

'I've come to discuss something with you,' Mọremí said hesitantly. 'I'm worried about school.'

Mọríebá froze. 'Have they been bullying you? Are you having academic problems?'

'No, no, Anti,' Mọremí laughed. She had no doubt that her aunt would deal with anybody that dared bully her. 'I'm worried about the school fees.'

'Bah! How much is it that you're worrying?'

'You're paying in dollars, Anti, the money runs into millions of naira! And that's not counting all the clothes, and the shoes and the food.'

'I can afford it,' Mọríebá said dismissively. 'I grew up in poverty. Before the age of ten, I learnt how to take care of myself. I lost both parents before I turned five, and I'm sure you've heard the story of how I was passed around like battered luggage before your grandmother finally took me in. I worked for this money, I, Mọríebá Alágbàdo.' She pounded her chest. 'I know the name of wealth and I use it. My wealth is not dependent on the vagaries of the Nigerian economy. Are you familiar with the Yoruba word àgbàná?'

Mọremí shook her head.

'Àgbàná is the spirit of wastefulness. According to legend, when this spirit possesses your money, you end up destitute, but I'm so rich that if àgbàná enters my money through one end, it would emerge from the other end confused. I can live anywhere in the world and still remain a very wealthy woman. I'm far from poor, so you have nothing to worry about. But, more importantly, I enjoy spending money on you and Kudirat. Money means nothing if you can't share it with those you love.'

Mọremí decided to try another tack. 'Do you know how much my grandmother left to me?'

Mọríebá paused, then got up and fetched her phone from the table and started rifling through it. 'I'm not so sure.' She picked up a pair of reading glasses and placed them on her nose. 'Ah, here's the list. She left about forty million naira, in her various accounts. She has four houses at Bodija and one shopping mall at Gate. She has two other houses somewhere in Ikoyi and another one in Lekki.'

All the facts and figures Mọríebá was throwing around didn't mean much to Mọremí, but it was reassuring, so she forged ahead. 'Do you think Olórí Ẹbí has spent all the money?'

'I know he has been collecting the rents on the houses and shopping mall.' A faint smile crossed her face. 'But he doesn't have access to the money in the banks. They have strict rules about relatives and papers and such like that.'

Mọremí was impressed by Mọríebá's openness. She doubted that most adults discussed their financial status with seventeen-year-old girls. 'Here's the thing, Anti ... Do you have access to the papers to the house and accounts?'

The question gave Mọríebá another pause. 'Actually, I've been so preoccupied with finding the will that I haven't even thought about the title deeds, but I think I know where all those things are stored.'

'I want us to find all those papers, Anti. I want you to use my grandmother's money to send Kudirat and I to school, and then invest the rest for us. That way I can at least stop worrying about burdening you with our school fees. Kudirat and I have discussed this, and we've decided that we should spend an extra year in school, maybe take one of their advanced classes while we sit for JAMB or apply to one of those medical schools abroad.'

Mọ́ríebá gave her a hug. 'Your head is correct! Your head is correct like the thrift collector of Somolu.'

Mọ́remí lifted her head off the pillow and looked straight into her aunt's eyes. 'My head is not correct, Anti Mọ́ríebá, but I have decided I will no longer be a victim, no longer a pawn to be pushed around by people. I am taking control of my money, of my life, and that's how it should be.'

Mọ́ríebá touched her cheek tenderly. 'You're now an adult.'

They made arrangements to go to her grandmother's house at Idi-Ikan on Saturday morning. Mọ́remí planned the outfit she would wear with meticulous care. She chose and discarded so many clothes that Kudirat started teasing her about how vain she was.

'Or is there somebody at Idi-Ikan you're hoping to impress?'

'I don't want anybody to recognise me,' Mọ́remí said, trying to make her understand. 'You see, all those people – they know me. Those children that we all played with when I was growing up will be there, staring at me.'

'Why is that so important? It's their eyes? They can use them to do anything they like.'

'The staring in Lagos I can take: they look at me as if I'm a rarity. But these ones, they know me as Mọ́remí, the richest girl in the neighbourhood, now returning as the girl who was a housemaid.' Mọ́remí hung her head as shame flooded her face pink. 'They'll all be laughing at me.'

She finally settled on a pair of baggy jeans, an oversized t-shirt with a hoodie and a pair of Timberlands. She was nervous throughout the drive to Idi-Ikan, but her worry was for nothing. The neighbourhood was deserted, except for a few naked children playing hopscotch in front of the house across from her grandmother's.

Iya Ruka met them at the car. She screamed and hugged Mọremí.

'Mọremí, my Mọremí.' She hugged her again, and pushed her hoodie off. 'See how tall you have grown, even taller than me.' She turned Mọremí around. 'What have they been feeding you in Lagos? Heey God, I thank you o! So I will still see you on this side of heaven?'

After fussing over Mọremí for a few more minutes, she fished out the key to the house from a cloth bag tied around her waist and opened the gate.

Mọremí held herself stiffly, afraid she might shatter if she allowed herself to absorb how decrepit her childhood home had become. The front yard had been overtaken by weeds, and as for the main house itself, it looked like an old man who had given up on life. Peeling paint, dark patches. The wooden windows that used to be thrown open to let in light and air were tightly shut.

'Sorry about the way grass is just growing anyhow,' Iya Ruka interjected into the silence. 'We are only cutting it once in a year, when we want be do party, àbí when we want be do meeting.'

Mọremí swallowed a smile at Iya Ruka's habit of speaking English; at least that one thing had not changed.

'We need to do something about this, Iya Ruka,' Mọríebá said. 'This house was meant to be lived in, not deserted like a graveyard.'

'Ah, last year I axe Olórí Ẹbí to let me be coming to be live here and be take care of everytin. My husband he yaff marry new wife, and she is a trouble woman. But Olórí Ẹbí didn't gree. He pain me well-well.' Iya Ruka unlocked the main door and pushed it open.

'Thank you, Iya Ruka, we'll take it from here.' Mọ́ríebá reached out for the keys.

The woman hesitated, and cleared her throat.

Mọ́ríebá smiled at her. 'Don't worry, I brought something for you. I'll give it to you before we leave.'

The woman returned the smile and dipped her knees before dropping the keys into Mọ́ríebá's open palm.

The musty smell of a house dying from neglect clogged Mọ́remí's throat, alongside memories. The first time, she'd stepped into the house hesitantly, just as she was doing now. A sombre five-year-old who didn't say much. Her first real birthday party had been thrown lavishly for her there, cakes, candles, party games. She had finally learnt how to smile, laughing as her grandmother tickled her. In the small parlour, she'd spent evenings on her grandmother's lap, having her hair matted, reading or being read to. Nights of watching Yoruba Nollywood films that her grandmother had been so fond of on the old colour TV.

She stepped into the big parlour. The pictures were still there. Sepia-coloured photos of ancestors past, scowling down at her through dirty glass from their lofty position in the skies above. She took another step into the room and looked at each photograph until she encountered her mother's full-coloured picture. She was so young, and happy. She grinned into the camera; the world was her oyster. There Mọ́remí was, wrapped in her mother's arms.

Another shot of her mother with a younger Olórí Ẹbí. She was grinning up at him while he scowled at the camera.

Mọremí picked the last frame off the wall. It was her mother at around eighteen years old. Gone was the naughty laughter, the happiness. Her face was drawn, ashy, with something like desperation lurking within her eyes.

Mọremí started as she felt a touch on her shoulder.

It was Mọ́ríebá. 'We will return another day. The house will be cleaned and repainted. Let's go and find what we came here for.'

In her grandmother's room, thick dust had settled everywhere, the damp making Mọremí's nostrils itch.

Mọ́ríebá knelt on the floor, unworried about getting her clothes dirty. 'She kept papers in a locked briefcase underneath her bed. Maybe she had a copy of the will in that briefcase. It should've been taken for safekeeping at her bank.'

Mọremí joined Mọ́ríebá on the floor as she started pulling out boxes of shoes, a suitcase full of clothes, more shoeboxes and finally a leather briefcase with broken locks.

'Aunty Mọ́ríebá,' Mọremí whispered as a memory dislodged by grief nudged her mind, 'I don't think we'll find papers.'

Mọ́ríebá looked up at her. 'Why?'

'Olórí Ẹbí took them.'

Mọ́ríebá expelled a sigh of disgust. 'When? Are you sure about this?'

'Yes Aunty. It was the day after Alhaja's burial. He was carrying boxes overflowing with paper. I met him as he came out of grandma's room.'

'Shit!' Mọ́ríebá stood up, then beamed. 'I bet he didn't find this though.' She headed off towards the wardrobe and started pulling out clothes. She unceremoniously dumped piles and piles of expensive materials on the bed. Mọ́remí wasn't surprised that none of Alhaja's clothes had been touched: nobody wanted the personal effects of a woman who died troubled.

After emptying it, Mọ́ríebá peered into the wardrobe. 'Come, let me show you.' She beckoned to Mọ́remí, and they both peered in at a bare wall. Mọ́ríebá placed her palm flat on the wall and slid a panel open, revealing a square-shaped hole.

Mọ́ríebá stepped back. 'I think you should do this; after all it belongs to you.'

Mọ́remí inserted her hand into the hole and pulled out a stack of five hundred naira notes, and then another stack, and another one. Just when she thought there was nothing else in the hole, her palm touched something hard and leathery. She pulled it out. It was a pouch. She pulled open the strings that held the mouth shut. Inside the pouch were three passbooks, a chequebook, her mother's and grandmother's passports, three gold chains and a thick gold ring.

Mọ́remí slipped the ring on her thumb. It fitted her perfectly.

MADAM CHERIE COCO...

Olórí Ẹbí paced the length of his spacious bedroom and studied, once again, the interlocking patterns of the wooden floor. Night after night, ever since that infernal girl! Sent from the pits of hell! Mọ́ríebá had come to see him about her damned business proposal! He had lost his sleep, his peace of mind.

He'd had it all neatly tied up: Mọ́remí sent to Lagos, the deeds to the properties and the will in his possession, rents flowing into his account, a deal in the works to sell the Lekki property. Now that fucking witch wanted to take it all away. She was out to ruin him!

The only things left were the bank accounts. How to bypass the fucking fussy official rules of the bank and get Alhaja's money out? To make matters worse, the stupid old woman had not used just one bank, but three damned banks, all of them greedy, none of them willing to cut a deal, fucking cowards! It had been 'bring one paper' after the other: affidavits, statements of accounts, signatures, death certificates, letters of authorization.

He had tried to figure out a way of declaring Àmọ̀pé dead, but had been meeting 419s and sheer incompetents.

He was tired. He needed sleep. Maybe his head would clear, maybe he'd be able to think better. The best he'd been able to manage was two hours interrupted by night-mares of Mọ́ríebá chasing after him with a machete, or his debtors coming to his office to disgrace him, or having to sell the only property left to him, his father's house. *The shame, the disgrace! She wants to open my yansh in public!*

He swept his hand over his head, gathering all the ill luck that might be hovering there, and snapped his fingers in the direction of the window. *A head attracting ill-luck does not belong to me.* He placed both hands on his head and blessed himself. *My head the praised, my head the worshipped.*

After a few more prayers, he calmed down somewhat and pulled open the drawer of his bedside cabinet, fetched a small bottle full of sleeping pills and swallowed four dry. The medicine had been recommended to him by the new doctor Wálé had sent him to see. The man had told him to take only two and warned him about how strong and addictive the pills were. Olórí Ẹbí laughed.

The doctor might be well versed in the white man's medicine, but he knew nothing about the spiritual, of witches, mothers of the night, who would tie hundreds of wrappers in flight. Those who ate your arm through your brain, mothers of the earth who consumed your heart through your kidneys. Women who drank human blood for sport.

If Mọ́ríebá wasn't a witch, how had she convinced poor, mad Tọ́lá to give her Mọ́remí's guardianship? How had she persuaded a woman well known for being antisocial to come out of her room, talk less of her flat? How had she managed to hide her from everybody for nearly three months?

A year before Alhaja Àdùkẹ́'s death, Bàbá Lálúpọn had informed him that Mọ́ríebá was a Yemoja initiate. Olórí Ẹbí had thought little of it, because he knew there were more fake initiations than real ones. But by this point, no one could convince him that Mọ́ríebá wasn't only a Yemoja initiate, she was also a witch, a proper one! The type they burn at crossroads.

Olórí Ẹbí grabbed the bottle of schnapps sitting on the cabinet, unscrewed the lid and gulped down a quarter of its contents in one long swallow.

The only thing that can quench this fire is a bigger conflagration. I have the matches and a keg full of petrol.

The alcohol burnt its familiar route into his gullet. He lay on his bed and shut his eyes, waiting for the slowing down of his heartbeat, the soft cloudiness that inked up the eyes. He was really, truly tired.

I just want to sleep, I need to sleep. Stop thinking, Raufu, if I can just stop thinking for a moment.

That woman, Iya Ruka or whatever her name was, had come yesterday around 7pm. She came with gleeful eyes and shining teeth that had been stained brown from eating too many kolanuts. Her goitre bounced; it danced a jig around her neck.

She'd come to thank him and to ask him to help thank Anti Mọ́ríebá. For the great and bloody wonderful Anti Mọ́ríebá had told her that she could move into Alhaja's house. Not only that, the amazing and freaking marvellous Anti Mọ́ríebá had given her some money to buy more sewing machines.

Oh, wasn't she a sweetheart? Wasn't she a hero? Shouldn't she be given a national award for being the most bleeding wonderful and damned marvellous Anti Mọ́ríebá ever liveth?

Olórí Ẹbí had looked at the woman with distaste. The acid in his guts burnt its way to his throat, bitter. That was how he had felt. Bitter and betrayed!

When he had given Iya Ruka the keys to Alhaja's compound, hadn't it been to help her? Not only would she have unsupervised access to the house, to take whatever she wanted, whenever she wanted it, she would also collect a stipend from him for the job. She had only been asked to clean up, once a year, around the time of Alhaja's remembrance. Nobody had questioned her about how she ran the place. But how had she repaid him? By opening the gate to that Mọ́ríebá and Mọ́remí!

'Couldn't you have informed me?' he yelled at the woman.

'But ... but, sir,' the woman had blabbered, 'I thought you already knew. Aren't they your daughters?' She had peered at him through sly, laughing eyes. 'Moreover, the house belongs to Mọ́remí, and nobody in their right minds would lock a landlord out of their own premises!'

That had been when he snapped. He had jumped on her with a fury that surprised even him. Olórí Ẹbí was not generally a violent man. Yes, he could be cold, calculated, evil even, but his violence had never been directed at women. Even in his former life as Raffie the Razor, he'd never raised his hand to hit a woman. He had his ways of dealing with women, better ways than merely beating them.

But he hadn't been able to control himself with that stupid woman. He had beaten her until she curled into herself like the cur she was. It had taken the trio of Ìyàwó, Quadri and Lékan to restrain him.

They should have allowed me kill to her. At least I would have rid the world of one damn ugly woman!

He knew the person to blame for his loss of control. *I-know-her-name!*

'Who told you the house belongs to Mọ́remí? Who told you that, you cross-eyed, goitre-infested excuse of a woman? In the days of yore, I would have sacrificed you to Ògún, because you're nothing more than meat to the gods!'

All this he had been yelling at her while Ìyàwó and Quadri had tried to put the woman together. They gathered her torn clothes off the floor and hurried her through the door, while Lékan held him bound in a nervous embrace.

Olórí Ẹbí's palms itched as they remembered the satisfaction of slapping Iya Ruka, punching her, poking her in the eye. Briefly, he felt a stirring of guilt, but he pushed it aside. Iya Ruka was beneath contempt. The person deserving his ire was nowhere near. Mọ́ríebá!

Èṣù had obviously ignored his pleas. Olórí Ẹbí hadn't been bothered at first: he'd simply gone ahead and called the attention of other Órìṣà. After all, there was a whole pantheon of them.

He had offered alligator blood, dog meat, kola – he even killed a whole cow for Ọya of tumultuous weather. He'd tried every damn thing Bàbá Lálúpọn had instructed him to proffer as sacrifices, but so far nothing had worked. Mọ́ríebá was still strutting about town like she owned the earth, throwing parties that made the news, her guests printed in full colour in many gossip magazines.

When he had gone to her house to retrieve Tọ́lá, and Iya Tọ́lá and Wálé had rained insults on her, instead of getting offended, she had merely smiled and offered them food. The fucking witch! Did she even know how to cook?

Olórí Ẹbí's thoughts roiled within him as the hands of the luminous clock hanging on the wall opposite his bed crept slowly, oh so slowly. He followed every tick. 5:00, 5:01, 5:02 ...

Someone was banging his head with a hammer. He opened his eyes. The clock said 6:23. The banging continued, as he realised it was his door. He flung aside the bedclothes and went to pull it open. It was Lékan.

'What is it now?' he asked wearily. He felt every single day of his fifty-four years, from his head to his littlest finger.

'Good morning, Bàámi.'

'Get to the point.'

'There are two men and four police officers downstairs. They are asking for you.'

Olórí Ẹbí's first instinct was to jump through the nearest window. 'Police ke?' He straightened up, noticing he wasn't dressed properly. 'Tell them I'll be down in a moment. Take them into the parlour.'

'I asked if they would like to sit down, but they refused sir.'

'Just go and stay with them, except you want me to come downstairs naked. Is that what you want?' He shut the door with a bang that echoed the collapse of his bravado. He leaned his head against the door, his palms clammy.

Is there going to be no end to this haunting? Did I do something to anger Èṣù? Why is ill luck following me about like a fart follows its owner? Is Àdùkẹ́ haunting me?

He sat at the foot of the bed and cradled his head in his arms. The last time he'd had anything to do with the police was twenty-three years earlier, when he had been in the first flush of his youth.

Olórí Ẹbí and his friends had been on a heist that had gone horribly wrong. It had, like previous ones, been meticulously planned. The insider was a well-known man who had brought successful deals to them in the past, but that last one had been a trap.

The husband and his wife had been prostrate on the floor, the money already taken out to the getaway car. But Sule, as usual, had been high, and wanted to mess around with the family before they left. He had just ordered the man's houseboy to start fondling madam's breasts when the police had barged in on them.

Luckily for Olórí Ẹbí, he had been rummaging through the fridge when the distinctive shock waves of police assault rifles set his alarms off. He'd gone into overdrive, squeezed through the kitchen window and jumped over the fence at the back of the house. The only thought in his head at the time had been that he would never repeat his experience with the police anti-crime division. He had been bewildered when he found himself in his father's house at Alágbàdo the following day, standing in the middle of his childhood home, surrounded by the debris of a long-abandoned compound.

No, it can't be that! I've not been back to Alábẹ́rẹ́ since then! It's twenty-three years ago!

He hurried into his clothes and was soon threading the stairwell with heavy steps, so that those waiting for him would know he did not fear them.

Four uniformed policemen and two in plainclothes were waiting for him. One stepped forward and handed him an envelope, while another pushed a clipboard towards him.

'Please, sign here, sir.'

'What am I signing? You can't just barge into a man's house and order him to sign papers! You can't come into my house and start threatening me!' Even as he was shouting, his bowels threatened to dislodge their contents.

'We are sorry, sir,' said one, whose bowtie looked like it was strangling him. 'My name is Murdoch, and I'm a clerk from the high court. The letter is a restraining order. You can look through it, but you do need to sign here to show that you received it.'

'You should have said all that before starting to act like a commando.'

Since they were not here to arrest him, Olórí Ẹbí thought it prudent to get rid of them quickly. He stretched out his hand for the clipboard and signed hurriedly, then stalked off to the sitting room and waited until he heard the front door shut behind them. He then looked at the thick envelope clutched in his fist. It was an officious-looking document bearing the logo of an Ibadan high court. He attempted to read it, but the small lettering made his eyes ache.

He pulled open the door and shouted for Quadri. He handed the letter to him. 'What are they saying?' Five minutes later, Quadri was still reading and shaking his head with what Olórí Ẹbí suspected was amusement.

'When will you finish reading this thing?' Olórí Ẹbí snapped impatiently. 'Why are you reading this thing as if it's a love letter? Just tell me everything in one sentence!'

Quadri folded the document neatly and replaced it in its envelope. 'The long and short of all these, Bàámi, is that the court is ordering you never to go near any of Mọ́remí's property again, and that henceforth all rents would be paid into one account that has been opened for her.'

Olórí Ẹbí had suspected that this day would come, since that witch refused to die. He just hadn't thought it would be this soon. He had assumed he would at least have some time to gather his arsenal. Could she have copies of the title deeds? The reason he had been confident that his scheme would work was Alhaja Àdùkẹ́'s aversion to documentation. She had delegated handling of her lawyers to him while he was living with her. He knew there were no extra copies of her documents anywhere ... surely?

If Mọ́ríebá had found the will, she could find the title deeds.

'So, what are you going to do now, Bàámi?' Quadri asked quietly.

'Get out of here!'

Olórí Ẹbí paced a familiar path on the floor. Quadri's question went round and around his head. *What are you going to do now?*

Olórí Ẹbí thought long and hard. He considered pulling out his joker. It wasn't over until it was over. He still had one more card to play. There was a saying about people in glass houses and stones, yes?

He fished his phone out of his pocket and placed a call to Madam Cherie Coco.

'Razor,' said a voice made hoarse by too many cigarettes.

He could picture her. Cherie with a cigarette dangling from her dark lips, those lips that used to do things to him in the days when jungle dey mature. Her skin bleached to the endodermis by way of a special chemical bath she took about three times annually and her refusal to leave her house during the daytime. Her overflowing curves seated comfortably in a giant recliner she had specially made. The phone clenched in her fist, knuckles that had stubbornly refused all attempts at bleaching contrasting with the rest of her.

He hated that she still called him by his old name, a name he had given up along with his guns and machetes. But there was nothing he could do about it. They went way back, had eaten palm oil together, had drunk wine from the same calabash ... He decided to let it slide, as usual.

'I have a job for you,' he whispered. He threw the doors open to check that none of his children were eavesdropping.

'Why else would you be calling me?' Madam Cherie Coco drawled. 'To tell me you want to marry me?'

She laughed, a deep laughter that reflected her greedy appetite for life. Making a mockery of those days when Razor had been so desperate to marry her. He had been one of her many lovers, but he had assumed, naively, that she would settle for him because he was the only one allowed to spend the night in her home. He remembered that same laughter on the day he had returned from Alágbàdo and had snuck into her house at Alábẹ́rẹ́. He had told her of his plans to straighten out his life, to make her his wife.

'I should give up my career and come and marry you?' she had roared. 'I'll lend you a coin, honey. The police are searching for you, they've been here twice.'

Olórí Ẹbí had a word with his feet.

Since then, although he had given up on the idea of marrying her, he had not stopped using her to carry out certain jobs. Madam Cherie Coco was a professional to the core, a man!

'I want you to do a setup for me. Her name is Mọ́ríebá Alágbàdo.'

'Are you talking about Mọ́ríebá Alágbàdo the business mogul, or someone else?'

'We are talking about the same person,' Olórí Ẹbí snapped in annoyance.

'You must be kidding me,' she laughed. 'Do you even know the woman you're asking me to set up?'

'Oh, yes, I do. You may not know this, but she's my sister's daughter, and she grew up in my house. I know her secret, Cherie, that's why I'm calling you.' He lowered his voice. 'She likes women.'

Cherie sighed loudly into the phone. 'That shouldn't be too difficult. How does she like them?'

'In their late twenties, tall, bookish, dark-skinned. She likes them very pretty. I want pictures – better still, videos, as many as possible.'

'You're going to pay heavily for this, Raufu.'

'Don't I always?'

SEASON FIVE:
WHAT LIES BENEATH
(2012–2013)

FUGUE

Rita ran downstairs to meet Wálé, as she had been doing for the past three weeks. Mummy Tobi was upstairs, making dinner and getting the children ready for bed.

Rita smiled at him as he alighted from his car. 'Welcome darling.' She leaned in for a kiss.

'How are the children?' he asked, as she took his briefcase from him.

She smiled at him playfully, flirtatiously. 'They are fine. They're looking forward to going to Kẹ́mi's place for the weekend.'

He frowned. 'Tọ́lá, I don't like the idea of the children going away again. Didn't you just return from Ibadan?'

'Haba, it's Christmas time,' she said, as they climbed up the staircase. 'Kẹ́mi wants them to get to know their cousins. They'll be back home by Sunday.'

'I still don't like the idea.'

Rita pushed open the door to the apartment. It was replete with the smell of vegetables lightly steamed in locust bean, smoked fish, palm oil, bell peppers and onions – Wálé's favourite soup. Mummy Tobi was magic in the kitchen. Her chubby fingers would measure out precise amounts of ingredients while she danced to the songs coming out of the small CD player she had installed in the kitchen as soon as she started working for them.

Wálé had not been pleased about the music. He had not been pleased that the woman had been sent to them by Móríebá. But more than that, he hated that Mummy Tobi treated him with a cold indifference. She would smile at him politely, never responding directly to any of his instructions. But the woman was magic in the kitchen.

Wálé drew in a deep breath as he shut the door behind him. 'I'm suddenly very hungry. What are we having with the efo?'

'Amala.' Rita followed Wálé into their room. She took off his socks, his shoes. She fetched a bowl of warm water from the bathroom, and washed and massaged his feet.

They had neither discussed Ibadan nor the events that had led up to it. Rita was a good and obedient wife. She had returned from Ibadan with her twelve yards of wife material intact. She rose early in the mornings, took long, languorous baths. She dressed in the clothes he bought for her, all ruffles, pleats and flounces. She wore waist-length weaves, natural hair imported from India that was rumoured to be stolen from altars of Indian gods. She attended to his every need, obeyed every command, fussed over the children. Being a good wife was a chore Rita enthusiastically threw herself into.

That night after dinner, she curled into Wálé as they sat on the couch watching TV with the children. He pushed her away. It was too hot for cuddling, he said, but Jésùtitófúnmi should come and sit next to him.

'I'm a big girl now, Daddy. It's only babies that cuddle with their dads.' Jésùtitófúnmi had decided she would no longer tolerate nonsense from her dad. Her relationship with her mother had changed too. They spoke frankly, openly, about what had happened. They talked about her siblings, how to protect them, for Daddy could not be trusted.

Rita had taken her for a check-up in Ibadan. There had been no physical marks of that night or the nights that led up to it. But Jésùtitófúnmi still woke up in the night, sweating and crying. Rita hardly ever slept. She sat with her daughter and held her until she fell asleep again.

Jésùtitófúnmi caught her mum's eyes, Rita nodded. She rose from her seat and smiled at her daddy. 'I think we should go to our room now.'

That night, after the lights were out and the rest of the house was asleep, Rita curled into Wálé again. There was electricity: PHCN had been generous, but Wálé hadn't. He had turned his back on her. She spooned him.

He was out first thing the following morning – a doctor's life, you know, always busy, always on call. But she'd checked his schedule – he wasn't on call till 1pm.

'Come home tonight, I have a surprise for you,' she whispered as she handed him his briefcase.

When Kẹ́mi came for the children a bit later, she looked around in amazement. 'You've had the apartment repainted!'

'I chose the colours and painted it myself,' Rita said shyly. She showed Kẹ́mi around the pastel apartment, whorls of cream, blue and lilac. On the sitting room wall you could almost see the face of a woman emerging from the whorls. It was Tọ́lá's face, hiding itself in plain sight, like she was doing in real life.

Kẹ́mi peered at the wall. 'This is nice!'

'Come, let me show you something.' Rita pulled Kẹ́mi after her, through the kitchen, where Mummy Tobi was making magic with beans, crayfish, palm oil, pepper, plantain and ABBA.

The winner takes it all
The loser has to fall

Rita pushed open the door to the room off the kitchen, the room that still smelled faintly of Mọ́remí and Kudirat, but more strongly of paint and turpentine. She had turned the room into a jungle. The painting ran from floor to ceiling on every wall: thick bushes, trees, vines twining themselves around the trees.

She pulled the blinds shut and switched off the light. There were red eyes and blue eyes and black-brown shiny eyes peering out at them from the jungle.

'I'm speechless,' Kẹ́mi said. 'I didn't know you could paint like this, Tọ́lá.'

'It's Rita.' She smiled at Kẹ́mi as she switched the light back on. 'This is Rita. Tọ́lá can't draw a crooked line, but I can paint.'

Kẹ́mi's expression did not change. 'You're a fantastic artist ... Rita.'

Rita beamed at her sister. 'Thank you so much.' Kẹ́mi understood, and that was more than enough.

They returned to the sitting room. Kẹ́mi sat down. 'So, where are the children?'

'They've gone to buy some things from the super-market,' Rita said. 'Ngozi, my neighbour's housemaid, is such a gem, she's been coming around to help with them since we returned from Ibadan. The funniest thing is that she's stealing from me.'

'What? You know this and you're allowing her into your home? I sent my last housemaid away because she was stealing milk. I mean, powdered milk, for heaven's sake!'

'Ngozi only steals medicine,' Rita laughed. 'She steals my contraceptives and multivitamin pills. I let her. On all other counts she's a very good girl.'

'Talking about medicine,' Kẹ́mi said, pulling a small envelope out of her bag, 'the pills you asked me to help you check. They're all depressants. Where did you get them from?'

Rita was not surprised. 'I found them in the medicine cabinet.' She scrutinised the list Kẹ́mi had handed her. The names corresponded with the names of the antidepressants Wálé claimed had been recommended for her at the hospital.

Blue pills, pink pills, aquamarine pills, round pills, square pills, push-you-under pills, they are benzodiazepines, Zyprexa, Seroquel ...

Tọ́lá helped Rita pull herself together. Even in her hidden state, she helped Rita to stay grounded. Rita was the Sàngó to her Ọya. Rita was Tọ́lá, half of a whole.

'Rita! Rita!' Kẹ́mi was shaking her.

Rita blinked. 'What?'

'You went out for a few minutes.'

'Sorry.' She lifted up the sachet of 'contraceptives' she'd been using religiously for close to eight years, and no longer wondered about her emptiness. 'So, this is a depressant too.' She turned the medicine around and tried to read the small print. 'I wonder why that girl has been stealing the medicine.'

'Housemaids steal the most mind-boggling things. I think it gives them a sense of power, to take something that their boss thinks is important.' Kẹ́mi laughed. 'On the other hand, there's no telling what people can get high on.'

'Thanks sister.' Rita folded the paper and placed it in her pocket. 'What about that psychiatrist I asked you to help me find? Dr Adejana.'

The children burst into the sitting room, sweaty and out of breath. Ngozi was hot on their heels. They were carrying shopping bags full of snacks and toiletries. A few months ago, Rita wouldn't have been able to afford all these things, not by herself. Heat rushed up her cheeks. Nobody had ever loved her or cared for her the way Mọ́ríebá did. Mọ́ríebá's love was an active thing, it made her heart beat erratically, as it was doing presently. Rita pulled herself together and focused her attention on the children.

'Stop running around, you're going to hurt yourselves.'

'Good afternoon, Aunty Kẹ́mi.' Jésùtitófúnmi ran to her aunt and hugged her. Kẹ́mi pulled her onto her lap and tickled her.

Rita scrutinized Ngozi's face. The girl looked animated, not like someone who was taking depressants. Tọ́lá suddenly remembered Kudirat and Mọ́remí quizzing her about contraceptives a few years earlier. Rita banished the thought. Surely, it can't be ...

'Me too! Me too! Tiku me, tiku me, tiku me too, Anti!' Jésùwálayẹ́'s voice intruded into her thoughts. He was struggling to pull his sister off Kẹ́mi's lap.

Kẹ́mi shooed them off. 'Okay, children, go and pack your bags.'

'Our bags are already packed. Let's go and get them.' Jésùtitófúnmi grabbed her siblings and ushered them towards their bedroom.

'Aunty, I will help them take their bags downstairs, but I have to return home, my Oga say I shull come.' Ngozi leaned confidentially towards Rita and whispered, 'You know say my Oga no well.'

'Ngozi, thank you so much.' She exchanged a look with Kẹ́mi. The two women grinned at each other.

The children and their bags were packed into Kẹ́mi's car.

'About Dr Adejana: she works at Yaba Psychiatric Hospital. Do you want to book an appointment with her?' Kẹ́mi asked, as she started the car.

'No, not yet,' said Rita, her mind already on the night ahead.

WAR GAMES

Wálé didn't get home until midnight. Mummy Tobi was long gone, always leaving at 7pm sharp – another thing Wálé didn't like about her.

Rita met him at the door. He reeked of alcohol. He stared at her like he had never seen her before. He probably hadn't.

She was wearing a school uniform, belonging to either Kudirat or Mọ́remí. The uniform was tight on her, in the armpits, across unfettered breasts that jiggled underneath the thin cloth, across her butt and riding up on her hips. She had her hair matted backwards, a style called kòlẹ́sẹ, her face inexpertly painted.

'Why are you dressed like this?' he asked, his eyes leaving butterfly touches on her lips and breasts. They caressed the flare of her hips and lingered, longingly, on the blood-red high-heeled shoes on her feet.

Rita shifted, pushing her breasts forward. Wálé backed off a little.

'Remember the games we used to play when we were newly married?' she asked.

'But you didn't like playing those games.' His gaze was back on her face, on the black lipstick smeared on, the eye pencil drawn thickly. His eyes questioned her.

'I have decided I like them now.' She grabbed him and hauled him closer. 'You haff been a fery naughty boy.'

Rita had never seen him so unsure before.

'What game is this?' He tried to shift out of her grip. She responded with a hard slap across his cheek.

'Don axe me question! You haff been a naughty boy!'

'But wait—'

She didn't. She hauled him across the sitting room into their bedroom.

He was babbling. 'Safe word ... prepare toys ...'

His words dried up as Rita threw the bedclothes off, displaying the line-up she had for him. She pushed him hard against the wall. Wálé smiled, that sharky smile she hadn't seen on his face since the early days.

'Don't open that your dirty mout and be tawkin to me!' She kissed him, hard. She pinned his arms above his head. Desire coursed through her as she drew in his tongue, bit his lips until his eyes rolled into his head. She would conquer him today. She stepped back. 'Off your clothes!'

He straightened away from the wall, the shit-eating grin back on his face. 'So, you finally came to your senses. I should have sent you to Ibadan earlier.'

His words plunged a knife into the open wound of her heart. She gave him a resounding slap that sent his head snapping back. 'If you open dat your dirty mout again, I go show you pepper! Just off am!'

She turned her back to him, squeezed back the tears that had sprung into her eyes and pulled herself together. She looked grimly at the toys that used to give her horrors.

Tie me up!

Tie me down!

Whip me harder, you coward, whip me!

Leather whip, handcuffs, ropes, dog collar, chain, strap-on. Wálé had tried everything, in their early days, to convince Tọ́lá to play his games.

Sex is a power game and I want to be your slave.

He wanted to be whipped, gagged, humiliated. But like the baby she had been, Tọ́lá had stubbornly refused to participate, paralysed by the fear instilled in her by her mother about how dirty sex was and how whoreful women who participated enthusiastically in the act were.

Rita, on the other hand, did not have any problems playing power games in the bedroom.

She had had time to practice in the past year. In darkened rooms, with masked men that smelled of dirt and desperation. She knew all about desires that could not be discussed openly. She had got drunk on the power that came with having total control over someone else's pleasure, the power that came with getting paid for it.

She knew about trust, safe words, boundaries. But Wálé's sickness had nothing to do with his BDSM fantasies. He did not deserve boundaries, or safe words. That night was not about pleasure – it was about punishment.

She turned to face him. His shirt was a pool of white

on the floor, his red tie streaked across it. 'Undo your pants, slowly.'

Wálé looked into her eyes as he took off his belt, unzipped his fly and stepped out of his pants. His boxers were rolled down his hips. His turgid penis sprang out and nodded at her.

Rita snapped the whip she'd been hiding behind her back. 'Kneel down!'

Wálé fell easily into character. 'Aunti, please don't beat me. I promise to be a good boy.'

'You be stubborn boy!' She cracked the whip through the air. 'I say kneel down there!'

He knelt on the floor, a bit awkwardly.

'Now raise your hands up.'

'But that's not how—'

'Shut up!' Rita raised her voice. 'Turn around and bend over!'

He did, getting on all fours. Rita swiped his butt with the whip.

'You like this, don't you?'

'No, no, I don't like it!' Thwack!

'You wan make I stop?' Thwack!

'No, no, please don't stop!' Thwack! Thwack!

'You be useless man, you no get respect for your elders!' Rita picked the dog collar off the bed and locked it around his throat. 'I go tish you respect today.' She picked the handcuffs off the bed. 'But first, I go arrest you for naughtiness.'

She leaned close to him. 'Shebi you want make I handcuff you.' He nodded. She backhanded him. 'You can't talk, abi?'

'Yes,' he choked out. 'This thing is a little too tight.'

She knelt beside him, her breasts close to his face. She'd not taken her bath that morning so that she'd smell ripe for him. He drew in a deep breath.

'You like it, don't you? You like my smelly armpits.' She lifted her arm, tearing the uniform in the process, to expose her unshaven armpit and the side of her left breast. She leaned in closer to him, and he lifted his head and sniffed.

'Because your housemaids, they used to smell, those ones that would punish you and fuck you!' She bared her teeth at him as she snapped the cuffs on his wrists. 'You like being fucked by housemaids, don't you?'

'Yes, Aunty Tọ́lá.'

Thwack, the whip went, thwack! Thwack! He cried out.

'I am Rita! You're really a worm – despicable, dirty, the lowest of the low.'

'Please don't beat me too hard, Aunty Rita, I'm sorry.'

'Do you want me to stop?' Thwack thwack! He was hard. His penis had grown longer, thicker.

'I can see that your one-eyed snake is nodding,' she chuckled. She took the rope off the bed and wrapped it tightly around his ankles.

'What are you doing?'

'Shut up! You've been a naughty boy and I go punish you today!' Rita was a broken record.

'But that's not how it's done—'

She swiped the whip across his back, and watched as a welt appeared on his skin. 'Don't you ever tell me what to do again!' She grabbed the collar, and his neck snapped back. She tightened the collar a little more and smiled as he winced.

Wálé slumped on the floor. Rita went and turned up the music, fetched her reefer and a bottle of vodka. She smoked and took a pull from the bottle. Wálé started coughing as the smoke thickened, so she loosened the collar a little and poured some vodka down his throat. She lit the wrap of smack and held it under his face, his eyes clouding over as he sucked it.

'Get back into position.'

Wálé struggled back to his kneeling position.

Rita took another shot of vodka and picked up the whip. 'You are a dirty boy, that's why your housemaids used to fuck you!'

Thwack! Thwack! Thwack! Thwack!

'Are you ready to take your medicine now?'

He nodded.

'I don tell you say make you no dey nod again!' Rita suddenly felt a rush of desire. Her nipples tightened and she went damp between her thighs. 'You want your medicine now?'

'Yes.'

She slapped him so hard he dropped to the floor. She leaned towards him, so he could see the burning hatred in her eyes. 'Yes who?'

'Yes, Aunty Rita.'

Rita reached for the strap-on. She had ordered it off the internet the week after she had returned from Ibadan. It was thick, a whopping fifteen inches of plexiglass. It was ridged. It curved wickedly, a scimitar.

She dangled it in front of his face. 'You want some of this, don't you?'

She moved the strap-on closer to his lips. His tongue snaked out and touched the tip; she pulled it away. He stretched his neck and tried desperately to touch the tip of the dong with his tongue again.

She pulled her pinafore up and bent over him so that he could smell her essence. His tongue reached for her clit. She allowed him to tongue her a little, but when she started enjoying it too much she slapped his face and pushed his head away. He watched her as she strapped the dong on. He was panting like a puppy. She held his head back and pushed it into his mouth, and he slobbered all over it.

'Suck it, suck my dick, you dirty whore.' She pulled the dick out of his mouth and stood in front of him while she slathered lube all over it. His face was wet with tears and mucus. 'Did your housemaids fuck you with this?'

'They used candles, Anti Rita,' he sniffed.

'Me I go fuck you with my thick dick, I go fuck you wella.' She fetched the whip again. Thwack, thwack, on buttocks that bore the memory of previous lashes. She spread the lube over his buttocks. She gentled her touch as she got to the butthole. He was moaning.

'Shut up! Shut up dia! You want make I stop? If you want my dick, you go take am quietly! Stop screaming like a bitch on heat!' She slapped his ass.

'I'm your bitch, Anti Rita, I'm a dirty boy, I want to be your bitch, please,' he sobbed. He got into position, his butt up in the air, his chest on the floor. He was clenching his butthole, his cock rigid, like it would burst at any moment, spilling his seed all over the floor.

She was poised at the edge of his hole. He was pleading, begging her to start, to stop, to do something, please, please, please ...

She entered him in one fluid motion, shouting in triumph as she slid home. She could feel her penis, its thickness, his tightness, the wall of his hole as it clenched around all fifteen inches. Wálé was moaning underneath her ... *my bitch, my fucking bitch.*

She thrust into him, hard.

Rita rode Wálé. She rode him like a horse, she rode him as she had ridden so many men in whorehouses, tiny cockroach-infested rooms at Omídun, in Bariga, on Lagos Island.

He shouted as he came and slumped on the floor, panting from exhaustion.

VOYEUR

Kudirat was in Móríebá's dressing room, her favorite part of the house. A space where she unleashed her imagination and dreamt dreams of a future that was coming.

Sometimes she simply sat on the rug, staring at her reflection in the mirror, Narcissus. She would study the lines of her face, marvelling at how her skin had cleared up. Sometimes she snapped photographs for her Instagram page, posing, puckering her lips.

She spent hours on YouTube learning how to apply make-up, to highlight, glow up. She was a slay queen and she intended to wear that crown for as long as she wanted.

Sometimes she just lay on the floor listing all the changes a few months had wrought in her life.

Nobody knew she used the room. It was her secret, one thing she didn't share with Móremí.

She'd gone into the dressing room that morning to reflect on school, how she now rubbed shoulders with people she used to envy and admire as they drove past her in their shiny cars. Now she was the one being driven around in shiny cars, but she didn't know how to behave.

She knew she would never turn into one of them, so affluent they didn't know anything about reality. Teens who spoke the language of entitlement and privilege without an iota of self-awareness.

She took a couple of pictures and uploaded them, then laid back on the rug and started imagining what Europe would be like. Mọríebá was taking them on a trip, and since the day she'd told them, Kudirat hadn't been able to sit still. Her heart jumped at the slightest noise. What if something bad happened and the trip had to be cancelled?

She would take offerings to Aunty Mọríebá's shrine. She would plead with the Órìṣà to stave off all evil.

She was still deep in contemplation when she heard a noise. She jumped off the floor and was about to step out of the dressing room when the door that led into the bedroom was pushed open. She froze at the threshold as Chinwe and Mọríebá stumbled into the room, giggling and shushing each other. They looked drunk.

Chinwe was Mọríebá's young friend. She was in Ibadan for her youth service and had nowhere else to stay, so Mọríebá had offered her a room. She had been living with them since November, a quiet mouse of a girl who always had her head buried in a book. The girl tried to be nice, but Kudirat had the impression that she was a loner.

Why is Aunty Mọríebá kissing Chinwe?

Kudirat could not tear her eyes away from the two women kissing each other feverishly a few feet away. They were so into each other, they didn't even sense that she was there. Mọríebá's full lips slid over Chinwe's, their tongues touching. They'd come up for air, look into each other's eyes, smile and then start again. Mọríebá slid her tongue over Chinwe's lips into her parted mouth, her hands gliding up Chinwe's back, those long fingers splayed over Chinwe's buttocks. They moulded the plumpness. Chinwe reached round Mọ́ríebá, her hands caressing Mọ́ríebá's back. The women danced, one step forward, one step backward.

Kudirat was frozen to the spot, saliva pooling in her mouth. Her mind was filled with the image of the two women. Chinwe slid her fingers into Mọ́ríebá's hair to pull her closer. Mọ́ríebá kissed Chinwe's throat, her shoulders. She slid the thin straps of the blouse off Chinwe's shoulders. Chinwe was wearing a brown, lacy bra that matched her skin tone. Mọ́ríebá took her time, kissing the plump mounds created by the push-up bra. Chinwe moaned as Mọ́ríebá dragged the blouse down and reached around to unclasp her bra, cupping both her bra and her breasts and feathering kisses on them. In spite of the air conditioning, a light film of perspiration glistened on Chinwe's face.

By the time Mọ́ríebá dipped her head lower to take one of Chinwe's stiff nipples in her mouth, Kudirat felt damp between her legs. She clasped both hands to her mouth, frozen to the spot. Her eyes were fastened on the glistening nipple. She had never seen anything so beautiful.

Kudirat had seen her parents having sex before, in the middle of the night, when they thought she and her brother were asleep. Bàámi would be on top of Màámi, grunting away. She had also watched a lot of porn on her phone and with friends at school. Porn made her uncomfortable, giggly. Nothing had ever turned her on so much that she wanted to lie down and touch herself. She wanted to grind her hand between her thighs. She wanted to sigh and moan as Chinwe was.

Mọ́ríebá was on her knees, kissing down Chinwe's stomach towards Chinwe's panties, barely a string between her legs. Her hands splayed over Chinwe's buttocks, squeezing them. As Chinwe's knees buckled, Mọ́ríebá lifted her off her feet and carried her towards the bed, away from Kudirat's greedy eyes.

Kudirat snapped out of her trance. She backed into the dressing room, slid to the floor bonelessly and tried to sort out her feelings. The first thing she needed to do was sort out how to get out of that dressing room without being discovered. She sent a heartfelt prayer to Ọya for guidance and fetched her phone from the pocket of her gown.

As she unlocked her phone, several messages came in all at once. She quickly muted the ping! ping! All the messages were from Mọ́remí. She opened the chat and typed furiously.

> **Where the fuck are you? I've been searching for you all over the house**
>
> *12:15 pm*

> You have to help me, I'm in Aunty Mọ́ríebá's room. I'll explain everything to you later. Please just find a way to get Aunty Mọ́ríebá and that Chinwe girl out of her room
>
> *1:24 pm*

> **What is going on?**
>
> *1:24 pm*

Please don't ask questions now, you have to think of something that's important enough to get Aunty Ọríẹbá out of her room

1:25 pm

Kudirat crawled into the darkest recess of the dressing room and waited to be rescued.

THE DENIZENS OF ALÁBẹ́Rẹ́...

Olórí Ẹbí switched on the ceiling fan as he entered his room. He threw the damp towel that had been tied around his waist on the bed and got dressed quickly.

Today was not a day for dawdling. In and out! No time for chit-chat.

He picked a tiny oblong package up from his bedside cabinet and slid an object wrapped in a red cloth out of it. A black thread was wound tightly around the cloth. He whispered instructions to it.

'You will go ahead of me, Olúgboùn – the one that bears words in the air. You will tell Sule that everything I say is the truth, for the truth depends on the bearer of words, not on the facts. He will agree with every word that comes out of my mouth, for I have become the bearer of the truth. He will follow my orders. You are Olúgboùn, the one that carries messages through the air, and I, Raufu, the son of Adetoun, am your master, for I have made sacrifices to you. So it is. Àse!'

He spat at the cloth thrice and put it in the pocket of his agbádá. He pulled out a drawer and took another package wrapped in fresh green leaves from it. He unwrapped the package, fished out a cowry shell nestling inside and spoke to it. 'Gbètu-gbètu, the handmaiden of Olúgboùn, carry my words into the heart of Sule, the son of Bọ́lọ́mọpẹ́.' He placed the cowry carefully in the recesses of his right cheek.

Even while he was carrying out the rituals, the shadow of doubt that had been stalking him for over a year hovered. After all, the Óríṣà appeared to have completely turned their backs on him. On the other hand, the ways of the Óríṣà were unfathomable: sometimes one lost battles but in the end won the war. Moreover, these rituals gave him boldness, and he needed all the confidence he could get.

As he descended the staircase, he called Lékan.

'The car is ready, Bàámi,' said Lékan, appearing at the bottom of the stairs.

Olórí Ẹbí floated out to his car on a cloud of brilliant white dry lace. On his head was a purple abetí ajá that perfectly matched the colour of his pointy-toed heelless slippers. He stood still for a moment and revelled in the shininess of the brand-new Hummer he had bought after his old jalopy died.

One did not curl up and die in times of crisis. It was important to show one's enemies that they had failed.

The fact that he had got the Hummer on credit was not something he worried about. Providence and, lately, Mọ́ríebá, had a way of covering his ass. In spite of the fact that the girl was stubborn, hard of hearing and an arrogant witch, she'd never neglected her duty of ensuring he was cared for, the way Alhaja had done in her lifetime.

As he climbed into the luxurious interior of the car, his excitement dampened as he recollected his desti-nation, his mission.

The truth was that if there had been an alternative, Olórí Ẹbí would have taken it, but that letter, coupled with his near-empty bank account, had forced his hand. After collecting rents from his sister's properties for seven years, he had realised how piddling the amount he was getting off the family lands was. He had no intention of returning to dancing at the edge of poverty.

As the car snaked its way out of the narrow potholed roads of Idi-Ikan, onto the wider potholed road leading to Beere, an old man dashed into the road and was nearly hit by an okada. Olórí Ẹbí suddenly felt a fear that the old man could be him. His discomfort was taken over by a fierce determination.

'We are going to Alábẹ́rẹ́,' he grunted. He did not ask if Lékan could find his way to Alábẹ́rẹ́. He expected all his boys to be able to make their way, even blindfolded, to places angels fear to tread. How else would they learn to take care of themselves?

Alábẹ́rẹ́ was home to thieves, drug addicts, drug peddlers, sex workers and their pimps, pickpockets and their Fagins. This illustrious line-up included other bottom feeders of Ibadan that kept the not-so-obviously-crooked members of society in check. Olórí Ẹbí had founded Alábẹ́rẹ́ together with Sule, Cherie Coco and four other boys. If truth be told, Sule had discovered Alábẹ́rẹ́ and the others had joined in making the place what it eventually became.

The boys had met one another at a motor park in Molete, where they spent their days as conduc-tors-cum-pickpockets, their nights sleeping in parked or vandalised buses. Sule had grown tired of the harassment they suffered from bus drivers and of having to hide from gangs seeking homeless children to traffic for body parts or the sex market. He had disappeared one day, returning that evening to ask the others to pool their money.

Five teenage boys had moved into one room in a face-me-I-face-you house that had neither a toilet nor a bathroom. They took their baths in the backyard, whenever they bothered to, and shat into polythene bags, which they threw into nearby bushes. But it had been their home, somewhere to lay their heads, somewhere to hatch plans about how they would take over the world.

They met Cherie Coco in Alábẹ́rẹ́, their landlord's daughter. A tough muscular girl who had bullied the boys into allowing her to join their pickpocketing expeditions almost as soon as they'd moved into her father's house.

Within four years, Alábẹ́rẹ́'s population had grown to a few hundred teenagers and a few older people. Before long, 'respectable' people were moving out of the neighbourhood, making room for pimps, drug dealers, sex workers of all genders and a few other nutjobs. With them had come the trade in machetes, body parts, double-edged axes (code-name Ake UTC), homemade guns and ammunition.

Cherie had refused to move out with her dad, who had, by then, become so scared of her that he had not protested too much. Some people claimed he had been relieved that she decided to stay.

The larger Alábẹ́rẹ́'s population grew, the further up the food chain Olórí Ẹbí (the criminal formerly known as Raffie the Razor), Sule, Cherie and the other boys had climbed. By this time, Alábẹ́rẹ́ had attracted the attention of older crime lords, people who had been running Ibadan and its environs from time immemorial. It was a ripening mango that had to be plucked before it became the meal of bush birds. Gang wars had broken out, with different factions wading in to claim territories. But the teenagers were wild, they wouldn't give up their turf. They had fought back with their machetes and axes and guns. They had fought back with their wits.

The government had eventually waded in, levelling everything and everyone in sight. They had all gone into hiding, only to return quietly about a year later. Soon Alábẹ́rẹ́ was once again abuzz with perfectly executed armed-robbery operations, prostitution, drugs, begging rings, fights, kidnapping, guns and human trafficking. Hardcore Fújì was the background music to their violence.

Raffie the Razor had bought his place among the legends with bullets and blood, until the failed heist had revealed the coward in him and sent him scuttling to Alágbàdo, then to Alhaja Àdùkẹ́'s house in Idi-Ikan, where he had metamorphosed, once again, into Raufu Alágbàdo.

After thirty minutes, Lékan emerged onto a dirt road bordered by houses in various stages of decrepitude. He pulled to a stop behind a high fence that seemed to have no beginning or end.

'Bàámi, do you want me to come along with you?'

Olórí Ẹbí ignored his son and walked determinedly towards the fence.

Alábẹ́rẹ́ was a solid square, with the well-fortified houses of the four major gang lords forming a barricade around a fiefdom built out of roofing sheets and hardboard. It was impossible to drive a car into Alábẹ́rẹ́: you either walked through the alleyways or passed through the house of one of the warlords.

It had been more than twenty years since his uncere-monial exit from Alábẹ́rẹ́, but Olórí Ẹbí knew how to gain entrance. He pushed his hand into a hole in the metal and felt for the mechanism. There was a faint click, and Olórí Ẹbí stepped back as a small section of the fence opened with a loud grinding noise. He squeezed through the narrow opening, which ground to a close behind him. It had been his brainchild – a free service provided when they had kidnapped a Lebanese construction mogul.

The compound in which he found himself was huge. The main house was further down. On his left and right were bungalows, and row upon row of beer cartons.

Dark clouds were gathering in the skies, a portend of heavy rain or something more sinister. Olórí Ẹbí rubbed his tongue against the cowry shell in his cheek. Striding towards him from the house were three muscular men with rifles slung over their shoulders.

'Agba ki in wa l'oja,' Olórí Ẹbí called out.

The tallest and darkest of the men stepped forward, right arm extended.

Orí ọmọ tuntun á wó!

Orí ọmọ tuntun á fà'ya!

Olórí Ẹbí grasped the arm and the two men did a complicated dance that included chest bumping, arm groping and finally the snapping of fingers.

'Welcome back,' said the man in a soft voice that jarred with his hard, scar-ridden face and missing eye. 'Chairman has been expecting you.'

He led the way and Olórí Ẹbí followed. The two other security guards fell in step behind them.

'It's good to be home, Chuks,' said Olórí Ẹbí, as nostalgia and trepidation hit him with the same intensity. It occurred to him how much danger he could be in. These men did not forgive, they did not forget. He grasped the talisman in his pocket and squeezed it tightly.

'Things have not changed much around here,' he observed as they approached the one-storey building. He felt some satisfaction that the house had been extended in a higgledy-piggledy fashion. The extensions had obviously not seen a single stroke from an architect's pencil. In spite of their power, the gang lords still lacked a sense of aesthetics.

'Things should not change all the time.' Chuks paused and glared at him. 'Raffie the Razor.' Olórí Ẹbí's former name was a curse on his lips. 'You know, it's not all of us that have the luxury of running away in times of trouble.'

Olórí Ẹbí winced as he caught the shade thrown by Chuks.

'We wan sabi say the tins we leave behind, when we dey inside wall, go dey when we return.' Olórí Ẹbí clenched his jaw. He would not allow a mere henchman to ruin his mission. What does Chuks know about brotherhood and loyalty? He hadn't even been there in the early days. Those were the days when jungle dey mature!

As they drew closer to the main house, the door was pulled open by a tiny girl, a pistol in her fist. She stared openly at Olórí Ẹbí, who stared right back at her. She was dressed in a pair of combat trousers in the greens of the Nigerian army, and a singlet that clung to her breasts. She reminded Olórí Ẹbí of Ìyàwó when she had been younger, before she started popping out the babies. He wondered if she would be as sweet.

They passed a room full of people laughing, the smell of alcohol and marijuana strong in the air. Chuks led him up a flight of stairs and down a long corridor, eventually turning into a room that was cool and blessedly quiet.

As Olórí Ẹbí shut the door behind him, the hum of

an air conditioner filled his ears. Sule dropped the phone
he was fiddling with and widened his arms and lips in an
expansive welcome gesture. 'It is good to see you, Razor.'

Sule was sat at a huge mahogany table covered with
laptops and phones. He was a man of diminutive dimen-
sions. His face was that of a child: pink lips, a delicate nose
and shell-shaped ears. Whenever he bothered to smile,
like he was presently doing, two cute dimples appeared in
his cheeks. However, he made up for his angelic looks by
being deeply, darkly and truly evil.

'Same here, Sule, same here.' Olórí Ẹbí was a bit
annoyed that Sule still looked that good. He was dressed
in a pair of torn jeans, a t-shirt and a pair of loafers,
and beside him Olórí Ẹbí felt crude, like an overbloated
elephant that had seen better days. Sule led them to
another part of his office with comfortable chairs.

'You just left us without a backward glance, but it's
alright man.' He flicked Olórí Ẹbí's agbádá. 'You're now a
proper civilian, complete with agbádá and a flourishing
stomach.'

'This, Sule,' he smiled, as he rubbed said stomach,
'is a sign of good living. It is only the person with a big
stomach that the money would be given in big Ghana-
must-go bags.'

The two men laughed as Chuks took an unopened
bottle of schnapps from the minibar in the corner and put
it on a tray with two shot glasses. He placed the tray reverently on the glass-topped table in front of the men.

Sule showed Olórí Ẹbí its unbroken seal, then handed
the bottle to Chuks, who opened it and served the men.
Olórí Ẹbí laughed to himself. If Sule wanted to poison
him, a mere seal would not stop him.

'To old friendships, and running away to fight another day,' he toasted Olórí Ẹbí, and downed the contents of his glass in one gulp.

Olórí Ẹbí refused to take the bait. He smiled and swallowed his schnapps.

'And to what do we owe the pleasure of your visit?' Sule asked after refilling the glasses.

'I came to see how the old place is doing.'

Sule raised an eyebrow and the two men laughed.

'It took you twenty years to come and check how we've been doing.' Sule coughed. 'Tell me another lie, Razor.'

Olórí Ẹbí smiled back.

'I do get reports about you, man,' Sule continued. 'I heard you're doing quite well, that you have a house full of sons.'

'It is Elédùà's doing.' Olórí Ẹbí downed his drink. He wasn't there for small talk. 'Sule, I need a favour from you.'

Sule smiled. 'Now we are getting somewhere.'

Olórí Ẹbí did not care for his sarcasm, but he had business. He owed nobody an explanation. He knew those men. In his shoes, they would have done the exact same thing. 'I'm looking for my sister's daughter, and I've gathered from reliable sources that she's now living in your kingdom.'

Sule leaned forward and poured some more schnapps into Olórí Ẹbí's glass.

'Her name is Àmọ̀pé.' Olórí Ẹbí ran his tongue around the cowry shell in his cheek. 'She does crack when heroin is not available. I heard she moved here about four years ago.'

'Àmọ̀pé.' Sule fingered his chin. 'That name sounds familiar. Chuks!'

'My Chair?' Chuks, who had dematerialised after serving the drinks, suddenly reappeared.

'Do you know of any Àmọ̀pé?'

Chuks was the registrar. He knew every single soul who lived in Alábẹ́rẹ́. He knew their real names, code names, family lineage, how much they earned, how useful they were and where they came from. He knew when it was time for them to depart from Alábẹ́rẹ́, usually head-first.

'Yes, I know Àmọ̀pé. It's that deportee that speaks like she's the Queen of England, but she earns her keep, so she's alright.'

'I want her back.' Olórí Ẹbí adopted a sad mien, the bewildered uncle whose heart had been broken by his favourite niece. 'She's my sister's only child, and we've been searching for her since before her mother's death over seven years ago. That girl has caused so much heart-break and sadness to her mother and the little, innocent daughter she abandoned.'

Sule gave him a long, hard look. Olórí Ẹbí touched the talisman in his pocket and rolled his tongue around the cowry.

'Ah, I remember Àmọ̀pé now, you used to bring her here when she was younger.' Sule eyes gleamed. 'Seven years is a long time. Why are you just coming here? You know there's no junkie I can't find for you as long as she's within Nigeria. So, what really happened?'

Olórí Ẹbí's patience was at an end. 'I want you to go and bring her for me.'

'Who are you to stroll in here after twenty years and start ordering me around?' Sule paused, and suddenly broke into an angelic smile. 'We should be celebrating how far we've come since the last time we saw each other, not fighting. Chuks, fetch Àmọ̀pé and call Bashiru for me.'

Olórí Ẹbí released a pent-up breath as Chuks left the room.

'Àmọ̀pé is actually a nice girl. I remember her quite clearly now.' Sule added quietly, 'Poor thing, what you did to her though.'

The men recited Alábẹ́rẹ́'s motto together, sotto voce.

The sins of the mother shall be visited on the daughter the granddaughter, the great-granddaughter, forever and ever amen.

'I remember your rich half-sister – that must be Àmọ̀pé's mother. So she's dead. I wonder how you managed to off her without pulling a hit.' Sule downed another tumbler of schnapps. 'Or maybe I shouldn't. You're still handy with poisons, I suppose, cowardly shit, but whatever rocks your boat man.'

Olórí Ẹbí cursed Èṣù under his breath. For a minute he had taken his mask off, allowed Sule under his skin. He couldn't let himself be vulnerable with the enemy.

'Yes, poor Àdùkẹ́ died. We woke up one morning and she was dead,' said Olórí Ẹbí, back in character. 'But thanks be to Allah that she did not suffer for long. She left quietly. May He grant her eternal rest.'

'I'm sure you're also thankful that you know her daughter is here.' Sule drew closer to him. 'So, tell me Razor, why do you want her now? What changed? Seven years is a very long time. Is it the signatures? Was there a will?'

Olórí Ẹbí narrowed his eyes. 'I did not come here to be cross-examined, Sule. I came to fetch my niece.'

'Mmm, you want your junkie back, your rich junkie. Does she even know that her mother is dead?'

'How much do you want?' Olórí Ẹbí growled.

'Half of everything.'

'You must be out of your mind.'

'Ah, the money must be even more than I imagined.'

'I'm not here to play games!' Olórí Ẹbí's mind worked furiously. That the gbètu-gbètu had not worked was clear. He waved a mental fist at the Mothers, those who killed you slowly all the while laughing with you.

'Neither am I.' Sule waited a heartbeat and then laughed, he laughed so hard tears coursed down his cheeks.

Olórí Ẹbí stared at him. The problem with people who smoked too much marijuana was that it affected their brain eventually. He never touched the stuff. No matter how badly he hungered for a high, he stuck to alcohol, which was way better.

Sule stopped laughing as abruptly as he had started. 'It's alright, Razor, I'm not as greedy as you.' He patted Olórí Ẹbí's arm. 'I know you too well: the next thing you'll do after leaving this place is to go and hire somebody to kill me, or find other devious means of throwing sand in my garri.' He shook his head ruefully. 'I like a quiet life. My bullets have better uses.'

Olórí Ẹbí unclenched his fists.

'Here's the deal.' Sule looked at him from behind glinting glasses. 'You take your niece and we'll take ten million naira when the deal, whatever it is, is done.'

'Highway robber,' Olórí Ẹbí shouted in relief. 'The one and only Sule, thief exemplar!'

Sule burst into laughter. 'You don't need to sing the praises of my lineage.'

'I can't promise you ten million. You'll definitely get eight. I don't even know the worth of my sister's properties.'

'We can help you find out. You know we have the means.' Sule's smile was oily.

'No, thank you very much, I can do that by myself.'

Olórí Ẹbí held out his hand and Sule shook it.

Èṣù grabbed a bottle of schnapps off the cabinet and joined the men in a celebratory drink.

A CRY-CRY FILM...

Mọremí was lying across her bed, face down, chin on the pillow, long fingers holding open the book she was reading. Kudirat was lying down beside her, one pillow tucked underneath her chin, another on top of her legs. She was reading too. On the floor was a plate of digestive biscuits and two glasses of orange juice. The only sounds in the room were the whispery turning of paper and the quiet hum of the air conditioner.

They were supposed to be reading for their WAEC exams, which started in a couple of weeks. But they were tired of reading academic books and staring at the screens of their iPads. They'd sat for their IGCSCEs the previous month and had passed with flying colours. Kudirat with slightly more colours than Mọremí. The girls had agreed that Kudirat was a show off: she had not needed to score all As. She wanted to show the other students that just because she had spent the better part of her life in government schools it did not mean she was dumb. Her results were a love letter to their condescension and mockery.

Mọremí had nothing to prove to anybody. All she wanted was to be left in peace to read and travel and, maybe sometime in the distant future, write about her adventures. Although she was going along with Kudirat, pretending an interest in medicine, she was doing it only to keep herself occupied until she laid hands on her inheritance.

Mọremí picked up a biscuit and chewed it slowly as she read *The Secret Lives of Baba Segi's Wives* by Lola Shoneyin. She wriggled in enjoyment. She'd just turned another page when Mọríebá's chat head popped up on her phone.

> Sweetheart can you kindly come downstairs immediately? And tell Kudirat not to follow you or try to snoop
>
> *11:45 am*

Mọremí giggled as she read the message.

Kudirat peered over her shoulder. 'Oh, so me, I'm the snoop now, abi?' She laughed and rolled over. 'The matter that we don't want the kingpin to hear, it's the kingpin that would end up solving it.'

> I'll be down in a minute
>
> *11:45 am*

> I'm in the sitting room
>
> *11:45 am*

> Okay Aunty
>
> *11:46 am*

She rose from the bed. 'Whatever, just don't follow me or do that sitting-on-the-staircase-and-eavesdropping thing you do. Kingpin indeed, when you look more like a safety pin or an office pin.'

Kudirat threw a pillow at her. Mọ́remí dodged it, stuck out her tongue and escaped through the door as another pillow sailed her way.

She was still giggling when she got downstairs. She skipped towards the sitting room, which was off to her right, and stopped cold at the door. Her face turned stiff.

Sitting down in a pool of yellow jacquard lace was Olórí Ẹbí. The stones that dotted the lace shone even brighter than the afternoon sun pouring through the glass door that led to the patio. His cap was red, his smile white, his cheeks dimpled, his tribal marks a work of art. He sat prettily like a bride about to walk down the aisle, conscious of how good he looked.

'Ah ah, Mọ́ríebá, why is this one here?' he chuckled.

Mọ́remí was staring at him as one would a snake, with repulsion and fascination.

'Good afternoon sir,' she said. She dipped her knees and crabwalked to where Mọ́ríebá was seated, afraid of turning her back on him. He was the kind of person who would sneak up behind you and bury a knife in the small of your back.

'Good afternoon, good girl.' He bared his teeth at her. 'I can see you're looking more and more like your aunty every day. See, both of you are even dressed the same way, jeans and baggy t-shirts.'

Mọ́remí knew when she was being mocked. She turned her back on him, knife or no, and leaned towards Mọ́ríebá.

'Please sit down,' Mọ́ríebá said stiffly. 'Raufu Alágbàdo has something to say to you.'

Olórí Ẹbí looked taken aback for a moment, but he recovered quickly enough, the amiable smile back on his face. 'I've already told you everything, and I don't think that children should hear that kind of thing. Our discussion is strictly for adults.'

'I don't think so,' Mọ́ríebá said coldly. 'Mọ́remí turned eighteen last week, so she is no longer a child, and since it's her grandmother's property we are talking about I don't think it is right that we should discuss it behind her back.'

'Nobody hears bad news from the mouth of a diviner,' he muttered, as he glanced at the shiny watch on his wrist. 'See how time flies when you're enjoying yourself.' He jumped out of the chair. 'I think I'd better leave now.'

'Sit down.' Mọ́ríebá's words were crisp and dry. They bore the chill of harmattan wind. The hairs on Mọ́remí's neck sprang up. Mọ́ríebá picked up the remote control on the low stool beside her and deliberately pressed 'lock'. The click of bolts sliding home was like a hammer.

'The doors are locked, and they won't open for the next fifteen minutes,' Mọ́ríebá said. 'Enough time for us to discuss this important matter that you brought to my attention this morning.'

Mọ́remí was staring at her aunt. She'd never seen her that way before. Her face was a mask of fury, her eyes shone with tears. She moved as close as possible to Mọ́ríebá, quietly.

'It's your choice,' Olórí Ẹbí said stubbornly

Mọ́ríebá turned her attention to Mọ́remí. 'I have something to tell you. I should have told you before now, but I didn't think it was important. I thought I should give you enough time to get to know me and to start healing from the brutality that the man standing over there exposed you to for some years.'

Mọremí took her aunt's hand in hers. 'You don't have to tell me anything.'

'What's all these rubbish?' Olórí Ẹbí snapped. 'Mọríebá, open the door this minute or there'll be hell to pay.'

Mọríebá ignored him, her eyes still on Mọremí. 'I'm a lesbian. I know you know what that means.'

Mọremí shrugged.

Olórí Ẹbí sucked his teeth loudly. 'Ah! The things that these Oyinbo people have done to us is madness. See these ones behaving as if they are in one of those cry-cry films they are always showing. Maybe they'll soon start singing like those Indian film people.'

Mọríebá stared at him blank faced all through his tirade. 'Okay, I think it's done talking.' Olórí Ẹbí fell quiet and stalked back to his seat.

Mọríebá picked a folder off the table and handed it to Mọremí. 'Open it.'

Mọremí hesitated. She knew something bad had happened. She didn't want to know what it was.

'I said, "Open it!"'

Mọremí flipped the folder open. The first thing she saw was an eight by eleven full-colour picture. Mọríebá was lying on her back, stark naked. Between her thighs was another woman whose back was turned to the camera. The second shot showed Mọríebá fucking the same woman doggy style with a black strap-on. The next one was of her suckling on the woman's breast. Every photograph showed Mọríebá naked, her face captured in different grimaces, her body in different postures. The other woman's face was always averted, but Mọremí identified her as Chinwe. It was in the curve of her cheeks.

'Ah, you no longer have any shame. How can you be showing these kind of things to a young girl? Isn't there a law against pornography? Don't you even feel a twinge of conscience?'

Mọremí was confused. Of course she knew her aunt was gay, but why was she showing her these pictures?

'Now, take a good look at the bastard sitting over there.'

Mọremí didn't look at the bastard, because he was not important. She closed the folder and watched her aunt, who had tears streaming down her face. 'He said we should stop asking after your grandmother's properties, that he has all the deeds to the houses. He said you can keep the money but he's keeping the properties. He said we should have the court injunction rescinded.'

Mọríebá's lips were trembling. She couldn't talk any longer. Mọremí took the remote from her slack fingers and pushed the button that would open the door.

Olórí Ẹbí stomped out of the room. Neither of the women looked at him. Mọremí hugged her aunt.

'He has videos, he has more pictures,' Mọríebá blubbered into Mọremí's t-shirt. 'It was Chinwe, it must be her. I knew something was off when she left without telling anybody and her phone couldn't be reached. She stole some of my jewellery, but that can be replaced, that's why I didn't say anything.'

Mọríebá eventually straightened up and wiped her face with a handkerchief she fetched out of her pocket.

'It's alright, Aunty M.' Mọremí placed her forehead against her aunt's. She looked into her eyes and saw the hurt in them.

'I'm not crying because he threatened to publish those things in the newspaper, I'm crying because he's trying to tear our relationship apart. All he cares about are those houses. Why is he so desperate? He's frivolous and a poor manager of wealth – that was why Alhaja tied up my grandfather's inheritance so he wouldn't fritter it away. Part of the money I used to start my business was taken from his estate. All the grandchildren come into their share once they reach twenty-one years of age. If it was up to Raufu, there wouldn't be a dime of that money left.'

One thing Mọremí was good at was listening, so she did.

'If he told me he wanted money, I would have given it to him. Lord knows I've bailed him out of trouble enough times. He went and bought a jeep on credit earlier this year. I've paid for the damn thing and he doesn't even know.'

'Heey! Anti Mọríebá!'

The two women looked up. It was Kudirat.

'Did you see Olórí Ẹbí? He just left now,' Kudirat said. She fell quiet and walked over to where they were seated. 'What is it? Tell me what happened.'

Mọremí asked Mọríebá a question with her eyes. Mọríebá nodded. Mọremí handed Kudirat the folder.

Kudirat glanced at the first picture, then tossed it on the floor. 'He's trying to blackmail you abi?' She smiled mirthlessly. 'We will handle this.'

SEASON SIX:
THE TROUBLE WITH
BEING [2013-2014]

LA PETITE MORT

If I were Ṭọ́lá, I wouldn't have been able to handle this. I'd be a mess, I'd be so damned scared. I'm sure that by now I'd be thinking that I'm a monster. That I've crossed the boundary of being human. Like Ògún wielding my vengeful machete, or less? Subhuman, an amoeba maybe.

But I'm not Ṭọ́lá. I am Rita and my work is never quite done. That's the trouble with being. Ṭọ́lá is human, soft, kind, forgiving, empathetic, depressed, powerless!

Me I be Rita. I'm unforgiving, vengeful and petty as fuck.

Rita was practising breathing – breathing through her mouth that is. She was doing it the way she'd read about such things in books. Like, if your house was on fire and the whole place was filled with smoke, right? You were advised to flatten yourself on the floor and breathe through your mouth. Because smoke was lighter than air, or was it denser? Whatever. The point was avoiding smoke inhalation while the firefighters literally walked through hell to rescue you. Rita was not in a smoke-filled room, but she believed that a fire breaking out might be the solution to this problem called a police station. The stink of the cell was bad enough to burn her throat worse than mere smoke inhalation, and then there were the tiny and not-so-tiny insects crawling all over her, making her itch in places on her body she hadn't even known existed.

She had started the breathing experiment around midnight and was getting strange looks from her cellmates, whom she ignored. The air stank: of unwashed bodies, urine, faeces, desperation. She kept her face as close to the floor as possible, to inhale a somewhat stale but better air.

Maybe it's my imagination. Don't I stink just as badly? How long have I been here?

She sniffed the air low to the floor again and sniffed her armpit. She was still making comparisons between her stink, the stink of the room and that of the air close to the floor, when the sound of iron bars being pushed open reached her ears.

She noted, from the corner of her eye, that some of her cellmates ran over to the gate, probably hoping somebody had come for them. Poor fools! They complained bitterly as they were roughly shoved out of the way by two policemen.

'That's her over there,' a familiar voice said from beyond the bodies clustering at the gate.

Rita held her breath as she craned her neck to see if it was the same policeman who had been at the flat, with so many others, yesterday? Whatever. After Mummy Tobi had made the call.

His voice had ordered her movements throughout the day.

Wear something!
Stand over there!
Sit down there!
Don't touch anything!
Take off your belt!

Rita had been a bit shell-shocked really, so she dumbly followed all his orders, as dumbly as Tọ́lá would have.

Honestly I didn't know people died that messily!

She'd assumed it would be like in the movies. In movies, people died prettily, their limbs arranged just so, their eyes shut neatly. They didn't drool or pop their eyes out at you, except in some Nollywood movies, but even those badly acted deaths were still prettier than the horror of yesterday— or was it the day before? And the actors didn't spend an inordinate amount of time clawing at their throat. The horror! The horror of his long, lingering death. The way he had been struggling, screaming silently because the collar had been too tight, cutting off his voice as well as his air supply.

She had been studying the faces he was making. Thinking about how he was wasting the little bit of air he had left by struggling so hard. He should just have died quietly. There had been no need for all that drama, it hadn't saved him anyway, but Wálé had to be a drama queen till the bitter end.

Rita had chosen to see his death throes as the ultimate ecstasy. Didn't the French call it the little death? La petite mort!

'Convess, convess now! How did you keel your horzeband?'

Who said that to me?

'What did you do with this tin?'

'Why do you use this rubber penis for?'

'Hey you!' The policeman who had opened the door yelled in her direction.

Rita tried to remember who he was. Hadn't he been in a dark room with her yesterday wearing an absurd pair of sunglasses?

Oh ... it isn't him, it's the other one, who had threatened to bring out the 'inszrumens of tawshur' if I don't cooperate.

Rita decided to stand up, but she had to hold her breath first. Twenty, nineteen, eighteen, seventeen – her throat started to burn – fifteen ... twelve, ten, nine ...

'Hey you on the floor! Come here before I count to three!'

'I'm already counting down, stupid!' She jerked away violently as the young lady who had been sitting dejectedly beside her *(All day? All month? Everywhere is so damn dark!) touched* her arm. The fleeting, butterfly touch felt like a hammer against Rita's skin. She jumped off the cold floor and made for the exit. The other inmates made way for her, their eyes hungrily envious.

'Your arms!' the policeman barked.

'My arms?'

He clasped a pair of cuffs on her wrists with a fluidity that she admired. 'Go with him.' He used his chin to point at another policeman, who was standing off to one side in the passageway.

A babble of voices sounded again as he relocked the door. Rita followed the other policeman down the dark and narrow passageway. The whole place stank of unwashed bodies, but she resisted the urge to go down on all fours to breathe in the air close to the floor. She wouldn't want them to think she was crazy.

They finally emerged into a room flooded with sunlight. Rita took a deep, appreciative breath as her eyes got used to the light.

Kẹ́mi and Mọ́ríebá and her mother stood staring at her from the other side of a counter. They looked dreadful. She wondered why her mother in particular kept making faces like someone who had lost a dear relative. She wanted to smile at them, but her mouth felt filthy, so she kept her lips in a straight line.

'There she is,' Iya Tọ́lá announced unnecessarily.

'Are you okay?' Kẹ́mi asked.

'No, I'm not.' Rita lifted the corners of her lips.

'You will be fine,' Mọ́ríebá reassured her. 'We've come to see if we can make your stay here as comfortable as possible.'

Rita shook her head. She did not want to be comfortable. She needed to hold Tọ́lá off for as long as possible, so she wouldn't come and ruin things or bear the pain. Tọ́lá was delicate.

'The DPO will see you now,' said the policeman at the counter.

Kẹ́mi smiled at him. 'Thank you, officer. Which way are we going?'

'Come through.' The policeman indicated an opening beside the counter. Kẹ́mi rushed through and wrapped Rita in an awkward hug that surprised her.

Gosh! To be loved unconditionally.

Iya Tọ́lá joined them and looked at Rita through mournful, long-suffering eyes full of patience. Tọ́lá was her cross, and she would bear it. Rita side-stepped Iya Tọ́lá's attempt to touch her, and Iya Tọ́lá clasped her hands to her breasts as silent tears flowed down her cheeks.

The DPO's office was cramped, there was barely space for them and the table, itself overflowing with papers. On the wall behind the DPO were two framed pictures, one of the state governor and the other of the president. One was smiling, the other looked as if he was being given an enema.

'Please, please, sit down.' The man smiled as if they were there on a social visit. 'Mrs Alágbàdo, thanks so much, I got the package that you sent to me.' He directed his words at Móríebá.

Móríebá and Kẹ́mi squeezed into the two spare chairs in front of the table while Iya Tọ́lá and Rita took up positions in different corners of the room. The policeman was dismissed.

The DPO dragged a folder towards him and flipped through it. His lips moved as he read the contents. After a while, he sniffed and looked up at Móríebá. 'Who's this?' he used his chin to point at Kẹ́mi.

'This is Kẹ́mi Lawanson. She's Tọ́lá's sister, and the other woman is Tọ́lá's mother.'

Rita looked at Kẹ́mi Lawanson. Tọ́lá's sister. Yes, of course.

'This report says your sister killed her husband on the 5th of February.'

'I'm sure it also said that it was under unusual circumstances,' said Móríebá.

An embarrassed silence circled them.

The DPO cleared his throat, and snuck a look at Rita. 'Yes, yes. It says here that they were using sex toys.'

'Those are BDSM instruments, sir,' Kẹ́mi said.

'Yes! Whips and dildos and collars!' He fell silent as he scanned the report again, his lips forming the words, his eyes growing rounder until they seem to fill his face.

'I honestly don't know what to say,' the DPO continued. 'Of course we've heard of cases like this. I mean, there's nothing new under the sun.' He tittered nervously. 'Even though I don't think there are many cases like this in Nigeria, you know ... or maybe the families handle it quietly. She's going to be charged for manslaughter, you know?'

'Yes, sir, we do,' Mọ́ríebá sighed.

'Although I'm sure that there are laws for all these things in more advanced parts of the world, but this is Nigeria.' He spread his hands and got caught up studying them.

'We came to tell you one little thing, sir.' Kẹ́mi adopted his confidential air. 'Tọ́lá is under psychiatric care at Yaba, and she's not been taking her meds. She has an appointment with the doctor tomorrow.'

The DPO took his hands off the table and shifted his seat back. 'Why didn't anybody tell me this before? You mean we've been here with a mad woman? We even locked her in a room full of other people!'

'Sir, she's not a mad woman, she suffers from depression and a medical condition called DID, dissociative identity disorder. At least, that's what it says in her file here.' Kẹ́mi pulled out a file and pushed it towards the DPO. The man shifted back again, as if the file's madness might be contagious. 'Her doctor wanted to come here with us today, but she had an emergency and had to return to the hospital.'

Rita wondered where Kẹ́mi and Mọ́ríebá had got the file. She'd never been to Yaba before. She couldn't recall ever being there.

'This is a different case entirely!'

'No, it's not, sir,' Kẹ́mi said gently. 'We know she can't be bailed and we don't want to get any civil society organisation involved. All we are asking for is that Tọ́lá should have her own cell, and that her doctor can come and see her tomorrow – you know how these hungry human rights activists behave!'

'I've never had this kind of wahala before.' The DPO stared accusingly at all the people in the room. 'I don't like all these people shouting about human rights coming into my station. They never mind their own business.'

The room fell quiet as they all contemplated how irritating human rights activists could be.

'Sergeant Limba!' The DPO had started sweating profusely.

The sergeant stepped into the room with a smart salute.

'Can you make arrangements for an empty cell?'

'And if a small mattress can be arranged for her, we'd really appreciate it,' Mọ́ríebá added sweetly.

'Mattress?' The word was a question thrown at Sergeant Limba.

'I'll see what I can do, sir!'

'Clean mattress,' Kẹ́mi shouted after Sergeant Limba's retreating back.

'One more thing: your sister has refused to give her statement.' The DPO dared a look at Rita. For a fleeting second she contemplated doing the Haka but settled for a scowl, like a normal human being. He quickly looked away.

In order to establish that she was normal, Rita decided to say something. 'I'm ready to give my statement. It is mine, the statement is mine, but I'll give it to him, although I don't get why he wants it.'

'Good, good.' The DPO shuffled the papers on his desk. 'I will tell the sergeant to take down your statement before you're removed to your cell. I don't even know if mental people can give statements. All these evil spirits running around my station now ehn? We have to do special prayer.' He looked up. 'Madam, you will have to pay a pastor to do it.'

'It's alright, sir.' Kẹ́mi raised placating hands. 'We are ready to do anything to make her stay here comfortable.'

The DPO gave Rita another nervous look. 'I'm sorry, you won't be able to give her any medicine while she's under arrest, but her doctor can see her tomorrow, under supervision of course.'

'You're very kind, sir, and your kindness will be repaid tenfold,' said Mọ́ríebá.

'I know,' the DPO smiled. 'Sagent Limba! Remove the suspect to give her statement immediately!'

I just want some vodka.

'Me too, my darling, I would like to drink some with you,' Èṣù said as Rita brushed by them on the narrow passageway. Rita looked at them and smiled. They smiled back.

FUCKING LITTLE LIAR

Mọremí, Mọ́ríebá and Kudirat were in the sitting room of the mini flat in the basement of the house. They were waiting for Ortega. Mọ́ríebá was not too enamoured of the idea. She had rejected so many other plans that the girls had gone ahead and invited him in spite of her protestations. That Ortega was a thug, and just because he had once hired parents for Kudirat didn't mean he was right to handle this.

'Ah, but Aunty Móríebá, it's only a thief that can track the footsteps of another thief at a garbage dump,' Kudirat had said.

According to Ngozi, who had been delegated to investigate him, Ortega was presently the right-hand man of the president of the National Union of Road Transport Workers, a legalised criminal arm of the government.

'This doesn't mean he's knowledgeable about the workings of the underworld,' Móríebá had insisted.

But things had changed. The text that had landed in her phone the previous evening had her hands tied.

'Is your friend coming or not?' Móríebá had been antsy since they arrived at the flat five minutes earlier.

Móremí's tone was placatory. 'He should be here anytime soon. He called me when he got to the toll gate.'

'That boy might not come,' Móríebá insisted. 'I told you he's not a real criminal.'

'How many criminals do you know, Aunty M?' Kudirat teased her.

'I know Olórí Ẹbí and now I know Chinwe and the people who have joined the blackmail-of-Móríebá-Alágbàdo-to-an-inch-of-her-life gang, and I think you, Kudirat, have the makings of a criminal.'

'That was a low one, Aunty M,' Kudirat said in mock annoyance.

Móremí's phone rang. 'Hello. Ortega? Yes. The black gate. Tell Mallam Sule your name. We already told him you're coming, he'll bring you here.'

The three women fell silent as they waited for his arrival. Kudirat jumped out of her chair as soon as the bell rang.

'Ortega.' She pulled the door open. 'Mallam Sule, thanks, you may return to the gate now.'

Ortega had changed in the past couple of years. He had grown taller and filled out. His once thin, gangly body was muscular. He wore jeans, a t-shirt and high tops, and had a laptop bag slung across his shoulder. He looked prosperous.

'It's so good to see you.' Mọremí found, to her surprise, that she meant it.

'You too, you girls are all grown up,' he said as he hugged her.

'This is our aunt, Mọríebá Alágbàdo.'

'Pleasure meeting you, ma'am.' Ortega shook the hand that was held out to him.

'I'll get you something to drink while the girls fill you in.' Mọríebá hurried out of the room.

The girls knew their aunt felt awkward discussing it all with a stranger.

'I heard what happened to Tọlá and her husband, that was some crazy shit, man.'

Mọremí didn't want to talk about Tọlá. She was still trying to sort out her feelings about Wálé's murder. 'About as crazy as the story I'm about to share with you.'

Kudirat handed him the folder. He pulled out the first picture and then took the others out one after the other. He examined the pictures closely. Mọremí scrutinised his face. When he was done, he returned the pictures to the folder and leaned back into the chair.

'Somebody is blackmailing our aunt.' Mọremí moved to the edge of her seat so he would understand the urgency of the situation. 'This same person is also in possession of some documents belonging to me.' She told him all about the will, Olórí Ẹbí and Mọríebá.

'The other girl in the pictures, that one with her back to the camera, tell me about her.'

'Chinwe Orlu,' said Kudirat. 'We really don't know her very well. She was Aunty M's friend. We suspect she's the one that took the pictures. She disappeared just before Olórí Ẹbí came to blackmail Aunty M.'

Mọ́ríebá returned with one of the maids, who was carrying a tray of drinks. 'Please help yourself.'

'I have a few questions concerning the pictures, ma'am.' His voice was cool and polite. 'Where did you meet the lady in the pictures? Do you have any idea how they were taken?'

'Aren't you too young to be in this line of business?' Mọ́ríebá blurted out.

Mọ́remí held her breath, but Ortega smiled.

'If you don't want to work with me on account of my age, Ms Alágbàdo, I'll totally understand, but I can assure you that I'm damn good at what I do.' He rose from his seat. 'Kudirat, Mọ́remí, please do keep in touch.'

'Wait, stop!' Mọ́ríebá was out of her seat too.

'You have nothing to worry about, ma'am. Everything that has happened so far in this flat stays here.' He gave her a reassuring smile.

'No, it's not that,' Mọ́ríebá said sheepishly. 'I was out of line.' She stood toe to toe with him and looked into his eyes. 'I'm sorry. I will answer your questions.'

Ortega shrugged and sat back down.

'I met Chinwe at the mall, the one at Dugbe. I had dashed in to pick a couple of things for some friends. I was in such a hurry that I bumped into her as I exited the supermarket, spilling all her belongings. I was shocked when she burst into tears. She looked so helpless, so vulnerable, standing there in her loafers and glasses, that after I helped her to pick up her things I offered to buy her a drink. We ended up having lunch and that was when she told me this long story about how she was a youth corper and that it was her first time in Ibadan. She said the government hadn't paid their allowance and her flatmates had thrown her things out. She looked so sad and brave. I offered her a place in my house.' Mọ́ríebá paused. 'It wasn't all innocent really. I was attracted to her from the get go.'

Her gaze was averted. Mọ́remí wondered, again, why Mọ́ríebá was so ashamed, what she'd done wrong.

'She made the first move.' Mọ́ríebá's voice had deepened. 'I wouldn't want to take advantage of someone who's so vulnerable. She came knocking on my door in her transparent nightgown, saying she'd had a nightmare. I suspected that she wanted more than comforting, my instincts were screaming "no". But I was attracted to her, and it is so hard for LGBT people in this country to find love ...' She trailed off.

'I allowed her to make all the moves. That girl was good! I mean, she was a good actress,' she added hurriedly.

When Kudirat did not crack a smile, Mọ́remí swallowed hers.

'She never accepted any money or gifts from me. She would buy me little things: the dark chocolate I love so much, she would bring me wine, the type I used to drink before I got rich enough to afford good ones. I honestly thought she loved me. And we only made love, had sex, in my bedroom. We couldn't risk even looking at each other intimately outside of my bedroom.' She laughed ruefully. 'The fucking little liar.'

'Did you ever meet any of her friends?' Ortega asked, as he pulled an old Nokia phone out of his pocket.

'No, she never brought anybody home. She usually left early, for her job, and returned in the afternoon. She was shy, bookish – until that day in my bedroom.' Móríebá sighed into silence.

'That's not all, Ortega,' Móremí said. 'Aunty Móríebá got a text message yesterday, and that's why you're actually here.'

Móríebá handed her phone to Ortega.

Yu hav noting to fear from yr uncle. He can't use computa. He hav one copy of the pix. I hav e-copies of pix & video. They are save for now. Await fourda instrutions.

'Bad grammar,' Ortega said after reading through the text. He returned the phone to Móríebá. 'Very unprofessional. I mean, it works for internet scams, but not blackmail gigs.'

Móremí smirked.

'We suspect that Chinwe sent it,' said Kudirat.

'Let me get this straight: there are two sets of people blackmailing you?' He looked at Móríebá, and she nodded. 'The first person is a family member and he's in possession of some documents belonging to Móremí, and the second is the guy who the first one hired to film the blackmail material?'

'Yes. We didn't even know about the second person until yesterday,' Móríebá said. 'Olórí Ẹbí is such a dunce. I mean, really? He probably believes in the lie that there's honour among thieves. The way his mind works. It defies logic.'

Ortega picked up his phone and dialled a number. As it started ringing he switched on the speaker.

'Ortega how you dey now?' a gravelly voice came over the phone.

'My Chair,' Ortega responded, grinning widely.

'You don reach Ibadan?'

'Yes, my Chair. Baba Fryo, you're on speakerphone. I'm with a couple of pretty cool chicks I was in school with, and they need our help.' He smiled up at the girls. 'Mọ́remí, Kudirat, say hello to Baba Fryo. They need me to do some work for them, so I'll be needing a contact person here in Ibadan.'

'That's no big deal,' Baba Fryo said. 'The go-to man is Sule Alapawura. I'll send you his number and tell him you're coming to see him. Don't go to him with empty mouth.'

'No lele, thanks so much, my Chair.'

'You're a good son to me,' Baba Fryo said and ended the call.

Ortega looked up at the girls who were staring at him wide-eyed. 'That's my chairman. He's a very nice man, you heard him?' He had barely finished talking when his phone beeped. 'Ah, here's the number. Do you girls know Sule?'

Mọ́remí and Kudirat shrugged.

Mọ́ríebá cleared her throat. 'I don't know him personally, but I've heard about him around town. That guy is dangerous. Isn't he the kingpin of Alábẹ́rẹ́?'

Ortega nodded, and they listened as he made another call, ending it with a promise to bring the consultation fee.

'That was quick.' Mọ́ríebá was rather impressed.

'We told you, Ortega is our man.' Mọ́remí and Kudirat grinned at Mọ́ríebá.

'Sule said we should see him around 6pm. I think Mọremí should come along with me. If I'd known it was this kind of deal I would have brought one of my boys. You do have a baseball cap?'

Mọremí grinned back at Ortega and nodded.

'Ma'am, may I ask about your budget?' Ortega's voice was all business.

'I'll deposit a million naira into your account.' Mọríebá sounded anxious. 'Would that be enough?'

Ortega smiled. 'A million should do, for now. One more thing, ma'am: I'll need to stay around till this business is over, maybe get one or two boys in with me. We'll need to beef up your security and sweep your house for hidden cameras.'

A panicked look flashed across Mọríebá's face. 'No, please, don't.' She shook her head. 'I've spent most of my life trying not to become a prisoner to my wealth.'

Ortega smiled reassuringly. 'Madam, you won't even notice they are there. It's for your safety. We are not going to do anything heavy.'

Mọríebá's phone rang. She looked at the caller ID and sighed. 'Sorry, I have to take this call.' On her way out past Ortega she said, 'You can make use of this flat for as long as you want. Your boys are welcome too. Just don't throw any wild parties.'

'Don't worry, ma'am. The partying will come after we've completed the job.'

THE MONEY-MAKING MACHINE

'Catch!' Olórí Ẹbí tossed a little black bag at Àmọ̀pé. She stretched out one arm but missed it, and then got on her hands and knees to trawl for it on the floor. He stared at her with a mixture of pity and disgust.

Àmọ̀pé was all skin and bones, her head close shaven. Her dark skin had a grey tinge to it, and there were dark spots all over her thin arms. Her face though, her face was still smooth, with intelligent eyes that had seen everything. Thick, curvy lips and an aristocratic nose that turned up at the tip.

I, Àdùkẹ́ Olatorera Alágbàdo, being of sound mind and body, to my only daughter, Àmọ̀pé Omobolanle Alágbàdo, I bequeath all my worldly goods, which would be administered by her until her daughter, my granddaughter, Mọ́remí Asake Alágbàdo, turns twenty-one. Underlisted are the aforementioned properties:

A three-storey building: 28 Moruwa Close, Lekki, Ajah Roundabout, Lagos.

Three semi-detached houses: nos 4, 5 and 6 Awosika Avenue, Old Bodija, Ibadan.

Two semi-detached: nos 34A and 34B, Moroway Drive, Ikoyi.

One bungalow: SW8/166/897 Idi-Ikan, Ibadan.

Àmọ̀pé whimpered as she drew the small sachet containing the brown sugar out of the bag. She rubbed it against her cheek and smiled blissfully, her eyes lit up like those of a child who'd just been handed a bag of sweets.

The elders have a saying that once you own a slave, you own all their earthly possessions. Not that I'm saying that Àmòpé is my slave.

'Thank you my dear, darling uncle.' She sat on the bare mattress, tightened the ankara wrapper around her chest and dragged a small leather bag from one corner of the room.

The room itself was a tiny square that had been a storeroom in its former life. Olórí Ẹbí had placed her there because he didn't want her in the main house. Junkies would steal and sell anything they could lay their hands on when the biting need for a high hit them. He didn't want to wake up to an empty house.

The room was sandwiched between the main house and the outdoor toilet. He thought it apt, since she could no longer be considered human, and only human beings were allowed to live in a house. Àmòpé belonged to a new species created by heroin. She was a zombie, a half-dead thing well on her way to being flushed down the toilet.

'Àmòpé, Àmòpé, Àmòpé, how many times did I call you?'

'Three times, my darling uncle.'

She looked at him with eyes snapping with impatience, but Olórí Ẹbí forged on. 'Remember our deal that you will clean up in preparation for our return to the bank the week after next.'

... however, this will only be in effect if the said sole heir was declared drug free by independent doctors from Union Bank, Zenith Bank and High Street Bank.

'Don't worry, Uncle, I got this.' She sniffled as she laid out the tools of her trade neatly, reverently, on the stool in front of her: a syringe, a lighter, a candle, a spoon and a long rag. 'Like I told you yesterday, I'm not feeling too hot, and I only need to eat very well, but I'll be fine.'

'Isn't that what you said last week? This is getting too long. I really can't afford to keep supplying you if you won't help me.'

She paused and looked at him, eyes brimming with tears. 'Please uncle, don't do this. You know I'm a very sick woman, you know this!'

'I'm sorry, mai dia.' Olórí Ẹbí touched her shoulder with the tip of his fingers. 'It's not that I don't understand. All you need is to be clean for a week, then we'll go for the test. After that you can continue.' He pointed at the sachet she was still holding.

She wiped a line of tears. As she measured the heroin carefully onto a strip of paper, she paused and looked up at Olórí Ẹbí, who was still standing by the doorway, her face a big question mark. 'May I have some privacy please?'

Olórí Ẹbí opened his mouth in surprise. He clapped his hands and was about to say something derisive but swallowed his words and stepped out of the room, shutting the door quietly behind him.

'Ah!' he ejaculated as he made for the main house. 'So, beggars are choosers! See this small girl ordering me around.'

He tried to remember the last time someone had spoken to him in that tone of voice, but failed. Mọ́ríebá didn't count. She was an ill-mannered girl, and rudeness was the trademark of children who hadn't been raised properly. 'Because I want to eat beef, I am now forced to call a cow my elder brother. A junkie! A mere beggarly prostitute telling me to give her some privacy in my own house! Why am I even surprised?' He fumed as he stepped into the main house. 'She is her mother's daughter after all, a useless bunch of women.'

Another useless woman, L'Ẹgbǎ, had been snooping around his house the other day. She had come from the direction of the backyard claiming that she was looking for Ìyàwó. He wondered if that snoopy woman had learnt that Àmọ̀pé was here.

'Bàámi, the car is ready.' Lékan was standing right in his path, beaming.

Olórí Ẹbí glared at his son with ill-concealed annoyance. The boy had been on at him about one of his friends who had a 'deal' that only came 'once in a lifetime'. But Olórí Ẹbí knew his son: he was thicker than two bricks. He spent his days mooning after women and his nights drinking. If it had been Quadri that had brought the deal he might've considered it seriously, but this was Lékan! He had decided to indulge him, to prove to Lékan once and for all that he was a fool, and maybe prevent him from bringing more lame ideas.

Olórí Ẹbí listened to his prattle about money-making machines and shady deals by the government all the way to the office. He had been involved in too many scams not to recognise something that smelled like one.

So, when an expensive-looking young man, with regal features, creamy skin and curly hair walked into his office, he was taken aback. The man's expensive perfume filled the corners, it filled Olórí Ẹbí's senses. The perfume reminded Olórí Ẹbí of how Mọ́ríebá smelled each time she came into his house – of generational wealth and international travel and a soft life. Except in this case the wearer was male. It suited him better than that brat.

'Bàámi, this is the Mahmoud I told you about.' Lékan's grin split his face in two.

'Please, please, sit down.' Olórí Ẹbí's heart started beating unusually as his eyes became entangled with Mahmoud's. Unspeakable images filled his head. His cheeks flushed hotly as Mahmoud gave him a slow, knowing smile.

'Lékan! Go to the secretary's office and bring your ... our visitor a proper chair befitting a man of his status.'

'I won't like to put you to any trouble, sir.' His voice had a deep timbre that made Olórí Ẹbí's hands tremble.

Olórí Ẹbí took hold of himself and cleared his throat. 'It's no trouble,' he said, trying to mimic the well-rounded vowels that had just caressed his ears.

Lékan was back in the room with a chair. Olórí Ẹbí was horrified to see how grimy it looked next to the beautiful young man. He cringed as Mahmoud sat on the chair in his immaculate babariga, and suddenly realised that he hadn't painted his office in the past two years. A ratty blind was fluttering behind him; a 2008 calendar was off to his right.

Haba Raufu get a grip!

Mahmoud went straight to business. 'I'm sure Lékan has told you about the deal.' Olórí Ẹbí leaned towards him with rapt attention, his arms resting on the table.

'It's quite simple, sir,' Mahmoud continued. He drew a card out of his pocket and pushed it across the table with his long fingers. Olórí Ẹbí picked it up and pretended to read it, glancing at Mahmoud's well manicured nails. 'I'm Mahmoud Abubk'r ibn Traore. I work with the CBN as a store manager.'

Mahmoud pulled a phone out of his pocket, fiddled with it and gave it to Olórí Ẹbí. Lékan hurried to his father's side and showed him pictures of Mahmoud shaking the president's hand, Mahmoud and the CBN governor at what seemed like a party and finally some chunky machines, the likes of which Olórí Ẹbí had never seen before.

'The party in power is preparing for next elections, and you know very well that this costs a lot of money. Last year the government decided to change Nigeria's currency notes and bought these machines, but when they realised that the cost of production might be too risky in Nigeria, they changed their minds and decided to print the new currencies in SA.'

Olórí Ẹbí wondered where SA was, but he nodded in agreement. Far be it for him to behave like a bushman in the presence of this ... this prince.

'We are looking for trustworthy individuals who can handle this deal for us.'

Olórí Ẹbí asked the only disquieting question on his mind: 'Why me?'

'Luck sir! Whichever god you worship is obviously on your side.' Mahmoud smiled at Lékan fondly. 'I met Lékan at a party thrown for me by my cousin and we hit it off immediately. Seeing how street smart he is, I told him about this deal and he said you were an ideal candidate.'

Olórí Ẹbí considered his son with new respect.

'You are well known in this community. And all the people we have spoken to assured us that you are a discreet and trustworthy person.'

Olórí Ẹbí arched an eyebrow.

Mahmoud raised his hands in defeat. 'Alright, not everybody thought you are trustworthy, but they can swear that you're very discreet,' he smiled. 'We also carried out a thorough investigation through the secret service, sir.

We know you are one of the founding fathers of Alábẹ́rẹ́ – Olórí Ẹbí opened his mouth like a fish – 'and we also know you left the place and became a businessman, a honest one living off the rents of your properties and managing your family's wealth.'

Olórí Ẹbí did not allow Mahmoud to see how pleased he was by that remark.

'You were chosen for your ruggedness and determination. We also know that with your background this kind of deal won't be strange. The fact that you do not have any political affiliations also weighs heavily in your favour.'

Olórí Ẹbí stared at the young man for the longest time. He weighed his words, his options. This might be the deal that would seal his fortunes. Everyone knew that politicians were a bunch of crooks. *If not for Alábẹ́rẹ́ I would have been a big man by now ... kai!*

'There's really nothing more to say, sir. I'll give you time to decide whether you're in or not.' Mahmoud drew an envelope out of his pocket and gave it to Olórí Ẹbí. 'I'll give you a week to check out my background, sir. Here are my details. You also have to understand that this is a secret: you'll have to be discreet.'

'You don't need to tell me that,' Olórí Ẹbí assured him.

'If I don't hear back from you by the end of the week, I'll know you're not interested.' Mahmoud rose from his seat and extended a hand across the table. 'Have a good day, sir.'

He was nearly at the door.

'Wait,' said Olórí Ẹbí, 'you didn't tell me how much this would cost me.'

Mahmoud fished a card out of his pocket and handed it to him. 'I hope to hear back from you soon. Lékan, please see me off.'

Olórí Ẹbí took a look at the number on the card. Eighty million naira. He got out his phone from the voluminous fold of his agbádá and placed a call to Sule Alapawura. He would know what to do.

YABA LEFT

Kudirat wanted to weep as she watched Tọ́lá being dragged forcefully from behind the counter by three burly policemen.

'There is really no need for this violence,' Mọ́ríebá shouted, as she and Kẹ́mi ran towards the men. Another policeman blocked their path.

The female officers gathered near the doorway, craning their necks to watch the spectacle and to discuss in loud voices how they suspected all along that the woman was truly crazy, because no woman in her right mind would ever kill her own husband. They talked of witches, of women who ran naked in the streets without any prior notice to their poor husbands.

'Serving notice before losing your mind must be nice,' Kudirat muttered. She moved away from the officers and blocked out their chatter.

'Leave me alone. Tell these people to leave me alone,' said Tọ́lá. The eerie thing was that she wasn't raving or shouting. Her voice was even, like she was making a statement of fact. 'You think I can't fight you all off with just one finger?'

A policeman tried to wrap the chain he was holding around Tọ́lá's ankle, but a well-aimed kick caught him on the chin.

Kudirat winced as he went down. She wondered where Tọ́lá got her strength. Despite her arms being cuffed behind her back, Tọlá jerked, she kicked, she heaved like an erupting volcano. Kudirat didn't know that tears were pouring down her face until she felt saltiness on her tongue. She wiped her face with her t-shirt as another policeman emerged from the passageway and tried to grab Tọlá by the throat.

Kudirat decided she would no longer watch. She ran out of the police station and through the gate towards Mọ́ríebá's car, but it had been locked. Across the road, just in front of the police station fence, was a woman selling sweets and kolanuts from a long bench. The woman monitored the small tray of goods as seriously as the women selling gold in Balogun market. Kudirat crossed to her side of the road, smiled at the woman and bought some Tom-Tom sweets. 'Please, ma, may I sit down beside you?'

The woman gave her a suspicious look but nodded. Kudirat sat down and unwrapped the sweet, but she didn't put it in her mouth. She couldn't.

What had happened to the woman that she used to know? Yes, Tọlá hadn't been totally sane, but this Tọlá wasn't the woman she'd lived with for so many years. There was a wildness to her that had nothing to do with her mental illness. Kudirat felt like she was seeing a different person. It was in the way she held herself, erect. It was in the line of her face, in her eyes. The person appeared much taller than the Tọlá she'd known, which might be due to her losing so much weight. She was slimmer now, slinkier. There was an aura of danger that clung to this new Tọlá, like a leopard – the type that would snap you in half with one bite.

Kudirat and Mọ́remí had talked a lot about Tọlá and Wálé, and how mean and heartless he had been. But in all their imaginings of the end of their relationship, Tọ́lá murdering Wálé was the last thing they'd thought would happen. In fact, if any murder was to occur, it would have been more likely that Wálé would kill Tọ́lá and pass it off as suicide.

She remembered the day Jésùtitófúnmi had whispered dreadful words into her ears about Wálé. Words she could never repeat to anyone, not even Mọ́remí. Words that should never cross the lips of an adult, never mind a child. Wálé was a virus that destroyed everything it came in contact with.

Kudirat swore that no man would ever put her in such a position. She blamed the family for what happened between the Roberts. They shouldn't have forced Tọ́lá to return to him. Who baffled her were Tọ́lá's parents – her mother in particular. But then she remembered how easily her own mother had given her up.

'Kudirat!' Mọ́ríebá's voice jerked her out of her thoughts.

'I'm coming, Aunty M.' She rose from the bench and crossed the road.

They got into the car, but instead of turning the key in the ignition, Mọ́ríebá put her head on the wheel and started hyperventilating. Kudirat didn't know what to do, so she caressed Mọ́ríebá's back.

An ambulance was weaving out of the grounds of the police station, its siren wailing like a lost soul. Mọ́ríebá sat up straight and started the engine. She followed the ambulance as closely as she possibly could in the slow moving traffic heading out of Bariga towards Yaba. 'Where's Aunty Kẹ́mi? Why are we following the ambulance?' Kudirat asked.

'Kẹ́mi's in the ambulance with Tọ́lá and the doctor.'

'Is Aunty Tọ́lá alright?'

'I don't know about her being alright, but she's certainly calmer. The doctor gave her an injection; she said it would calm her down till we get to the hospital. Why didn't that bastard DPO call us earlier? He knew that Tọ́lá was sick, hadn't been sleeping or eating any of the food we've been bringing to her. What if she'd harmed herself? If Kẹ́mi hadn't gone there yesterday and insisted she must see her sister, she could've died!'

Kudirat was not used to listening, but she swallowed her words as torrents of anger and frustration flowed out of Mọ́ríebá.

'See why I did not want to involve the police in my own case? Isn't it the same useless way they would have handled it? People are so incompetent. So lacking in empathy and kindness.'

They hit a traffic jam, and the car slowed to a crawl. Ahead, the ambulance was still wailing, ineffectively, because there was no room to pass. Mọ́ríebá fell quiet.

'Everything is going to be alright, Aunty,' Kudirat said. 'You'll see, we'll all be fine.'

Mọ́ríebá's phone broke her silence. She handed it to Kudirat, who looked at the caller ID. It was Mọ́remí.

'What happened to your phone?' Mọ́remí asked. 'I've been calling you all afternoon.'

'My phone died. Aunty M and I are stuck in traffic. She says she'll call you back.'

'I wasn't calling to talk to her. I just want to find out how you guys are doing and how is Aunty Tọ́lá?'

Kudirat sighed. 'It's a long story. I'll tell you later.'

'By the way, tell Aunty M that Ortega has found the

woman that carried out the setup. We are going to see Sule Alapawura later today.'

Kudirat ended the call just as Móríebá found a space to park the car at the psychiatric hospital.

'So, what will happen to the children?' Kudirat asked as they alighted from the car.

Móríebá stared at her blankly for a second. 'They are coming to Ibadan with me. Kẹ́mi and I decided it is best under the circumstances. We've agreed that Iya Tọ́lá shouldn't be allowed near children.'

ASAS MOTEL NEAR MOLETE BRIDGE

Móremí stared at her reflection in the mirror and decided she might get used to her new look. Her formerly wild curls had been dyed black and dreadlocked. She was wearing contact lenses that changed her green eyes to brown. She pulled a face-cap over her head and straightened her t-shirt before finally turning away from the mirror. She picked up her knapsack from the foot of the bed and went down the stairs.

Kudirat and Ortega were seated at a spindly-legged table on the patio, their heads lowered over a laptop.

'I'm ready,' Móremí announced as she bounced through the sitting room towards them. 'What are you doing?'

'Uploading your article about the Emir of Daura,' Ortega said, clicking a button.

Over the past month, they'd been blogging furiously. This blog showed a picture of a middle-aged man wearing yards and yards of babariga and headgear to rival that of the Emir of Kano. He was sitting astride a horse, surrounded by a horde of people, their hands in the air.

The headline read 'Unveiled: The Emir of Daura, the 50th richest man in the world, is a Nigerian!'

'Have you seen Mukhtar?'

'Not today,' Mọ́remí shrugged.

Mukhtar was one of the laziest people Mọ́remí had ever encountered. He was either slouching about the flat or sleeping. But in action he was a chameleon. He could speak Hausa-inflected Queen's English, then pidgin speak from the streets of Warri in a blink of an eye.

'If we get downstairs and he's not there ...' Ortega allowed his words to hang in the air. He tapped Kudirat on the shoulder. 'Once it finishes uploading, please share it on the other platforms. Hopefully a couple of other bloggers will steal it before tonight.'

'Aye, aye captain,' Kudirat responded.

'Hey guys.' Mọ́ríebá stepped on to the patio. She looked drained. She had lost a lot of weight and had taken to lurking indoors. She googled herself constantly. Just that week, a girl's x-rated lesbian video had been uploaded to the internet. The homophobes had come out in droves, howling for her death.

As if that wasn't bad enough, the morality police had written article upon article about how Nigerian women were getting infected with lesbianism and how it sounded a death knell to the righteousness of a nation.

Mọ́remí had high hopes that it would soon be over. Mọ́ríebá had finally received the 'fourda instructions' from the blackmailers.

Cum to asas motel near Molete birge 6pm on d dot with 4 million Naira in raw cash. Put d moni inside Ghana mus go. Wait fourda instructions. Wear red cloth.

Mọ́remí never found out what Ortega would have done to Mukhtar, because they met him leaning against the Volkswagen bug that Mọ́ríebá had given to them to move around with. Mukhtar was smoking a spliff.

Ortega pulled open the door and folded the driver's seat. It took the three of them some time to manoeuvre the huge bag of cash into the car. Ortega put a tracker the shape and size of a matchbox deep inside the bag and zipped it up.

As Mọ́remí drove through the gate, Ortega dialled a number. 'Oga Chuks, yes, we're on our way ... Alright, are the boys in position? Don't worry, I go settle all of you nah. I've told you you'll get the money as soon as we've done the job.'

They fell quiet as Mọ́remí concentrated on navigating the usual hold up at the Challenge roundabout.

Ortega got out in front of St Anne's Grammar School. Mọ́remí drove further down, pulled up in front of Asas Motel and waited for the call.

Her phone beeped. She fished it out of her pocket and read the text message out loud to Mukhtar, who had just lit up the roach again and was studying the men furtively entering and leaving the whorehouse.

Carry Ghana-mus-go, be working down to the birge.

Mọ́remí forwarded the text message to Ortega as she and Mukhtar pulled the heavy bag out of the car. Mọ́remí wondered just how the blackmailers intended to carry all that money off.

Ortega had made fun of what he called their stone-age methods. 'If I were doing this kind of deal, I'd open a false account online, have you guys transfer the money to me and clear it out immediately.'

As they drew closer to the bridge, a young man dashed past them followed by a crowd of people shouting, 'Ole! Thief! Stop him!' They were still engulfed by the crush when a heavy-chested man grabbed the bag from them. It was gone. Mọremí turned to say something to Mukhtar, but he'd been swallowed by the crowd. Mọremí was borne along like a piece of debris by the tidal wave of human bodies and deposited near the motel. The crowd melted into the night. She was dialling Ortega's number when Mukhtar, looking as ragged as she felt, appeared beside her. He fished a crumpled pack of cigarettes from his pocket and lit up.

'Ortega,' she said, 'the bag was stolen from us.'

'Nice operation,' he said on the other end. 'Didn't think they'd do something like that. But don't worry, we are still one step ahead. Click on the Tracka icon on your phone and follow the money.'

Mọremí handed her phone to Mukhtar and jumped into the car.

'I think they are headed towards a place called Oke-Ado,' Mukhtar said after a while. 'Do you know the directions, or do we have to use Google Maps?'

Mọremí flashed his sarcasm a cold look and continued driving towards Oke-Ado. He fiddled with the sound system, Nigeria's hip-hop filling the small interior of the car. Mọremí wound down the windows to let in the cold evening air and let out their songs of war and the sickly sweet smell of maryjay.

They were soon at the night market that Oke-Ado was famous for. Lit with oil lamps and lanterns, Oke-Ado was a rumoured portal between the substantial and insubstantial.

Èṣù ported from the Volkswagen bug into the crowded market.

'Turn left,' said Mukhtar looking at the phone. 'The guys are in a place called Gbadebo Street, I'm with Chuks and his boys. Park in front of the high court.'

As Mọ́remí pulled up in front of the high court, two policemen approached. One pointed the weak yellow light of his torch into the car.

'Young man!' One of the policemen leaned into the car. 'Why are you parking here?'

Mukhtar leaned across. 'Ah please, oga, my brother and I are waiting for our older brother who went to see one of his friends at Iyaganku Quarters. He asked us to wait here for him.'

The other policeman went to the passenger's side and shone his torch on Mukhtar's face. 'Are you sure this one is your brother?'

'Yes, sir.' Mukhtar's voice was pure Eton, with a whisper of Hausa.

'Somebody has been smoking marijuana in this car!' The policeman shone his torch deeper into the car. Mọ́remí swore at Mukhtar underneath her breath. 'Step out of the car, let's see you.'

Mukhtar shrugged and pulled open his side of the door. He stepped out with a charming smile on his face. Mọ́remí turned off the ignition and did the same.

'Driver's licence!'

Mọ́remí pulled out her wallet and handed it over to him. Ortega had arranged the licence for her almost as soon as he taught her how to drive.

'Car papers!'

Mọ́remí opened the car and took the Ziploc bag containing the papers out of the dashboard. The policeman was still examining the papers when another car pulled up beside them. Ortega and Chuks got out.

'Officers.' Chuks smiled at the men.

'Chuks, Chuks. So, you know these boys?'

'They are my younger ones. Did they do anything?'

'Ah, no, we are just trying to make sure they don't do anything.' The policemen were all smiles and shaking hands.

'Mukhtar, abeg come and help me with the bags and laptops,' Ortega said.

Mọ́remí pulled open the door and folded the driver's seat. They piled the laptops, iPads and flash drives into the car.

'Una dey sell laptop?' one of the policemen asked curiously.

'Nooo,' Chuks laughed. 'My brother is an engineer. He's going to help me to fix them.'

They said their goodbyes and Mọ́remí drove off.

'So?' she asked as they emerged into Oke-Ado again.

Èṣù hopped back into the car. They stretched out their legs and watched, for that was what the Òrìṣà did, they watched over human beings as they unfolded their own destinies.

'We followed the money to a house. Chuks took over from there,' Ortega replied, one of the laptops open on his lap.

'Was there any shooting?' asked Mukhtar, craning his neck backwards.

'We didn't need to shoot: Chuks's boys outnumbered

them. They were taken by surprise, and gave us their phones and laptops. They hadn't even checked the bag.'

Mukhtar laughed. 'I'd like to be there when they find out that their money is 90% paper.'

'We can always drop you off so you can go and find out,' Ortega muttered.

Mọremí couldn't laugh. She was too nervous. She wanted to look at the computers now. What if none of them contained the videos and pictures?

'I hope no one is following us,' she said.

'Don't worry about that: the boys are holding them until we know we've got it.'

They were nearly home when Ortega shouted, 'Jackpot!'

Mọremí parked the car and Ortega was out in a flash, the still-open laptop in his hands. Mukhtar whooped.

'Kudirat, Aunty M,' Mọremí shouted, as she ran towards the front door. 'We've got the pictures!'

'There's still a lot to be done,' Ortega said as they sat round the dining table later that night.

The girls groaned.

'We have to wipe the memories of all the systems and clean up the memory banks too,' Ortega said, as they sat round the dining table later that night.

Mukhtar shoved a forkful of spaghetti into his mouth. 'Don't forget about the clouds.'

'What will you do with all those devices?' Mọríebá asked.

Ortega smiled at her. 'Nothing. You don't want to know about this, remember? By the way, ma'am, have you made the calls?'

Mọríebá smiled, a slow, wicked turning up of her lips. 'No one will give him tissue to wipe his butt.'

SEASON SEVEN:
THE MUGUNISATION OF
OLÓRÍ ẸBÍ (2014–2015)

THE BEST LAID PLANS OF MICE O' MEN

Olórí Ẹbí was in a foul mood. If anybody had told him that raising seventy million naira would be so difficult, he would have thought the person stupid. Not that he'd tried to raise that kind of money before, but a man of his social standing shouldn't experience such difficulties. Every plan he'd made had been torpedoed by the fools he'd surrounded himself with.

Àmọ́pé had been the first person to mess things up. After a week of cold turkey, which he'd ensured by locking her in the store room, he had got a shock at the hospital when she'd tested positive for heroin and some other substances he had never even heard of.

He hadn't bothered to return to the bank. He dumped Àmọ́pé back at his house and ordered Lékan to lock her up again.

As if that wasn't bad enough, Madam Cherie Coco had called to accuse him of setting her up. The long and short of it was that they'd lost Mọ́ríebá's pictures and videos to a bunch of gun-toting bastards. Madam Cherie Coco claimed he had done it because he hadn't wanted to pay the balance of her money.

Lékan popped his head into the room. 'Bàámi, Mahmoud is here. He just drove into the complex.'

Olórí Ẹbí ground the heels of his hands into his eyes. An ache had started just behind them.

'Do you want me to tell him to come back some other time?' Lékan's voice was full of sympathy.

There was nothing Olórí Ẹbí hated more than sympathy. He straightened his spine. 'Tell him to come upstairs,' he yelled. 'In fact, go and bring him to me.'

Lékan hurriedly left, shutting the door quietly.

Olórí Ẹbí opened his drawer and pulled out a sachet of Alabukun. He flapped the small bag, expertly tore the upper end of the sachet open and emptied its powdery contents straight down his throat. By the time Lékan returned with Mahmoud, Olórí Ẹbí felt fine, almost happy. The four shots of schnapps he'd quickly downed also helped.

'Mallam Mahmoud.' He rose from his chair and smiled at the young man, who was wearing a khaki brown jalamia. He was particularly glad that his office had had a makeover since the last meeting. The walls shone a lustrous deep green, the old calendar had been thrown out and a brilliant yellow curtain fluttered over the window.

'It's good to see you again, sir.' Mahmoud shook his proffered hand.

'Please sit down.' Olórí Ẹbí gestured to the newly upholstered chair.

Lékan fetched a bottle of water from the newly installed fridge and placed it in front of their visitor.

'My boss, the governor of CBN, informed me that you've called to make enquiries,' said Mahmoud, as he sipped some water.

Olórí Ẹbí took note of the delicate way he handled the bottle. 'I hope you are not offended, but you know eighty million naira is not the kind of money one wants to joke around with.'

There was no need to mention that he'd got Sule to look the boy up on the internet too. Sule had shown him pictures of the boy on that Facebook something and Instagram. The boy liked to take picture! He was always at one party or the other! There was even one picture he took with a man Sule said was the son of the president! Ah! The boy had money and wristwatches and perfumes! Children of nowadays were not shy about showing off their wealth at all!

Olórí Ẹbí liked the internet. He thought he might buy a laptop once this money thing was done. He would go to the internet and look at pictures. Ah!

Mahmoud laughed. 'If you hadn't done a proper background check on me, walahi, I would have thought we'd come to the wrong person.' He paused. 'So, is the money ready?'

Olórí Ẹbí knew the question would come. He'd thought of several ways of holding Mahmoud off till he raised the capital. A crazy idea slipped into his mind at that moment, and for once in his life, he decided to test the waters of honesty.

'I have a problem, my friend,' he started, before he lost his liver. 'I have not been able to raise the money.'

Mahmoud picked up the water and took another sip. He looked at Olórí Ẹbí through sad eyes.

'All the people I thought could loan me the money had one excuse or the other. I even tried to borrow the money with some deeds but the amount those shylocks are offering is way too low. I suspect it's the handiwork of my enemies.' Olórí Ẹbí leaned towards Mahmoud confidentially. 'I've been thinking that since you work in a bank, I mean the Central Bank ...' He lowered his head, his voice, his eyes trained on the younger man. 'I was thinking that maybe you can borrow me some money.'

Mahmoud made to say something but Olórí Ẹbí raised his hand. 'I am willing to part with deeds to my properties, and once this deal is done, you will have your money back within the month.'

'I'm so sorry, sir.' Mahmoud stood up without any more ado.

Olórí Ẹbí's heart flew out of the door ahead of the business deal, the deal that could change his life and shut up the mouths of his enemies.

'I really can't help you. I have already stuck out my neck bringing an unknown person into this mix, but how do I go back and tell them that you don't even have the cash?'

Mahmoud stretched out his hand and took Olórí Ẹbí's, patted the limp hand and made for the door.

Olórí Ẹbí was surprised by the mewl of pain he let out as Mahmoud's hand touched the door knob.

Mahmoud paused. 'Wait a minute!' His eyes were smiling. 'I think I have a solution to your problem. Do you know the Emir of Daura?'

Olórí Ẹbí shook his head frantically.

'He's my uncle, and sir, he's the fiftieth richest man in the whole of Africa. Do you have all the title deeds of the properties with you?'

Olórí Ẹbí nodded, not trusting himself not to say something to make the magic of the moment evaporate.

'Good, we'll look through the documents together and decide the ones you should give him.'

Olórí Ẹbí dashed back to his desk and bent underneath it.

'No need for stories, my dia,' he said, as he emerged from beneath the desk and plonked down a box of documents with an air of satisfaction. 'You can have everything.'

AROMENTAL

'I'd like to talk about your parents today,' Dr Kabir announced, in the voice of a teacher talking to a particularly slow student. Tọlá, who was seated across from him on an uncomfortable hard-backed chair, studied the table separating them. It was neat, books piled in a clean stack on one side and files on the other. But the gulf that separated them was wider than the table.

'Your parents?' said the doctor again.

Tọlá looked him straight in the eye.

He leaned back in his leather chair.

Dr Kabir was typical of the doctors she'd encountered in her lifetime, short and troubled as it had been. Young, arrogant, rude. That sneer she'd come to suspect was part of their medical training ('Now everybody, sneer. Not like that! Your lips must be set so, nose in the air! Pretend you know what the fuck you're doing!').

In times past, she had been seated on an uncomfortable wooden chair, a battery of students and social workers on the other side of a cavernous hall, Dr Kabir in the centre. Questions had been thrown at her in accusatory tones, judgemental glares that weighed her and found her wanting. She'd made a stink. She'd shown them the dark side of her 'madness'. So much so that the hospital had to summon the chief medical director, the policewoman in charge of her case, some bigwigs, her lawyer, Móríebá and Kémi. The outcome of that meeting had been one-on-one sessions with Dr Kabir instead.

And she'd paid dearly. Locked in solitary confinement, arms and legs strapped to a table, shots of medicine that knocked her out of the little mind she had left. But every single pain was worth it.

She was distracted by Dr Kabir's gleaming forehead. It reflected the sunlight pouring through shuttered windows. Tólá tried to spot her reflection in its depth.

'Yoruba people believe that the first sign of madness is excessive laughter,' she said abruptly.

The doctor made to say something but Tólá held up a hand and burst into laughter. He frowned at her as she lit up a cigarette.

'I don't care much about my parents. I already told you that my dad died. He was drunk driving. My mum though, she's a character. I'm trying to remember any time in my life that I loved that woman. I must have loved her once. All children do, but right now I can't remember when it was that I loved her, that I didn't fear her more than I loved her. She never wanted love from us. She wanted to be feared, she wanted to come back from her teaching job and find us all scrambling about the house putting things straight. She'd start honking loudly in her Peugeot 404 saloon as soon as she hit the turning to our street in case any of us was in a neighbour's house where we could

be infected by demons. She used to whip me every day
with a special prayer broom to keep the demons out of
me. She belongs to a particular church where women are
not allowed to do a lot of things, like wear jewellery and
certain clothes. She beat us, and my father beat her. She
said that wives must submit themselves to their husbands
as the church submits to God.'

Tọ́lá had stopped taking her pills. She'd tuck them into
the recesses of her cheeks, then spit them out as soon as
the nurses left her room.

'Mother did not like a lot of people, because she
believed everybody except her and her favourite pastor
was going to hell. For her, hell is real. For me, it was in
my home, it is in my head. I live there. I've lived there
since I was eight years old. I believe there's a devil. His
name is Olórí Ẹbí. The only difference between mother's
devil and mine is that hers is very good looking, not some
overweight Ibadan man who shouts his commands to the
four winds.'

Tọ́lá lit up another cigarette and studied it. 'I remember
the day I told my mum that my dad was molesting me.
She beat my demons out of me, all the while speaking in
unknown tongues. She called me a slut and said that she'd
suspected all along that I'd been having sex. She told me
about a certain light in my eyes that did not bode well for
my future. She said that God had sent me to her to test her
faith. It has always been all about her. Turns out she was
right about my evil future.'

'Do you still believe all the things she said about you?'
Dr Kabir asked.

She ignored the question. 'She decided it would
be better I was married off at an early age, before I did

something that would permanently ruin the family name. She warned me never to say anything about my father again to anyone, that she would make marks on my privates and add pepper to them, so that I would never forget.'

Dr Kabir fiddled with a tissue box. 'I must say that you have done very nicely since you were first brought in here. Discovering your painting skills is also helping to accelerate your recovery.'

Tọ́lá stared at him. 'I hardly have any education. The only thing I've done well is to give birth to three children, and I'm not even a good mother to them. At this point in my story, I'm not only officially a murderer, I've also been declared insane by a court and sent here. Now, let's picture, for one insane minute, that I "recover" and got discharged from this hospital. What are my chances of making anything of myself in the real world? Where will I live? What will I do with myself, Dr Kabir I-know-what-ails-you? Who will employ me, and to do what?'

She smoked her cigarette steadily until it burnt to the stub. 'No answers, sir?'

The doctor opened his mouth to say something.

'I really need to leave.' She stood up abruptly and left the room.

IT IS WITH GREAT RELUCTANCE THAT THE BUTTERFLY ENTERS THE BUSH

Mọ́remí and Mọ́ríebá pulled to a stop in front of Olórí Ẹbí's house and got out of the car. While Mọ́ríebá fetched a bag out of the back seat, Mọ́remí gaped at the freshly painted house gleaming in the afternoon sunshine. The neighbouring houses were faded, Olórí Ẹbí's a peacock among a group of peahens.

They opened the gate and walked to the front door. Mọríebá rang the bell. When nobody came to the door, Mọríebá adjusted the folds of her agbádá and rang the bell again. After waiting a few more minutes, they finally heard approaching footsteps. The door was thrown open by Ìyàwó, a snotty-nosed baby balanced on her hip.

Ìyàwó smiled. 'Anti Mọríebá, Anti Mọremí, good afternoon.' She stepped aside and allowed them into the hallway.

'Good afternoon, Ìyàwó, you're looking well,' Mọríebá said.

'Ah thank you.' Ìyàwó hesitated at the bottom of the staircase. 'I guess you've come to see your father.'

Mọremí and Mọríebá exchanged startled glances.

'Oh yes,' Mọríebá coughed. 'Can you kindly tell him we're around?'

'So, you haven't heard,' Ìyàwó said. 'Your father suffered a heart attack about two months ago. In fact we just returned from the hospital.'

Ìyàwó's insistence on referring to Olórí Ẹbí as their father grated on Mọremí's nerves.

Mọríebá made sad noises in her throat. 'We didn't hear anything, Ìyàwó. Maybe it's because we've been out of the country. But you could have dropped a message for us at my house.'

Ìyàwó shifted the baby to her other hip. 'Brother Tafa has been so kind, following us to the hospital and helping out, I thought somebody would have told you.'

'I'm sorry.' Mọríebá fiddled with the bag. 'Does that mean we won't be able to see him?'

'He's lying down in his room. I will go and tell him you're here.' Ìyàwó opened the sitting room door for them.

Móríebá sat on the closest chair to the door. 'It's alright if he can't see us. If you just fetch Àmòpé for us, we'll come and see him some other time.'

Ìyàwó froze at the mention of Àmòpé's name. 'I will tell Olórí Ẹbí you're here.'

A few minutes later, Olórí Ẹbí strode into the room. Móríebá again feeling his presence like the raw harmattan wind. He did not spare them a glance as he slowly manoeuvred himself into his favourite chair. After a few minutes of fumbling with his oversized clothes he finally looked at them, his old smile playing around his lips.

'Lákíríboto and her apprentice have come out to play.' He laughed at his own joke.

'You are a disgusting old man,' said Móríebá coldly. 'I thought they said you were knocking at death's door.'

Olórí Ẹbí bared his teeth at her. 'Oh, that's why you're here abi? You think I'm one foot in the grave. But you forget that I'm aníkúlápó, the one that holds death in his pocket, the one who never dies.'

'I know you have the medicine for death, Raufu.' Móríebá smiled mirthlessly. 'The same one your father, Saka, and his father, Amuda, used. Tell me, did they pass on the medicine to you from their graves?'

'You are a disrespectful woman who will never have children! You think playing mommy to other people's children will give you happiness? I'm so sorry for your sick, depraved and senseless life!' Olórí Ẹbí breathed heavily. His body shook with anger. 'Do you think that money can bring you happiness?'

Móríebá sucked her teeth. 'It is only the dead who

can be sure of those who will bury them.' She waved a dismissive hand. 'If money can't bring happiness, I wonder why you've spent the better part of your life trying to get it.'

Olórí Ẹbí looked fit to burst. 'So, Madam Lákíríboto, what brings your royal highness into our humble house?' He adjusted himself on the chair, and Mọremí noted that he listed towards his left side.

Mọríebá opened the bag she was carrying and pulled out a folder. 'I am here to throw you out of this house, which now belongs to me.'

Olórí Ẹbí straightened in his seat. 'What do you mean by that?'.

'Is the great aníkúlápó going deaf?' Mọríebá raised her voice, enunciating each word clearly. 'This house belongs to me!' She waved some documents in the air. 'So does your office complex, and the family lands in Alágbàdo. Look here,' she smiled, 'the title deeds to Alhaja's properties.'

The wheels turned and his eyes became slits. 'You set out to ruin me. You sent those scammers to me.'

Mọríebá shrugged. 'Stop whining, Olórí Ẹbí. You started the game. I simply finished it for you.'

'How dare you talk to me like that, you worthless woman!'

'I dare do anything I like.' Mọríebá was half out of the chair. 'I am not an idiot to be used and blackmailed by a stupid old man. I am ... I am Lákíríboto, that woman who haunts your nightmares!'

Olórí Ẹbí grabbed his chest and made a mewling sound.

Ìyàwó rushed in, a glass of water and some pills in her hands. She glared at the women. 'Please Aunty Mọríebá, can't you see he's a sick old man?' she chided them, as she fussed over her husband.

'Shut up, woman!' Olórí Ẹbí threw the half-drunk glass of water at her, missing her head by a few inches. 'Get out of here! You are very stupid and presumptuous! Who sought your opinion?'

Mọ́remí felt sorry for the woman as she scurried out of the room.

Olórí Ẹbí leaned back in the chair and shut his eyes. 'What do you want from me?'

'Nothing. I have taken everything you've ever had from you. You have nothing else I desire.' Mọ́ríebá shrugged off her agbádá and flicked the sleeves back on her shoulders in the classic 'one thousand, five hundred naira' gesture mastered by all affluent Yoruba women from birth.

He passed a hand over his brow. 'So, what are you doing here then?'

'We've come to fetch Àmọ̀pé, and then we'll be on our way.'

'I don't know what you're talking about.' His voice was a brick wall.

'We know she's here. We have proof!' Mọ́remí shouted.

He smiled at Mọ́remí. 'It is when a child does not recognise medicine that she calls it spinach. Let me tell you a bedside story, child.'

'We did not come here to listen to tales by moonlight,' Mọ́ríebá snapped. 'You either fetch Àmọ̀pé or I will find her myself, and man, you won't like it.'

'But you will listen to this one. After all, you have cornered a wounded lion, and it will break you in half with its powerful jaws.'

'You really are deluded, old man, lion ko, chicken ni!'

Olórí Ẹbí went on. 'There was a boy born into a big family. His father had been married several times to several women over the years. Some of the women still lived with him, while the others had died or divorced him. This innocent child was born by the youngest of the wives, a woman who had been previously engaged to another man.'

Mọ́remí shifted in her seat as Olórí Ẹbí's gaze seemed to pierce through her soul.

'She loved this other man deeply. He was the one her heart had been bound to since they were toddlers. They had plans, big plans: he was going to send her to school, she would become a nurse, or a teacher. She would become anything she wanted to be, and they would love each other till death.'

Mọ́remí knew who the story was about.

'But her dreams were cut short as she was forcefully married to a rich older man by her family because they owed him money. He would forgive their debt and she would provide him the much sought-after male child. Two years later, this woman gave the old man a son, and when her son was barely three years old, she died, she died of a broken heart. As it happens, under such circumstances the toddler was given over to be raised by his stepmothers, a bunch of women who were more wicked than witches. The boy was treated like a subhuman being. Although his father loved him, these women ensured that his life was hell on earth. They passed him among one another like an unwanted package. Sometimes they fed him, sometimes they didn't. Nobody paid any attention to him—'

Mọ́remí was beginning to find the story a tad melodramatic, so she was relieved when Mọ́ríebá clapped. 'Can we do this quickly? You bore me with this, your oft-repeated story that becomes even more wildly exaggerated with each new telling.'

'That's not all,' Olórí Ẹbí went on. 'When the boy – I – came into my own, that was when the family came crawling back. They wanted me to come and head them, I was rich enough now to be their son—'

'Liar!' A new female voice interrupted his flow.

Mọremí looked away from Olórí Ẹbí and her eyes tangled with those of a woman she hadn't seen in over thirteen years.

Àmọpé was thin to the point of emaciation, her hair a shock of grey tight curls on her head. She was wearing a pair of faded jeans and an old brown short-sleeved shirt. Stick-like arms pockmarked with scars poked out of the shirt, but her face had remained the same.

Mọremí recoiled. This was the woman who had brought her into the world to be used and abused.

'Why don't you tell them about how spoilt you were?' Àmọpé shut the door behind her and came into the room properly, arms folded across her chest. 'Tell them how the other children, except you, were sent to the farm on weekends. How the old man got you your own housemaid. You were his little prince! Tell them how you stole the little money your stepmothers had. How you dropped out of school and ran away to become a motor-park tout in Ibadan as soon as your father died. Tell them how my mother rescued you and took you in the first time you were accused of armed robbery. Tell them!'

Her voice broke. 'Tell them how you introduced me to drugs while you were living underneath my mother's roof.'

'Enough of the drama, Àmọ̀pé,' Mọ́ríebá said impatiently, as she grabbed her bag and ushered Mọ́remí to the door. 'We will have enough time to talk about all these things.'

'You are not going anywhere! Not with those papers!' Olórí Ẹbí sprung out of his chair with surprising speed and blocked their exit. 'You mere children think you can beard the lion in his den and get away unscathed.' He drew himself up to his full height and stretched out his hand. 'Give me those papers!'

Mọ́ríebá burst into laughter. 'You're joking, right? Old man, move out of my way.'

Olórí Ẹbí dipped his hand into the folds of his agbádá and pulled out a live tortoise that fitted snugly into his left palm.

Mọ́ríebá's eyes widened, then she doubled over in hysterical laughter and clapped her hands in derision. 'If your jazz is so powerful why hasn't it worked before?'

Olórí Ẹbí stretched the tortoise towards Mọ́remí, Mọ́ríebá and Àmọ̀pé in short, sharp thrusts, all the while chanting incantations at the top of his lungs. 'The ground underneath my feet pay attention to my words, the skies above lend me your ears. It is I, Raufu Mọ́tiléwá Agúntásọọ̀lò, the son of Arówóṣẹgbẹ́, who summons you this day. My words take charge of the elements for I hold authority on the palm of my hands.'

He stretched out his hand to the four corners of the room. 'East, west, north, south, hear the sound of my voice and lend me your ears. For it is what we tell the attentive leaf that it understands. It is what we tell the receptive leaf that it accepts. It is with great reluctance that a butterfly enters the bush.'

He used his left hand to fetch a tiny gourd from another pocket and tapped on the tortoise thrice. He threw some of the gourd's contents on the tortoise's shell and touched it with the tip of his tongue. The tortoise poked its head out of its shell slowly.

Mọ́remí was frozen to the spot. She didn't know if she was fascinated or repulsed. The room was heavy with an otherworldly presence as Olórí Ẹbí appeared to grow bigger and bigger until he filled the room, his head touching the ceiling. The tortoise cradled in his palm almost seemed to be grinning.

Somebody was calling her name, but the voice was coming from afar. Olórí Ẹbí was the only real thing: he filled her eyes, her senses. She stared at the tortoise as it drew her into itself, into the slow churning of its thoughts. Nothing else existed but Olórí Ẹbí's tortoise, his voice.

It could never be well with a never-do-well. Things never worked out for taboo breakers. The pestle could never find a place of rest ...

Mọ́remí snapped out of the spell as Olórí Ẹbí fell to the ground with a thud. Standing by the door, with a bewildered look on his face, was Quadri.

'What's going on here?' he asked, as Mọ́ríebá knelt beside Olórí Ẹbí's supine form, and fetched her phone out of her pocket.

'Hello, ambulance services? It's an emergency ... Yes, I know it's a private service, I'm a client. Come to number 3, Idi-Ikan.'

DELIVERANCE

Tọlá was standing in front of her easel, painting the man of her dreams. The man was black, a solid brick wall of darkness. He was tall and he was headless. An emptiness stood in place of his penis. His arms were outstretched, powerful: well-defined arms, nailed to an invisible cross.

Tọlá dipped her brush in the paint and slashed a trail of red down his torso. Her eyes were inside, seeing the line of blood trailing from his neck down to the empty spot between his spreadeagled legs.

The vision disappeared at the click-click of uneven heels. She expelled an angry breath, knowing without a doubt that she wouldn't be able to do anything further now. The other patients in the studio were dropping their tools and clearing out their workspaces. Clenching her jaw, Tọlá tightened her grip on the brush and focused on the canvas. The footsteps stopped beside her.

'Good afternoon, Miss Tọlá.' His deep voice set her teeth on edge.

'What do you want?' She dropped her paintbrush. She did not look at him.

'Remember I told you the senior pastor promised to come today?'

Tọlá squeezed her eyes shut and drew in a breath, ruing again the day she had smiled back at him. His name was Chizoba. He was a fine specimen of man, all white teeth, yellow skin and muscles that showed through his shirt. He reminded her of the men that had visited Rita in the darkened rooms of Isale-Eko. He smelled like them too, earthy, sweaty, pheromones clogging up the air.

He came to the asylum regularly with a bunch of other do-gooders who came to preach, or as he put it 'fellowship', with the patients. She had kept clear of them for a whole year. The women dressed in the long gowns and skirts discarded by Victorians on their way out of Nigeria. Scarves were bound tightly around their heads, creating deep furrows between their foreheads and eyebrows. They reminded her of her mother. They had the fire of fanaticism burning bright in their yellowed gazes. They looked like they'd never experienced an orgasm before in their lives.

Sometimes, when she watched them from behind her bedroom curtains, she would be tempted to spread her good news to them: about how they should consider spreading their legs and discovering that heaven was not as far from them as they imagined.

But a few months earlier, during one afternoon of weakness when she had been feeling the need for human contact, Chizoba had walked up to her in the corridor and flashed his pearly whites, and she had smiled back.

He had not left her alone since. He'd talk to her whether she responded or not. He would knock on her bedroom door, stalk her in the corridors, follow her into the studio. Whenever she bothered to pay him some attention, he would smile into her eyes and tell her the 'good news of Jesus Christ' and the bad news of the sordid world outside the asylum gates.

But she liked the way he would squint his eyes, his body poised as if he wanted to shove 'faith' into her head.

He painted her the picture of muscular Aryan angels with peace as wings, waiting to serenade her with their cherubic songs for all eternity. A heaven so white she had told him that nobody would let her in on account of her dark soul, and more so, because of her dark skin.

But he had said it was alright, that although none of the angels had black skin, that God, the one and only true God as he called him, the all-white God with his huge white ... well ... beard, would welcome her home with a hug.

He had told her that all she needed to do was to confess Jesus Christ as her lord and saviour, and her dark soul would become as white as snow.

'Shall we proceed to the fellowship now?' Chizoba asked.

Tọ́lá frowned and finally looked at him. 'I asked what you want from me.'

'You promised to attend the service if our senior pastor came visiting.'

She took a step towards him. 'I told you that I don't like church.'

'Is there any problem, Brother Chizoba?'

Tọ́lá's head whipped towards Nurse Lim, a giant of a man with deep tribal marks scored from the tips of his lips to his cheeks.

Chizoba stuttered. 'There isn't, only the senior pastor would like to meet with our new converts and I thought Miss Tọ́lá would like that.'

She sucked her teeth. 'What part of "I do not like" don't you understand?'

Tọ́lá had embraced her madness and found her voice. She would no longer be silenced.

A heavy hand descended on her shoulder. 'Calm down, Tọ́lá, nobody is forcing you to do anything against your will.'

Nurse Lim was being reasonable. Tọ́lá's shoulders slumped as the futility of arguing with them hit her. In the early days, she'd spent so many hours strapped down to a table, drugged to her eyeballs. She didn't want a repeat of that.

'My senior pastor is a very powerful man,' Chizoba boasted. 'The power of God is always with him, he might even deliver you—'

'Deliver me from what?'

'Relax, Tọ́lá. I heard they have really nice music, and there'll be cake,' said Nurse Lim.

To be in an asylum meant being offered cake as Ėṣù would be offered palm oil.

Ah, Èṣù. Tọ́lá gave them a sunny smile. 'Let's go then.'

The cafeteria was packed. Aside from the inmates seated on white plastic chairs, there were the doctors and nurses, nursing attendants and even some of the guards who manned the gates.

Tọ́lá stood at the back, Chizoba possessively by her side. She was his soul. He had won her.

The microphone spat static. On the podium a jerry-curled light-skinned man stood sweating profusely underneath his three-piece suit. Three hefty men in sunglasses stood guard in front of him. As he began preaching, the pastor's head bounced up and down as the enraptured audience shouted an 'Amen!' or 'Halleluyah!' to whatever it was he had been saying.

'Batsesheba! Rumunumu! Rumpelstiltskin!' the man shouted into the microphone. At least that was what Tọ́lá heard. She laughed as her eyes met the pastor's. She registered with faint surprise that she'd seen him on television before.

'You!' He pointed at her. 'Bring that young lady over here! Tha Lor' tol' me tudaay is your day of freedom!'

The congregation erupted into shouts of 'Halleluyah!' and 'Amen!' as she was half-pushed, half-pulled down the aisle by the ushers who had immediately run to her side.

As she was thrust forwards to the podium, the pastor raised his voice higher still. 'Bobirigiri, ripompolisti, orangey, limpopo, zambezi!' He pointed heavenwards. Tọ́lá looked up, expecting a rain of gold. 'Loose her, in Jesus' name!'

He jumped down from the podium and struck her on the forehead.

Tọ́lá blanked out. Rita grabbed the pastor's arm, flipped him over her head and heard a satisfying snap as she knelt sharply on his wrist.

'I am God,' she whispered fiercely. Then Rita ran.

She ran for the wide window closest to the podium and jumped through it. She ran past her hostel block, past doctors and nurses who ignored her. She ran past some inmates headed for the cafeteria. She ran until she got to the abandoned building where she'd hidden the things she'd need when the time was right over the past eight months. That time had come. She pulled off her grey uniform, put on the knee-length knickers, boots, long curly wig, sunglasses and a face cap. She grabbed the money she'd saved and placed the bundle in her pocket.

She took off at a rapid walk, not wanting to attract attention. They didn't seem to be following her. Within five minutes she was at the far end of the hospital compound, heading for the broken wall blocks that she knew could be moved. On the other side of the wall was a huge maize farm. She plunged into it, maize leaves and stalks scratching her bare arms and legs, but she didn't stop. She finally broke through to a tiny footpath and followed it. The footpath confirmed that she was right trusting Èṣù, because she knew there was a small village nearby. The pastor was right about one thing. *Tuudaaay is da daaay of my freedom.*

It had happened during her last time in solitary confinement. Èṣù had appeared to her as a woman/man. S/he had been indescribably beautiful. S/he had loosened the straps binding Rita to the table, helped her to sit up and offered her a sip of vodka, heavenly vodka. They had discussed a lot of things, but before they left, Èṣù had handed her a pen and paper and had told her how she would escape from the asylum. Rita had asked when she should leave. They had smiled and told her to be patient.

She half-slid, half-ran down the hill. A wider path seemed to run through the centre of the hamlet. She was soon surrounded by naked children, who stared at her open-mouthed.

'Good afternoon, madam,' Rita called out to a woman seated in front of her hut eating rice out of a pot burnt black by woodsmoke. 'Please, ma, I'm going to Abeokuta, can you show me the way?'

The woman took in Rita's shorts and shirt with one sweeping glance. 'You don't look like one of them,' she said finally. 'Sometimes we have escaped patients passing through. We have a phone number to call.'

Rita shrugged.

'I don't think you're one of them.' She pointed down the sandy road. 'Keep walking in that direction and you will get to the expressway, but it's very far. Do you want me to call my son to take you there on his bike?'

Taken by surprise at the woman's kindness, Rita replied shyly that she wouldn't mind.

'But you will have to buy fuel for him,' the woman said, and disappeared into the house.

Minutes later the woman reappeared as a Jincheng bicycle roared to a stop in front of the hut.

Rita climbed aboard, thanking the woman, and the young man drove her to the expressway.

'Wait here, madam,' he said when they arrived. 'Cars going to Abeokuta pass through here.'

'Where does the road on the other side lead to?' Rita asked.

'Ibadan.'

'So, if I cross to the other side, I will find buses going to Ibadan?'

'Yes, ma.'

Rita smiled at him and gave him a few notes from her pocket. The young man smiled in delight as he accepted the money. He thanked her and offered to help her cross the expressway.

'I'll be alright, thank you.'

Within five minutes, a car pulled up and a man wearing a sleeveless shirt stuck his head through the window.

'Can I give you a ride?'

The man smelled of sweat, pheromones and dark rooms. Rita flashed him her prettiest smile and climbed in beside him.